Before His Eyes

Before His Eyes

A Romance Novel by

S. Marie

Order this book online at www.trafford.com
or email orders@trafford.com

Most Trafford titles are also available at major online book retailers.

Printed in the United States of America.

ISBN: 978-1-4669-0327-2 (sc)
ISBN: 978-1-4669-0326-5 (hc)
ISBN: 978-1-4669-0325-8 (e)

Library of Congress Control Number: 2011960298

Trafford rev. 11/09/2011

 www.trafford.com

North America & international
toll-free: 1 888 232 4444 (USA & Canada)
phone: 250 383 6864 ♦ fax: 812 355 4082

CHAPTER ONE

"DOES MY HEAD hurt or what?!!" she thought. When she opened her eyes, there were two men and a woman dressed in scrubs working frantically around her.

"Doctor her eyes are open!!" the male nurse spoke urgently while attaching the blood pressure cuff.

The female doctor looked in her patient's face saying "Hello, I'm Doctor Jaime Edwards. You've had an accident and are in the Sydney Good Samaritan hospital. Do you know what day it is?"

The woman laying on the gurney responded quite hesitantly "I'm . . . not . . . sure."

The doctor asked, "What's your name?"

"Elsie . . . Elsie . . ." her face showing at first confusion, followed by panic.

A male voice stated. "Doctor, the patient's blood pressure is 210 over 120 and . . . what the?!!"

The patient was off the table, onto the floor scrambling towards the far corner. A bright red trail originated from her arm where the IV line had been established.

"Miss Endy please calm down. You've had a serious fall; your confusion is only natural. We can help if you'll let us continue our examination." the doctor was saying with more calm than she felt.

With the nature of Elsie Endy's fall, loss of blood and elevated blood pressure this could turn for the worse in short order.

Then Doctor Edwards turned to Nurse Jeffrey Osgood "get the gentleman that brought Miss Endy here—now!"

Using long quick strides, Jeffrey exited the examination room for the waiting room.

Once again focusing on Elsie, Doctor Jaime tried a second time, "Miss Endy do you remember anything about the fall you've had?"

Elsie curled in the far corner was starting to visibly shake.

As she responded the same shake was audible "no . . . no . . . Where did you say I was?"

Doctor Jaime moved closer to Elsie "you are in Sydney Good Samaritan."

"Sydney??" Elsie muttered to herself "you sound British or Australian".

Looking at the doctor and in a quizzical tone "Sydney, Australia??"

"Yes!—you remember where you are then." Doctor Jaime replied in hopes she had gained some credibility with her patient.

"Oh NO!! I would never fly that far?? I detest flying!!!" Elsie's voice defiant.

The door opened to Nurse Osgood and another gentleman's entrance. The gentleman was about 5'11" with a burly build, reddish-brown hair and hazel eyes filled with concern.

He spoke to the doctor "How is she Doc . . . ?"

He spied Elsie in the corner with what looked to be blood everywhere. He quickly walked in her direction only to be stopped dead in his tracks when she put her arms up in obvious fear of his determined advance.

As he crouched down in the spot he had halted, his voice became soft as if he was talking to a skittish colt. "Elsie, it's me Rusty. I brought you here after Tiara sent you for a tumble."

Rusty inched closer to her as he spoke.

Elsie's full focus was on his face; the rest of the people in the room disappeared into a blur.

When Rusty reached to touch her hand, she spoke quietly and evenly "You look and sound like Rusty Garnet the actor."

"Yes, that's right Mate. We're here on holiday so I could show you my farm". The sense of relief he felt was short lived.

"You all say I hit my head. Well I must be delusional if you expect me to believe an award winning actor, who could have any woman he wanted, would bring me to see his farm in Australia." Elsie spoke with such conviction it was as though she had physically slapped Rusty.

To further make her point, Elsie attempted to stand. However, her current condition could not to be ignored. As she reached her full height of 5'2", Elsie's eyes rolled back into her head. Rusty caught her before she sustained further injury from hitting the antiseptic tile floor.

Doctor Edwards gave succinct orders, "Get her on that table. Jeffrey—BP and pulse. Art—blood sugar level and get that IV re-established. Mr. Garnet, thank you, but it's time you left. We'll let you know as soon as we know."

Rusty was escorted to the door by Nurse Kimble. After the door closed behind Rusty, he turned to peer through the window. He watched for a few minutes while they assessed Elsie's condition. The IV line had been reinserted plus a bag of GLUCOSE, according to the label, hung next to the one marked SALINE. They were moving Elsie from the table to a gurney then rolling her towards the door. He moved out of their way.

In the hallway, the doctor ordered loud enough for Rusty to hear. "Art, I'll call Neurology while you're getting her X-rays. Make sure they do a full head to toe. Plus, I want an MRI head series. With all that bruising I want to make sure we have no surprises."

With that in motion, Doctor Edwards was heading for another exam room while Nurse Kimble pushed the gurney with Elsie and her over laden IV pole into the elevator.

Chapter Two

Oblivious to the fresh blood staining his shirt, Rusty glanced around the emergency waiting room for a seat. The only one available with empty seats around it was farther from the hallway. At least it was in direct line of sight of the elevator. He hoped being in the open like this, no one would recognize him. His ability to handle any fans in his current state of mind would win back the bad boy image he was glad had been proven wrong over time. How he hated the tabloids for sticking him with that title the first year Hollywood noticed him. It did pale in comparison to the outrageous love affair stories they spun from a single sighting of him with any attractive woman. And if the woman was famous too, it would inevitably lead to more headlines of jealous lovers followed shortly thereafter outlining their break-up. It was strange how those stories had eventually helped forge the relationship between Rusty and Elsie.

It had been two summers ago, around the middle of June. Rusty was returning to the states after three years at his ranch on a self-imposed exile. Prior to that, his career had been on a major high, he had fallen in love with Celeste. He'd brought a beautiful home on the coast in northern California. Preparations were under way for their elaborate wedding. What could be better? Or so he'd thought.

He had taken a hiatus from acting to spend quality time with his fiancée'. However, he was normally quite active. With Celeste focusing on her own career in show business, Rusty did very little except sit around on his laurels and eat. The tabloids had made a mockery of his increasing girth by likening him to Marlon Brando, the later years. Sadly, they'd hit the bull's eye with that one. Celeste and her career took off.

She didn't want to be tied down by " . . . a has-been who wouldn't even make an effort to uphold his image."

Her sneering commentary shattered his heart and trust like the crystal champagne flute she'd smashed onto their marble countertop to accentuate her words. It had taken a lot of time and soul searching for him to emerge from the wallowing self pity and depression that accompanied his return home to the ranch in Australia. Rusty managed to find and rebuild himself, not only internally, but externally. It had been serendipitous when Red Roget had invited him to his ranch in Montana to discuss a part in one of his upcoming projects. It wasn't as the star, but Red felt it was a pivotal character for which Rusty was a perfect fit. Not to mention, a way to rejuvenate his career. It had been five years since he'd acted in front of a camera.

Rusty didn't sleep much the night he flew into Montana. He'd been on airplanes for more hours than he cared to remember over the last few days. It was 5:30 in the morning when he gave up trying to sleep. A trip to Red's kitchen for coffee followed by an early morning ride might help clear the jet lag. He was fumbling around trying to find the coffee. Suddenly, a two-legged tumbleweed burst into Red's kitchen with two wolves in its wake.

When tumbleweed saw him, she smiled saying brightly for the hour "Good morning, you must be the guest Red mentioned would be coming in for a few days. Don't mind them. They're harmless, if you are."

Not waiting for response, she banged two stainless steel dog dishes onto the counter. This particular action seemed to be a signal to start a frenzy of howling and jumping.

"Sophie! Tycho! I'm getting your food—chill! Excuse me. I need to feed them before they wake the whole county." Her accent well-defined by the sarcasm.

It originated from one of the north eastern states. The dogs went into an impatient sit—furry butts hovering a mere inch above the floor—with tails swishing madly to a tune only they knew. The woman was scooping food out of a bin from a closet that looked to be the pantry. Food scooped and over to the sink for a little water. The dogs' eyes followed every movement.

Rusty thought for sure they'd lunge at the food when she faced them with a dish in each hand.

The woman calmly said "Sophie" placing a dish in front of the female dog that started eating in what could only be described as ladylike.

The male dog had gone into a full sit with eyes never leaving the second food dish.

"Tycho", the second dish had barely made contact with the slate tiles, he was gulping the food down.

Rusty may have been feeling jet lagged, but this tumbleweed was definitely a woman. His first impression of her gave way as he watched her turn from the dogs. She was on the short side, a tad over five feet. Her figure was reminiscent of Rueben's masterpiece with additional brush strokes on the top proportions. Noticing his perusal of her physical characteristics, she buttoned her over-sized denim shirt closed to hide the stressed tank top. Rusty was amazed. Having spent a sufficient amount of time in California, he knew women with bust lines like hers who'd put them right in your face, tell you how much they'd cost and offer a squeeze. Granted, the woman he was watching move about the kitchen didn't have one of those hard bodies with abs to die for. Yet, her curves presented a pleasant homey softness which he was thoroughly enjoying. The woman finished preparing the coffee pot. Hitting the brew button, she turned towards him. Rusty's gaze refocused on her face.

She started to talk matter-of-factly. "I believe Red told me his guest was going to be Rusty Garnet, the actor."

There was a momentary pause to allow Rusty to nod in affirmation.

She continued, "My name is Elsie. I've been here for the summer polishing a screenplay for Red. I seem to be the first one up and last to sleep thanks to the dogs. If you need anything, and Red isn't handy, let me know."

Elsie picked up the dog dishes to place in the sink. Rusty noticed she didn't seem to stop moving—nervous energy?

Now she was removing the clean dishes from the dishwasher and putting them in the appropriate cupboards. "Hope you don't mind my opinion—I think the part Red wants you to do is a win-win. It's not a lead, but it's a good part in a good movie; at least on paper anyway. It also fits in with your overall film portfolio—an impressive body of work of which you can be very proud. On a side note with no offense intended, you look a lot healthier than the last time I saw your picture splayed across a tabloid."

Finally, Rusty had a chance to speak. "Thanks, I'll take that as the intended compliment. So you're a fan."

Elsie bristled at his arrogant response. "Yes, Mr. Garnet, I think you've done some outstanding performances. It doesn't take a rocket scientist to guess how Tycho got his name."

Rusty had won an Oscar for his portrayal of the copper-nosed astronomer Tycho Brahe in the movie "Planetary Motion". Realizing this caused him to shift uncomfortably in his chair while he glanced at the dogs settling under the window. Tycho was the color of an old penny and gawky like a colt; whereas, Sophie in wolf gray moved with effortless grace.

"A yearling", Rusty commented in an attempt to steer the conversation.

"As a matter of fact, he turned two on the eleventh. He won't be fully mature till he's about four. He was shipped to me from California. With his red color everyone wanted me to name him Rusty, but it was a bit too trite for my taste" Elsie replied.

"Don't you think that's too much thought for naming a dog? They are dogs aren't they?" He needed clarification.

"They are Alaskan Malamutes. And as for naming a show dog, not really, that's only his call name. I won't bore you with his registered name."

Feeling like he was in the room with a fanatic, Rusty moved towards the doorway. The coffee pot beeped ready.

"How do you like your coffee Mr. Garnet?" Her tone sounded similar to a waitress in a corner coffee shop.

Rusty was perplexed. Was this woman a whacko fan or didn't give a rat's ass who he was? In some perverted way, he had to know.

"So Miss Endy", Rusty emphasized the formal, "isn't meeting one of your favorite film stars exciting for you?"

He sat at the table awaiting his cup of coffee.

Elsie smiled slightly. "Well, Mr. Garnet, and please do call me Elsie. As I was saying, it is interesting to meet you. As for anything else, I figure you eat, sleep, scratch your ass, et cetera like most people. Have good days and bad ones. Is it cool that you *were* one of *the* hottest actors in Hollywood—I'd be lying if I said no. But don't expect me to go all goofy, follow you around cooing and acting all girlie. I'm not in for that kind of nonsense. Not to mention, hardly your type."

Rusty thought he had her pegged "Please call me Rusty. I like my coffee with cream, no sugar. So you prefer sheilas and I should save my charm."

Her thumping down of the cream had him blundering on. "Hey, it's okay with me. That explains no ring, wild woman look, and snarky attitude. No big deal."

"Hold on a minute! Just because I'm not getting all wet for you, I must be a lesbian!" The tone in her voice had the dogs up and pacing.

The cup of hot liquid in her left hand had Rusty ready to join them. Coffee splashed agitatedly over its rim as she banged it on the table in front of him

"Hell's bells! You're only here for four days. Why am I bothering to get on my soapbox to explain away you're misconceptions? Particularly since I'll never see you again except in the movies." Her voice leveled. "You are Red's guest. I was merely trying to make you feel at ease with the situation."

Dismissing him with a look, "Sophie! Tycho! Let's go!" she swept passed him, then out the main door. The dogs vying for the position closest to her.

Rusty was at a loss. Should he be sorry he upset her? Or mad that she based her opinion of him from tabloid stories? Then again, he had based his opinion of her on her looks and a few comments. It was flattering that she named her dog after a character he had portrayed. Particularly since he felt it was his best work. Maybe he was wrong about her. Of course she had a point, in four days he'd be gone.

CHAPTER THREE

NEITHER ELSIE NOR Rusty mentioned their verbal encounter to Red. Over the next four days, they unintentionally got to know each other. Red preferred family style dinners. Thus, meals were scheduled to include all three of them. Elsie didn't want to appear ungrateful by using some lame excuse not to join the men. Red was notorious for picking a controversial topic for dinner conversation. Ironically, the deeper into a topic they delved; the more they discovered they all basically felt the same way. As the conversation would wane into dessert, Red would play devil's advocate on a new topic to keep the talk going. He also got a kick out of how opinionated they could all be; especially without the need for the inhibition removing effects of alcohol. Not that any of them were against imbibing, much the opposite. Rusty was surprised when Elsie joined them in the afternoon for a beer, a glass of wine at dinner, and brandy later in the evening. In her snifter, Red always poured amaretto.

Rusty's last full day at the ranch, a nasty storm blew across the state. Warnings announced on the radio and TV while they were at breakfast. Red had asked Rusty to join him in securing things around the house and barn. Meanwhile, Elsie was cooking up her own storm in the kitchen. She wanted to be prepared in case the power went out. Red had a generator for such emergencies, but she needed to feel useful. After lunch, Red wanted to get a mare due to foal next week in from the pasture. He and Rusty rode to the east pasture. Elsie had plans to run the dogs before crating them for the storm. After moving the crates to the lowest and most protected room in the house, she, Tycho and Sophie headed for the west pasture. They had only been gone for a half hour when she noticed the line of clouds moving southeast. It reminded her of a storm she had been through in Colorado. It sent a shiver of knowing down her spine.

"Tycho! Sophie! Move it!" She jogged towards the ranch house with the dogs chasing after her in play.

The day had been hovering around 80. The first blast of icy air hit her as they stepped onto Red's wraparound porch. When she opened the door to let the dogs into the house she looked back to see how quickly the storm had advanced. Another blast of cold air hit her as the thick dark gray clouds met the peak of the barn roof. This was going to be a bad one. In the house, she flipped on the TV. Putting the dogs into their crates, she draped a blanket over each to muffle any loud scary noises. The TV was showing a map of the state with Doppler radar.

Displayed along the bottom, scrolling in orange: "Severe Storm Warnings for the following counties . . ."

Like she needed that to know a severe storm was on top of them!

Her prominent concern was "Where were Red and Rusty?"

An earth-shaking crack of thunder followed by the unmistakable tapping of hail drew her to the window. Anyone who had been through similar storms knew it was not wise to be by a window, but Elsie was looking for the two men. She could clearly see the barn. Three dark blobs moved in from the east. Thank God! She went back the hall to fetch towels from the closet. When she returned with the towels, she peered towards the barn. This time she could barely see it. Another ear shattering thunderclap forced her away from the window. The tempo of the hail was amplified by the wind driving it under the porch roof against the side of the ranch house.

Red and Rusty got the mare settled into a stall and took care of the horses they had ridden. Neither one was relishing crossing the hundred yards that stretched between the buildings. Both of them being the chivalrous kind didn't want to let Elsie ride out the storm alone. Also, needing to see that she was in fact safe, not getting pummeled in the west pasture. They patted each other on the back as they exited the safety of the barn. Once the barn door was secure, they headed to house. Progress was slow from the littering everywhere of hail stones. It was a good thing

Rusty was behind Red. Red lost his footing and couldn't seem to get it back to walk. Rusty stumbled into Red by his third attempt. They steadied each other before moving forward. The trip seemed like an eternity. Rusty was going at a slower pace than Red causing the diminished visibility to conceal them from each other.

Elsie opened the door as she saw a shadow move onto the porch. She didn't care who it was, she stepped out to aid him into the house.

It was Red. "Elsie, thank God you're safe!"

Handing him a towel Elsie commented, "I was about to say the same thing to you. Where's Rusty?"

"Behind me. Sure hope he didn't get turned around." Red said peering through the same window Elsie had been using.

They didn't have any more time to ponder when a flash of light with a bone-crushing crack of thunder smacked the ranch house simultaneously.

As they were blinking in shock, a different cracking noise in combination with a muffled "oof" pulled their gazes outside. At the end of the porch, a section of roofing had come down. There appeared to be something underneath the debris.

"Oh God! That hit Rusty!" Red yanked the door open "Damn! I should've kept him in sight!"

On his way towards Rusty, Red slid off the porch. If the storm wasn't so bad, it might've been funny to see. Elsie stepped out to help. Red didn't let the fall from the porch deter him. He crawled to Rusty along the ground using the edge of the porch as a guide. He got to Rusty while Elsie managed to stay on the porch with a few more feet to go.

Both men saw her "Elsie get back in the house before you get hurt!!"

As if she was going to listen to them when she was fairing better than them?

Red tried shifting the section of roofing off Rusty. It wouldn't budge since it was still attached to the rest of the roof. Rusty was no help. He was trapped face down with only one arm free. Elsie noticed the roof post had snapped in two. Part of it was still attached to the roof. Where was the other part of the post?

Yelling as loud as she could "Red!! The post . . . by your feet . . . !"

He saw it and understood what she wanted. Use it as a lever to remove the pressure of the roof enough to allow Rusty to maneuver.

"Rusty you ready? Here goes!" Red grunted from the exertion.

The section of roof creaked as Red lifted it with the crude lever. Rusty started to wriggle out. His other arm freed to allow him the use of both arms. Or so he thought. When he put pressure on that arm, pain knifed through his hand. Looking down at it, he saw blood and shards of wood. Elsie realized he had stopped moving and why.

She grabbed the arm of the injured hand. "Rusty! Let's go!"

She pulled so hard she lost her grip on him and her footing which sent her flying towards the door. Nonetheless, it worked! Between her tug and Rusty pushing with his other arm, he was able to clear the fallen section of roofing. Red dropped the post to help Rusty the rest of the way across the porch into the house behind Elsie.

No sooner were they all in the house, "Red, do you have a first aid kit? But that probably won't be sufficient . . . I'll need gauze, wide tape, forceps, iodine, . . .".

Red didn't let her finish. "I have all of that in the vet bag we keep on hand."

He turned to go outside.

Rusty grabbed his arm with his good hand, "It's not in the barn is it, mate?"

"Yep." Red went back the way they had just come.

Another eternity seemed to go by while Red was gone. Elsie busied herself with getting Rusty to the kitchen table and collecting other things she would need to work on his hand. Rusty was relieved to be in the house. Elsie started to gently wash his hand carefully to not bump the protruding pieces of wood. With the blood rinsed away, they could see how severe the injury really was. By the time Red returned with the bag, Rusty's hand wasn't as bad as it had originally looked. There were only a few splinters of wood stuck in the palm of his hand. None of them were in very deep. The messiest one was a sliver slid under the skin on the backside of his hand.

"What can I do to help?" Red asked with a wince when he got a view of Rusty's hand.

Elsie smiled as she replied to his question "Get some hard liquor for all of us. Then I'll need you to hold him down so I can remove these pieces of lumber without getting slugged."

The two men were not amused.

Irritation noticeable in Rusty's reply: "I wouldn't hit a woman under any circumstance."

Red headed to the cabinet in the living room for the liquor; stripping his soaked clothing as he went.

Elsie responded softly to Rusty's curt remark. "It's nice to know you aren't one of those men."

Something in the way her voice cracked as she spoke caught his attention. He noted an odd look in her eyes while they waited quietly for Red. She wasn't flitting about keeping her hands busy. As he tried to decipher what it meant, he heard bottles clinking. Red returned with the requested bottle of booze. His clothing replaced by an Indian blanket wrapped around his waist. In his day, Red was an actor of whom shirtless scenes sent women into frenzy. Time had taken its toll. The wrinkles on his face made him look wizened; those on his chest and abdomen reminiscent of a rubber chicken. He handed one of the bottles to Rusty.

"Thanks mate. Nice get up." Rusty smirked.

To prevent Rusty from saying anything further Red stated sternly. "If you start laughing, I'll hit you over the head with one of these bottles. And since you are going to refrain from hitting the lady while she tends to your injuries, I'm going to see if I can get a fire going."

A chill was seeping into Rusty sitting in his cold, wet clothing.

He took a long swallow from the bottle "Come on mate, let's get this over with."

She carefully removed the pieces of wood stuck in his palm first. None were deep enough to require stitches. Scrubbed, swabbed with iodine and taped with a thick padding of gauze—all completed with firm gentleness. The back of his hand worried her—should she remove or tape it in place until they could get him to a doctor? Rusty sensed her hesitation. Elsie stood to fill the bowl with fresh water. Making the decision for her, he yanked out the sliver of wood.

"Elsie, I may have made a mistake." His voice sounded a pitch higher than normal as the blood gushed from his hand.

"Rusty what did you do?!" Elsie wrapped his hand with the rag she had been using.

The pressure she was putting on it hurt substantially. He tried to pull his hand away.

"Don't! I need to keep pressure on it to stop the bleeding." She growled at him.

He forced his hand to relax. With the other hand, he took another swig from the bottle. This time Red walked into the kitchen wearing clothing. His hair was still noticeably damp.

"The wind cut back enough to allow a small fire to burn. The hail has turned to rain. Maybe in the next hour the wind will die to where we can get a big fire going." The older man explained. "Damn, I'm cold. How's it going here?"

"Rusty decided to doctor the one himself. Now I have to hold the little boy's hand till it stops bleeding." Elsie responded sarcastically.

Rusty gripped the bottle tightly as he lifted it to his lips to keep from saying anything.

Red looked at them both oddly. "Power has been out since that one hit the roof. I was going to check the breakers, then crank on the generator. Hopefully, the worst has passed enough for us to get a radio or TV signal to see how bad the rest of the area is."

Elsie nodded. Rusty took another drink. With Red gone from the room again, Elsie unwrapped Rusty's hand. It had stopped bleeding. It was supposed to stay wrapped, but the wound needed cleaning. She was as thorough as possible without making it bleed excessively again. She wiped any fresh blood before bandaging it. With the wounds safely covered, Elsie found pink veterinary wrap for protection of the whole hand. Plus, it would limit Rusty using it in a way that might cause further injury.

"There you go—all fixed." sealing it with a kiss on his forehead. "You might want to see about getting out of those wet things now."

Rusty took another drink, leered and slurred: "Care to help?"

Taken aback, Elsie stood to put away the first aid supplies. It was then she noticed the already empty bottle of booze on the table. Red must've brought another bottle in with him this last time.

"If Red could keep you supplied with booze to ease the pain, he can just as easily help you out of your wet clothes." A shiver ran through her causing goose bumps everywhere.

She hadn't even noticed she had gotten as wet as the men. Being men, both of them had noticed. Thus, explaining why Red wouldn't stay in the room long and Rusty's gaze had focused on her chest the entire time she tended to his hand. Elsie escaped to her room. Morbid curiosity enticed her to glance in the dresser mirror before stripping off her wet things. She knew the peach seersucker shirt probably looked like wet tissue paper. Any remaining modesty deserted with a gasp when she saw the silky peach-colored bra underneath had responded to water in the same manner as her shirt.

She consoled her image in the mirror. "At least they saw Marilyn. A year ago, it would've been Two-Ton Tilly".

CHAPTER FOUR

IN HIS ROOM trading his own wet clothes for dry ones, Rusty was chastising himself for his lewd remark to Elsie. She didn't deserve that kind of treatment. Especially after the way she had ventured out in the storm to help, along with taking care of his wounds with gentle competence. At least she hadn't seen him pause outside her door. Her gasp followed by the clearly audible remark. No more alcohol the rest of the evening. Elsie appeared to be a nice person with whom he shared similar views on a number of subjects. Her love of animals reflected his own. Also, the way no topic seemed to be taboo or even of foreign nature to her was strangely enchanting. Red's opinion of her spoke well, too. She'd been here quite some time with Red where they shared an easy camaraderie. Red's reputation in Hollywood after turning director and avid wildlife conservationist had won him the title of an unwelcoming recluse. This in combination with the attitude Elsie wore like armor made the comfortable ease about the ranch house seem in contradiction.

"The two of them, make that three, including me", Rusty said aloud, "are perfect examples of not judging a book by its cover. Or believing the tabloids."

Elsie thought she heard talking when she left her room. Red was in the kitchen. Who was Rusty talking to?

She tapped on his door, "Rusty is everything alright?"

"Er um, yes I was looking for socks" Rusty quickly yanked on his sweatshirt prior to opening the door.

Elsie started to giggle.

"What's so funny?", then Rusty saw the tag of his sweatshirt sticking from under his chin.

Not only was it on backwards, inside out as well. With an exasperated sigh, he pulled the sweatshirt off. So much for not wanting to do anything else to make Elsie feel uncomfortable around him . . . Fumbling to get it righted with his hand's lack of mobility, Elsie took it from him. She fixed it, then helped him put it on the correct way.

Rusty thought to himself, "Can this get any worse? I proposition her to help me get my clothes off and here she is being gracious enough to help me get them on".

"Why Mr. Garnet, are you embarrassed?" Elsie asked with mirth lingering in her voice.

Rusty smiled when he saw her face beaming with delight. Their last night together was going to be pleasant after all.

"What's for dinner mate? I'm starving!" He asked maneuvering her out the hallway.

The storm had caused damage across the region. Some counties were still without power. Numerous injuries reported with plenty of property damage. Under the circumstances, Red's ranch and guests faired well. Well enough to allow Red to fly Rusty to the airport in Helena to catch his commercial flight to California early the next morning as planned. Elsie had taken the dogs for a long walk shortly after breakfast; conveniently not returning to the house in time to say goodbye to Rusty. However, she had given Red instructions, which he relayed to Rusty prior to parting.

"Elsie recommended you go see a doctor about that hand. Also, I wanted to apologize for you getting injured. I had hoped we'd discuss more how I envision this movie and your role in it. That is if you are even considering taking part anymore?"

"No need to apologize mate. You were a great host. I actually enjoyed the excitement. Thanks for inviting me. As for my involvement with the movie, the answer is yes. I'll have my assistant call for the shooting schedule. You said you'd be starting sometime around August 1st, right?" The men shook hands and parted.

After a few steps, Rusty turned back to Red. "Please tell Ms. Endy I'll be heeding her advice, on both counts. See you mate."

CHAPTER FIVE

Rusty was able to get an appointment with a doctor regarding his hand within an hour of arriving in Los Angeles. Being a celebrity had its perks. The doctor commended Elsie's first aid of the injury. However, he felt stitches were required for the back of the hand. Plus, he prescribed a course of antibiotics to prevent infection.

After Rusty settled in, he was on the phone to his assistant, Sherry, about the movie. He also asked her to get a Ms. Endy's address from Red when she called him. The next morning Sherry and Rusty were having coffee while they reviewed his schedule.

"Mr. Roget said he'd overnight everything in connection to the movie by the 30th. When I asked him for an end date, he seemed evasive. Not to question your judgment, but this is a supporting role rather than as the main character?" Sherry said putting sugar in her coffee.

"Sorry, I was so tired when I called you yesterday that all I wanted to think about was bed. I thought I'd give you the details at our meeting this morning. Red and I came to a very interesting agreement. Along with the character I'll be playing in the movie, I'll also be working on the production side with him. I expect you to review the details of the contract with your usual efficiency when it arrives."

"Are you sure Rusty? Rumor has it Red Roget is one of the hardest directors to work with. It's his way or no way. Not to mention, you can be equally stubborn. Do you both believe you are going to be able to agree on the final product?" Sherry's skepticism was undeniable.

"I was apprehensive when Red initially pitched the deal. Any misgivings I had were put to rest after spending time with the man. Heck, I've always wanted to try the other side of the camera. This makes it an ideal situation." Rusty didn't let Sherry in on the rest of his reasons.

Even though he lived to play roles where he molded his whole being into another persona to the point it was hard to recognize his own self, it was exhausting. It was time to be realistic. Great movies with great roles were few and far between. He'd certainly had a lion's share of them. Other actors added to the competition every day. How strange that Elsie's comment about his film career validated this decision.

Sherry waited till she had Rusty's full attention again before asking the question that she feared one day would come "Does this mean you won't be acting anymore?"

"Not right away. It does however mean, love, that your job will become much easier. Allowing you to concentrate on that family you and your husband have been waiting for the right time to have!" He replied with a bit of a chuckle to lighten the mood.

"This Ms. Endy whose address you wanted wouldn't happen to have anything to do with this decision would she?" Sherry felt the need to tease back.

Rusty gave her a scowl. "Not that it's any business of yours. She was also at Red's. She patched up my hand and I wanted to send her a 'thank you'. That's all. I'll probably never see her again. She's not even my type."

Did he sound defensive? Evidently, since Sherry quickly hid an amused smile behind a sip of coffee. She felt Rusty deserved to have a good woman with whom to share his life. Something Celeste hadn't been even from the start.

Concealing her continued delight "Mr. Roget would not give me Ms. Endy's address or phone number. You said she was at his ranch, why not send something there?"

Rusty's displeasure was evident "Red's place is too far off the beaten path. It would take days for something to be delivered. I'm not even really sure how much longer she'll be there." He stood to fetch his cigarettes.

When he finished lighting one, he came to a resolve. "Guess a verbal 'thank you' will have to suffice. I'll call Red's when we finish here."

Their meeting only lasted another few minutes. No one answered at Red's ranch when he called. He didn't bother leaving a message. He'd try back later. Unfortunately, Rusty didn't think of it again till it was too late to call with the time difference. He promised to do it first thing in the morning. Again, no one answered. Rusty hung up the phone deciding not to pursue the matter any further.

CHAPTER SIX

TWO HOURS LATER, Dr. Edwards was exiting the elevator heading for the waiting room. She could see Rusty Garnet sitting forward with his head in his hands. Yes, her patient Elsie Endy had been correct about who he was. Mr. Garnet had won so many of Hollywood's top awards; she was surprised he wasn't being mobbed for his autograph. But then again, she herself hadn't realized who he was until Elsie verbalized it. He looked like any other Australian rancher—worn jeans, faded shirt, minus the dried bloodstains, Southern Hemisphere tan, six day stubble, wind combed hair.

"Mr. Garnet, please come with me to discuss Ms. Endy's condition." She stated at reaching him.

When he raised his eyes to meet her gaze, she could understand why this man could play such a range of outstanding parts from a macho hedonistic slave to a genius losing his grip on reality. Rusty's eyes were filled with unshed tears that magnified his concern for Elsie. He stood without saying a word. The two walked in silence until the elevator doors closed.

"H-how is Elsie?" His voice was gruff from holding the tears in check.

"Mr. Garnet I won't lie to you. Ms. Endy is still far from out of the woods. She received a severe blow to the head. Tests indicate no skull fractures, but she does show signs that her brain has swelled forming a subdural hematoma. At this point, we don't want to go in and relieve the pressure unless it becomes life threatening. That combined with her low blood sugar and high blood pressure from the shock is a concern. I realize you got here as quickly as possible under the circumstances. With those conditions, it wasn't fast enough—she has slipped into a coma. The other injuries she sustained . . ." The rest of the doctor's comments were lost to him.

Elsie was in a coma. He couldn't breath; the rush of his own blood was all he could hear. The elevator had stopped.

Dr. Edwards was standing outside the doors peering in at him, speaking "Mr. Garnet this is the floor Ms. Endy is on."

When he didn't appear to move, she stepped back into the elevator "Mr. Garnet, are you alright?"

He shook his head "Sorry, you lost me after you said Elsie was in a coma."

"It's understandable. Situations like this are a lot to take in. I'll continue on the way to her room". This time they both stepped from the elevator.

"As I said before, the rest of Ms. Endy's injuries are not life th, er um, as serious." Not wanting to lose his attention again, Dr. Edwards relaxed her no-nonsense doctor repertoire. "Two ribs are cracked on her right side along with hairline fractures in her right wrist. Thankfully, there are no spinal injuries."

They reached the door marked 416.

"I need to warn you. We needed to attach monitor leads. Also, she has a lot of bruising. We need to watch for blood clots." The doctor added prior to leading Rusty into Elsie's room.

He looked around the room at all of the equipment.

The doctor marked a few things on the medical chart. "I have other patients to attend to Mr. Garnet. Do you have any questions before I go?"

"Not right now. Thank you", Rusty replied

Elsie's stillness was unnerving; the silence of the room, eerie. The only thing giving him reason to believe Elsie was still alive denoted by the constant beeping of the heart monitor. The tears he'd been holding back were brimming over. Rusty clutched Elsie's hand as he slid to his knees unable to keep his emotions contained any longer. An hour had gone by before his grief and anger had been spent. With a kiss on her unbruised cheek, he left to search for the doctor to find out where they went from here. A few feet from Elsie's door stood the nurses' station. He had walked by earlier without noticing. A familiar male nurse stepped towards him as Rusty approached the counter.

"Mr. Garnet, I'm Nurse Osgood. I was one of the ER nurses on Ms. Endy's case." He waited until Rusty had nodded before continuing. "This is Nurse Smythe."

Nurse Osgood indicated a woman much shorter than him, and whose matronly form hinted at her years of experience.

"She'll be handling Ms. Endy's care." With that, he got in the elevator leaving Rusty in Nurse Smythe's capable hands.

"Please call me Katie, dearie. Did you have any question regarding Ms. Endy?" Nurse Smythe patted his arm as she spoke.

"She prefers Elsie. If the doctor's not busy, I'd like to speak to her again." Rusty replied.

Katie's voice restarted her hand patting "Go use the men's room, around to the left. Splash some cool water on your face while I page the doctor."

She removed her hand from his arm to gently push him in the direction of the rest room.

Upon looking in the mirror, Rusty hardly recognized himself. His face was smudged with tear streaked dirt and blood stains. His shirt and arms had the same appearance. With a little soap and warm water, Rusty looked better. However, his shirt was destined for the trash bin. It would have to wait until he had a change of clothes. He just hoped it didn't smell as bad as it looked. In the corridor, he saw a gentleman in a white lab coat talking with Nurse Katie.

"Here is the gentleman that was with Ms. Endy when she arrived." Katie said to the gentleman as Rusty came into her view.

"Hello, I'm Dr. Gallagher. I've been assigned to Ms. Endy." Dr. Gallagher said confidently. "I understand you have some questions."

Quite some time later, Dr. Gallagher was entering the elevator while Rusty stood in the hallway trying to decide what to do. The doctor had explained how the blow to Elsie's head played a large part in her coma. As long as she wasn't suffering from severe seizures and her vital signs were within normal ranges there was hope. In cases like this, it was a matter of waiting for the body to heal itself. How long it would take for Elsie to awaken from her coma was an unknown. As such, Rusty needed to decide if he was going to stay here till she regained consciousness or go back to the farm for a change of clothes. Plus, he should call the states to inform Elsie's friends what happened. Not a call he was looking forward to making.

Still standing in the hall, Nurse Katie bustled up to him. "Mr. Garnet, there's a phone call for you. It's your brother. You can take it at the desk."

"Thank you Katie. Please call me Rusty." He took the phone Nurse Katie handed him.

"Caleb this is Rusty . . ." Caleb was calling to learn how Elsie was doing.

Rusty filled him in on her condition. Caleb might be his younger brother, but he remained level headed when it came to this type of situation. He told Rusty to stay at the hospital. He would make the arrangements for a hotel room nearby. In the morning, he'd bring a bag of clothing for Rusty and Elsie's palm pilot. Nurse Katie gave Rusty the direct number to Elsie's room where Caleb could call with the hotel information. Not feeling torn anymore, Rusty returned to Elsie's room to hold her hand until Nurse Katie chased him out for the night.

Hours later, Nurse Katie came into Elsie's room. The light on the administration phone designated the line in the room had been in use.

"Excuse me Rusty. Was that your brother with your overnight arrangements?" She asked softly.

Rusty nodded. His bloodshot eyes displaying the exhaustion he felt from the day's events.

"Visiting hours will be ending soon. You are tired and haven't eaten anything. Go get a good meal and a comfortable night's sleep. You won't do your Elsie any good if you both need a nurse. Come back in the morning, dearie. Just leave a number where you can be reached." The experienced nurse took charge of him, too.

Rusty didn't have the energy to argue with the nurse. Especially since he knew she was right. After copying the hotel information Caleb had given him, he handed it to Nurse Katie. He bent down to give Elsie a kiss on the hand followed by another on her cheek. Nurse Katie followed him to the lift.

"No worries, dearie. We'll take good care of your Elsie." Her words comforted him.

CHAPTER SEVEN

CALEB MANAGED TO get Rusty a room at a hotel within walking distance of the hospital. Rusty hadn't realized he didn't have his wallet until he went to use it for check-in. Trust his brother to think of everything. He had explained the situation to the hotel manager who was most accommodating. Along with his room card, Rusty was handed a bag of men's toiletries. When Rusty entered his room, he tossed his shirt into the trash and took a shower. He poured a drink from one of the bottles in the mini-bar. He was able to smoke a cigarette thanks to Caleb asking the manager to throw a pack of into the bag along with everything else. Towel at his waist, damp hair, drink in one hand and cigarette in the other—standing on balcony gazing at the stars reminded him of the second time he met Elsie.

It had been a few days prior to starting work with Red. Rusty had returned to Fresno rather than Los Angeles after a quick trip to the family ranch. He had plans to do some networking during those few days till he departed for Montana. He should have gone to bed, but his body was still on a different clock. It was close to midnight. With a drink in one hand and a cigarette burning in the other, he stepped onto the balcony. He hadn't considered what he looked like with the light shining from behind, wearing only a towel tied around his waist and hair freshly damp from a shower. Startled by clapping, he turned in the direction from which it came. Sitting in the dark on the balcony next door were two women. He couldn't see very much of them except their hair color. One was a platinum blonde the other a brunette. When he turned towards them, they stopped clapping to raise their glasses to him. He returned the gesture. Surprisingly that's as far as the women went. Their little flirtation complete, the women continued their conversation from where it had been interrupted by his appearance. He leaned against the front railing gazing at the stars.

Twenty minutes and another cigarette later, the two women called "good night" in his direction.

Before he could respond, their door shut.

The following morning Rusty decided to have his coffee on the balcony in the hopes of getting a look at the two ladies in the daylight. This time he put a robe on before venturing out. Luck was going his way. The blonde was drinking her coffee on the balcony, too. She didn't see Rusty right away, which gave him a few minutes of uninterrupted perusal. And they said Barbie's figure had impossible proportions. When she saw him, she waved her left hand. Flashing in the sunlight was a diamond ring and matching wedding band. It would figure. She faced the doorway. The brunette must have spoken to her. She looked at her watch and nodded. Waving to him again, she headed into the suite. They were probably on their way to check out. A pleasant diversion while it lasted. It couldn't have lasted very long anyway since Sherry was due shortly.

Sherry was as always punctual and organized. " . . . And don't forget about the benefit party in San Francisco at seven o'clock tonight. They were delighted when they received the RSVP saying you'd attend. You don't by any chance have a date for it do you? Either way, I indicated you and a guest."

"What? You mean you didn't arrange a date? You're slipping, mate." He scolded her.

She ignored his jibe by eating the brunch he ordered for them. After all, it was noon and he hadn't had anything other than coffee for breakfast. It was almost two o'clock till they finished reviewing everything prior to starting work on a new project. Noticing he was almost out of cigarettes, he escorted Sherry to the lobby on his way to buy a fresh pack.

On the return trip to his room, he spied the two ladies from the balcony standing inside the main lobby. Was that the brunette with her back towards him? Her hair looked ablaze with red highlights that went unnoticed in the moonless dark. Rusty had an impulsive urge to say "hello". They were hugging by the time he walked across the lobby to them.

"Hello Ladies!" Way to go Garnet; that was original.

The blonde looked up "Hello Adonis. What time is the next balcony show?"

The brunette started to turn toward him when a bellboy intercepted her by asking if he could take the dress bag she was holding to her room.

The blonde giggled "You two have fun; I have to run!", then she was gone.

Having politely disposed of the bellboy with a "no thank you", the brunette was able to give her full attention to Rusty.

"Do you parade around like that every night or was that a one night only showing?" It didn't take more than a few seconds for Elsie's face to go from a flirtatious smile to unmasked embarrassment when they recognized each other.

"Rusty if I'd have known it was you, we wouldn't have intruded upon your privacy last night. I'm so sorry." Elsie stammered.

Rusty chuckled. "No problem mate. It's good to see you again."

Regaining her composure, Elsie asked, "Aren't you supposed to be in Montana?"

"Not for another couple days. This is a layover to adjust my clock. How long are you here?" He queried with interest.

"This is my last day here. My flight departs tomorrow morning at six." She answered easily.

"Do you and your friend have any plans for this evening?" A woman on each arm sounded enticing to him.

"No, Kay went home. She's Tycho's breeder. We hadn't seen each other since he was 8 weeks old. Even though this was a business trip, I had to make time to visit with her. Her husband agreed to watch the baby while she came into LA for us to have a girls' night out. And that level of detail is going 'blah, blah, blah' in your head now isn't it?" She tried to cease her babbling.

The more she talked, the more entertained he became. "Since you don't have any plans, come to a party with me tonight. It's a benefit in San Francisco given to support a children's fund. It's not a formal soiree. Whatever you have in that bag would probably do quite nicely."

Her response was not forthcoming.

"Please mate? Do a friend a favor. Sherry, my assistant, indicated a guest on the RSVP. If I go without one, it gives fodder to another tabloid story of me dumping this or that starlet or vice-versa." Rusty could be very coercive when he played the sap.

Finally getting her wits about her, Elsie volleyed. "How will you explain me?"

"That's easy! You're a friend I wanted to thank for helping me. And this is my 'thank you'". He had it all figured out.

"In what way did I help you?" Suspicion crept into her voice.

"My hand." he said holding up the healed appendage. "I wanted to send you flowers or something to thank you more appropriately, but Red wouldn't share your address. Think of this as your 'thank you'—free food, free booze. You can even have my party bag."

Elsie tenderly touched the small scar on the back of his hand.

When she looked up into his face, she smiled. "Okay."

"Wonderful! I'm on my way back to my room. Let me carry that for you." Rusty took the dress bag from her to escort her to her room.

CHAPTER EIGHT

RUSTY KNOCKED ON Elsie's room door promptly at 5:10 pm. He was wearing a dark blue sport coat, khaki colored Dockers with a white dress shirt open at the neck.

When Elsie opened the door, he couldn't prevent a low whistle of appreciation from escaping.

She was wearing a Japanese silk brocade street length dress with a slit halfway up each thigh. Its ocean blue coloring reflected in her eyes and enhanced the fieriness of her hair. Her only jewelry sparkled delicately from each ear as the teardrop sapphires copied her eyes in response to his exclamation. The tiniest of giggles escaped as she reached for her purse in duplicating fabric. She also had a light hand when it came to her makeup, preferring to subtly enhance rather than renovate. Not only did she look lovely, she was also ready to leave. Without any conversation required, he placed her hand in the crook of his arm to escort her to the limousine awaiting them. Once they were on the road, he noticed her fidgeting with—the hem of her dress, her earrings, her purse, her hair, her shoes. Since it was a fairly long drive, he tried to ease her nervousness by asking about the dogs and sharing details from his short trip home. Each time they drifted into silence, her repetitive movements resumed.

"Elsie, are you uncomfortable going to this party with me?" He finally asked in a gentle tone.

"You have to not laugh when I tell you this." She made momentary eye contact with Rusty.

"I am very uncomfortable with going to any party whether I know most of the people or not. Oddly, having you as my escort diminishes my discomfort. Don't worry. I'd rather be a wallflower than a clinging vine.

This is a friendly excursion, not a date." Her honesty was a refreshing change for him.

"I'll admit that I usually don't relish going to these events either. Let me know if you need me to do anything to make it easier. I want you to have a good time." He reached over to give her hand a squeeze.

At that moment, they pulled up to the entrance of the pier where the party was located. After assisting her from the limousine, he kept hold of her hand as a comfortable gesture of support.

The first part of the evening, they stayed within arms reach of each other while they mingled. However, when she returned from a trip to the ladies room, she was unable to see him. By now she was feeling fairly at ease, unworried she accepted her third glass of champagne from a server. There was an area designated as a dance floor at the far end of the pier. Elsie navigated her way by the couples dancing to watch the sea lions lounging on the floating platforms.

Unexpectedly, a man grabbed her hand pulling her onto the dance floor. Not wanting to be rude, she started to dance with the stranger. It was a fast oldie so the dance floor was fairly full. As the song ended, she planned on slipping into the crowd to avoid further contact with her current dance partner. The start of a new song indicated the end of the previous tune. Elsie stepped into the throng of dancers. On her way to the other side, she noticed a waiter taking empty glasses from guests. She left the crowd to dispose of her flute. No sooner had she given it to the waiter, she was being pulled back onto the dance floor. It was a different man. She'd finish this dance, then go in search of Rusty. The last drink must've been enough to make her tipsy. During this song, Elsie got turned around. Instead of making her way back towards the pier entrance, she was on the far side of the dance floor again. Being gracious was thrown aside as she wove her way out of the dancing mass. At this point, walking along the rail seemed to be the safest means of escape. Unfortunately, the next song was a slow one. Most of the dancers dispersed to the edge of the dancing area to await a peppier tune; thus blocking her exodus. Elsie was beyond uncomfortable, on her way to fear that she wouldn't be able to locate Rusty. An arm slipped around her waist to draw her to the dance floor as a second slow song began. Hands curled into tight fists, she turned to deal with this brute. All tension released upon seeing it was Rusty who held her in his arms. She stepped closer to him as he moved her deftly around the dance floor. Her head came to a rest on his chest with a contented sigh.

He whispered, "This not being a real date, was it okay for me to do some rescuing?"

Not bothering to move her head "Thank you. I was starting to panic that I'd never get away from the crowd."

"When I saw you standing at the railing, I wanted to join you. I seemed to have as hard a time getting to you as you did trying to get off the dance floor. It's almost midnight Cinderella; ready to leave before your escort turns back into a rat?" He self mocked.

"Yes, but can we finish this dance?" She requested timidly.

He tugged her further into his embrace, their bodies touching shoulder to knee. Her soft feminine curves molding to his undeniable masculinity. The warmth and strength of him enveloped her in a luxurious cocoon. Rusty inhaled deeply the delicately enticing fragrance of Elsie as they danced. It was a light sweet fresh scent rather than a heady musk or flowery perfume.

As the song played its final notes, he led her off the dance floor. They paused their departure from the party long enough to give their regards to the hostess. He waved for the limousine driver as they exited the pier. Both of them were silent during the drive back to the hotel, languishing in the ease of each other's company.

Neither of them spoke until they were standing in front of her door.

She was the one to speak after the door to her room was unlocked. "Thank you for a delightful evening. The dance with you was an unexpected bonus there at the end. Good night."

She stood on her tiptoes to place a kiss on his cheek. Then she was in her room closing the door between them. He went to bed content with the welcome diversion.

He woke with a start a few hours later. Glancing at the clock, he saw it was 9:06. Damn! He had set the alarm for PM not AM. He had missed saying goodbye to her. They hadn't made any plans, but he felt like they had the start of a really good friendship. It would have been a nice gesture to see her off since they wouldn't be seeing each other for a while. Not to mention, he still didn't have her address or phone number. The light on his phone flashed. Calling down to the front desk, he discovered they had a message from Ms. Endy for him. It was delivered to his room with his breakfast. The note read:

Rusty,

Thank you again for a wonderful evening. My friends say I don't do things like that as much as I should. I suppose if they turned out half as nice as last night and were shared with someone like you, I'd have to agree with them.

If you're ever on the east coast give me a call-610-767-0924.

Good Luck with "Mountain's Majesty".

Elsie   email: EENDYMAL@juno.com

Chapter Nine

Nurse Katie told Rusty to get a good night's sleep. Alas, sleep would be elusive. The thought that he might never again experience the things that made Elsie special—her laughter, her sentiment, her odd sense-of-humor, her quirky habits, her temper, her honesty, her welcoming nature, her softness—a sampling of the many things that might only exist in his memories. He stubbed out the cigarette butt and drained the last bit of liquor from his glass before lying on the bed. Closing his eyes in an attempt at sleep, he drifted into the past again.

Overall the shoot for "Mountain's Majesty" had been going smoothly. They were miraculously ahead of schedule. The weather cooperated for the numerous outside shots. The cast got along famously. The production crew was A-one. Plus, against everyone's foreboding, Red and Rusty worked well together. They were more or less in agreement upon reviewing the approach to scenes and the results of what they had on film thus far. Until they discussed how a pivotal scene should be shot in the upcoming weeks. Depending on what they decided would determine how certain follow-up shots would be handled as well. Unfortunately, the two men coming from their usual different perspectives were unable to meet in the middle as previously. They had both presented their scenario to the other, but neither would budge from their own vision. Their disagreement so intense that neither one showed for coffee while the production crew held their 15 minute morning assembly. This issue could have a profound affect on the rest of the crew if they didn't come to a resolution relatively quickly. Not to mention, how it would impact on the final edit. Rusty knew that both he and Red were too close to the situation. Each felt they had too much riding on this to have it not go the right way; in this case, their own way. Maybe Elsie could help him find a way to get through to Red. She might have better insight on how to handle this predicament.

Rusty tried to contact her at various times that morning. He really wanted to speak with her before he had to be on the set with Red. He'd left a message each time with his business number. Only two people had his personal cell phone number—his assistant Sherry and his brother Caleb. Once Sherry had confirmed a caller, she would forward the call to his cell phone. If Sherry was not sure of a caller, she would take a message to relay to him the next time they spoke.

If nothing else, both Red and Rusty could be professional no matter how strong the undercurrent. Rusty did the afternoon's scene the way he was directed. Red's tone didn't hint at the misunderstanding existing between them. The crew unaware tempers were simmering below the surface. Prior to the final shot of the day, Red received a phone call. It must have been important since he asked Rusty to direct the final scene to take it. Red returned looking displeased as the crew was wrapping for the day. Before Rusty had a chance to extend an olive branch by asking if anything was wrong, his own cell phone was vibrating. Finally, it was Elsie. Ignoring the usual amenities, he explained to her the impasse at which the two men found themselves. Then without thinking, he asked if she could fly out to play mediator. Her tired sigh on the line had him realizing his faux pas. He tried to smooth it over, but she cut him off by saying she needed to think about the situation. She promised to contact him tomorrow.

The next morning went by with no call from her. Maybe calling with this dilemma had been a mistake. After all, he hadn't spoken to her since the party on the pier. Now to call her out of the blue to fix something which had no bearing to her was way out of line. Then expecting her to be at his beckon call by asking her to drop everything to fly halfway cross the country . . . The words "selfish bastard" rang in his ears. Berating himself was thankfully interrupted by the need to answer his cell phone. Rather than Elsie, it was Sherry with a message from Elsie. The message instructed him to avoid discussing anything related to the scene with Red until she contacted him again in the next few days. He should've been consoled that she hadn't completely blown him off like he deserved. Since they were ahead of schedule, Red and Rusty announced that after tomorrow's final shot, the cast and crew had three days off. Maybe it would give him and Red time to talk without affecting everyone else. While they were reviewing the dailies, Red told Rusty he made hotel reservations for the following evening for both of them. The cast and crew had thrown together a party to be held in town. Red felt they should be in attendance to keep the family feeling going.

With town two hours away, Red stated, "it made good horse sense" to stay overnight.

Perhaps a night of revelry might put both men in a better frame of mind.

The party had been pleasant enough. Rusty kept telling himself he wasn't having as good a time as the one he went to with Elsie because it wasn't on as grand a scale. Like the hoi polloi of a party ever deterred him from a good time. Red retired to his room around ten o'clock. Not feeling inclined to be alone to dwell on things, Rusty was one of the last to leave. When he woke the next morning, he called Red's room to see about breakfast and riding back to the ranch together. Much to his surprise, Red had checked out. However, the keys to his truck with a note had been left for Rusty. The note included a list of errands that needed to be run before he returned to the ranch. Rusty puttered around town following Red's instructions, then headed for the ranch house mid-afternoon.

CHAPTER TEN

THE EARLY OCTOBER evening turned chilly. Parking the truck in front of Red's house, Rusty saw smoke rising from the chimney. Red must be home if there was a fire burning in the fireplace. As Rusty carried parcels into the kitchen, sitting at the table wasn't only Red. Much to his surprise Elsie was there, too.

"Elsie, you came!" Rusty exclaimed excitedly.

Elsie glanced at Red, then at Rusty.

"Yes, I'm here." She said flatly. "I'm still trying to decide if this was a good idea. I suppose your timing could've been worse. You have exactly four days to get this disagreement resolved. Less if I get an emergency phone call."

Standing, she continued. "Now that I've had a nap, I'm going to take a shower. I've already heard Red's intentions for the scene. While he makes dinner, I'll listen to your version."

Rusty watched her until her door was closed.

Turning to Red "Uh, I should've told you I called her."

Red smiled "You don't need to explain. I did, too."

The men went outside to fetch the remaining items from the truck.

"Is it just my guilt or is she peeved?" Rusty asked.

"Yep, she burning mad at both of us for, how did she put it? . . . Oh yeah, 'acting like a pair of rutting bulls'. And somewhere in her colorful rant 'if she had wanted children, she wouldn't have dogs.'"

"I didn't see the dogs. Are they in her room?" Rusty queried.

"There's a topic on thin ice. It seems a couple of the dogs caught a nasty virus at a dog show. Tycho got deathly sick and some of the dogs in her friends' kennel contracted it as well. Plus, her friends had left for a week on vacation the day before the first one started showing any signs of illness. Her boy Tycho had to spend two nights at the vet along with one of theirs. The dogs have gotten over the worst of it. During it all, she spent a lot of stress filled sleepless nights."

Once the bags were on the kitchen table, they started unpacking them.

Red continued. "With the dogs so sick, they had to change plans on some upcoming shows; thus opening up her schedule. However, leaving the dogs this soon is fueling her irritation with us."

Rusty was confused with the information Red shared. "Why is she here then? For that matter, why did you call her about this? I called her looking for a sounding board."

"She asked me not to tell anyone who the screenplay was written by until we had the film in the can. With the way things turned, I felt it was time to pull her in." Red explained.

"And my phone call to her with the irrational suggestion to fly out added to your request of active involvement." Rusty summarized his part.

"She does have a personal stake with this her first motion picture. She doesn't want us ruining a solid piece of work over our prides." Red finished.

When she returned to the kitchen both men smiled in her direction.

The shower improved her disposition; she looked far less tense. "Rusty are you prepared to discuss your point of view?"

Rusty nodded. With a notebook in her hand, she led him into the living room to hear his version. Almost an hour later, Red announced dinner was ready whenever they were. Dinner was steeped in an apprehensive silence. She needed time to digest the two scenarios in order to find a solution everyone liked without diluting the story. After dinner was cleared, they all retired to the living room for drinks. Red selected some classical musical to combat their ongoing silence. After a period of time, Elsie had made them suffer enough over pulling her into their stalemate. She cleared her throat loudly to break the reverie they had fallen into watching the fire.

"Okay you two. First, both approaches are good. I understand why you can't agree. I'm not sure which way to go without reviewing the whole script again. However, there could be an easier, more productive approach to finding the answer. If it could be done?" She had their full attention.

"Would it be possible to put together a rough cut of what you have filmed so far to get a better impression of how the story is translating into film? You know, see and feel how the actors and you interpreted the story." Elsie waited patiently while they thought about it.

Finally, Red responded, "It will take us all day to piece it together. It would be a very rough version, especially with the scenes we haven't shot missing throughout the storyline."

Rusty chimed in. "For the missing pieces, we could put a placeholder with a little summary to keep a frame of reference as the story moves forward."

Red spoke to Rusty. "We have to make a list of the crew we need. Call them tonight to be at the editing building first thing tomorrow morning."

Looking at Elsie, he asked. "Will you be okay here alone tomorrow?"

"Just leave me a number where I can reach you and be back before dark. I'll be on edge with as black as it gets here without the dogs as an alertness gauge." Elsie said before taking another sip of her drink.

Red and Rusty went into the kitchen to make all the arrangements for the next day. Elsie stayed up well beyond the time Red and Rusty went to their rooms. Filled with the excitement of working on the rough cut, Rusty wasn't able to fall asleep right away. After a while, he heard her go into her room for a few minutes, then back out to the living room. He thought he should apologize for the way he acted on the phone the other day. Getting up, he pulled a shirt on to cover his bare chest. As he approached the living room, he saw that she had changed into flannel pajamas. She was propped—pillows behind her shoulders with her laptop perched on her raised legs—on the sofa. The classical music CD had been replaced with a soft rock CD. The fast clicking of the laptop keys could be heard.

"Excuse me Elsie." He interrupted her key staccato.

Startled, she jerked to a full sitting position causing the laptop to slide off her knees. She barely prevented it from crashing onto the floor.

"I'm sorry. I didn't mean to scare you." He apologized.

She looked at him wide-eyed while she placed the computer onto an adjacent sofa cushion.

"I wanted to apologize for the way I acted on the phone the other day. I couldn't believe what a selfish jerk I was." He stumbled through the overdue apology.

"Actually, 'selfish, inconsiderate prick' were the words I used when I hung up. I was going through hell with the dogs and you call me acting like your problem was the worst in the world." She pelted him with the full force of her anger. "Not a word from you for over two months, then I get a 'Henny Penny, the sky is falling'!"

Elsie was pacing the living room like the dogs had the morning they had met.

"Oooh, the gorgeous and famous actor called plain little old me. I should drop everything to obey your every whim what with the great gift you bestowed upon me." As intended, her sarcasm angered and hurt Rusty.

The worst of it, she was absolutely correct. He hated to admit, even to himself, thinking all of those things when she hadn't called him back immediately.

"I am here to resolve this issue, then I will be away from the likes of you. Maybe those tabloid stories aren't that far from the mark. I don't know why I thought you'd be different!" Her anger spent, she repositioned herself with her laptop in an attempt to dismiss him.

After a few moments of silence, Rusty spoke full of remorse. "You're right, I deserved that. I was sorry to hear the dogs had gotten sick. I know how much they mean to you".

Elsie's gaze met his full of defiance.

Finishing quickly, "I hope they are in good health for that special show coming up", with a hasty retreat to his room to prevent facing her fury further.

In the morning, Red roused by five o'clock to start the coffee while Rusty showered. When Red went to stoke the fire, he found Elsie asleep on the sofa. By the time he was done building up the fire, Rusty was on his way out the hall.

"Mornin' Mate." Rusty felt refreshed.

"Good morning." Red replied.

Scrunching his face, he whispered. "I want to bring wood in from outside so she has enough while we're gone, but I don't want to wake her. You think you could carry her to her room?"

Rusty pondered for a moment. "Sure, but somehow I don't think she'll be too happy with me if she wakes up in the process."

He carefully removed the laptop from its current location. After pulling the blanket aside, he hoisted her into his arms. She stirred enough to snuggle into his broad chest. Her bed was still rumpled from the nap she had taken yesterday afternoon. It allowed Rusty to slip her legs under the covers easily. As he was pulling the blanket into place, he noticed her pajamas had become partially unbuttoned. One creamy white mound was exposed to the circle of pink. Rusty was tempted to caress its smooth softness. Before his hormones made matters between them untenable, he tucked the covers around her neck and left the room. The two men disembarked from the ranch house by six o'clock.

CHAPTER ELEVEN

THE FEW CREW members they had contacted made it to the site by 7 o'clock. They were disgruntled about having their weekend cut short. When Red assured them it was merely a postponement of a day, they stopped complaining to focus on the task at hand. With the caterer off, they had to call an order into town by 10. By the time lunch arrived, they were ready for a break. Red and Rusty reviewed the first part of the cut while they ate. Pleasure with what they saw rejuvenated them for the rest of the afternoon. They lost track of time. It was close to 6pm when the phone in the edit room started ringing. Red answered it. It was Elsie wondering how much longer they would be. There was no problem. She was getting nervous alone in the middle of nowhere. Red covered the phone to speak to Rusty without her hearing. He thought it would take another two hours to clean up what they had, make the final compilation and copy it to a disc. It would take another hour and a half to review the cut before copying which didn't include any further edits. They agreed to not bother with the final run-through before making the copy. That still left her alone for another three hours—two hours of work plus an hour of drive time. It made more sense to have Red work the last two hours since he was familiar with the equipment. Rusty reluctantly agreed to drive the truck back to the ranch house to stay with Elsie. One of the crew would drive Red out before heading into town. Removing his hand from the mouthpiece, Red assured Elsie she would only be alone for another hour.

The ranch house was darker than Rusty expected as he drove up.

He was barely through the door when Elsie began chattering. "How'd it go? Where's Red? You didn't argue did you? Are you hungry? I made dinner. I already ate, but I can heat a plate for you. Do you want a beer or something else to drink with it?"

Elsie's babbling only served to accentuate her fidgeting. She must have been beyond nervous, well into scared. Who could blame her? He was getting itchy to reach the ranch driving in the pitch black on the desolate dirt road. After he took his coat off, he gently caught Elsie in his arms which stilled her instantly.

Speaking softly, "I realize you are probably disappointed it's me. I hope we can make the best of it until Red returns in a few hours."

He felt her tension ease.

"Yes, I am famished and would greatly appreciate a hot meal." Then he dropped his arms to allow her to move away.

Instead of darting for the kitchen as he expected, she stayed put looking up into his eyes.

She took a deep breath, then exhaled before speaking. "I'm glad it's you."

Rusty's eyebrows rose in a curious expression.

"About last night . . . please let me say this" when Rusty tried to interrupt. "I wanted to apologize for being hurtful."

Rusty couldn't let her continue, "You had every right to be angry."

"Rusty!" Her voice was no longer soft when she spoke, "I'm not apologizing for being angry. I'm apologizing for wanting to hurt you. Whether you were truly sorry or acting, I should have graciously accepted your apology."

Rusty felt they needed a change of topic. "No worries mate. Did you get much sleep after we left this morning?"

"I slept till about ten thirty. I take it I owe you the 'thank you' for tucking me into bed?" Her eye contact with Rusty faltered as her face infused with bright pink.

She must've wondered if her buttons had worked their way open before or after he had deposited her in bed.

"Yes. I tucked your covers around you to prevent you from catching a chill." He couldn't help smiling at the picture of her from this morning, which came to the forefront of his mind.

Elsie went into the kitchen to hide her embarrassment under the guise of putting together a plate of food for Rusty. It was mind boggling to see this response from her. The last time they'd been at the ranch with Red, she had sugarcoated nothing in their conversations. Judging from last night's thrashing that still held true. At times she had been clinically descriptive or as guttural as a horny truck driver. She was a divorced woman in her thirties who could intimidate a man with one look. Now here she was behaving *shy* over something so simple. Rusty shook his head in bemusement while he hung his coat.

During the meal, Rusty learned that Elsie could only stay a short period of time because she had entered the dogs in a Malamute only dog show in Sturbridge, Massachusetts at the end of the month. She wanted a little extra time to make sure they were healthy enough to go. She also needed the time to help Sara pack the RV for taking the three adults and seven dogs. Elsie's face became animated as she talked about her friends, Sara and Tom, and the specialty they planned to attend. After Rusty helped Elsie clean up, they went into the living room. She put another log on the fire while he selected their listening entertainment. They chatted for a short while prior to falling into a companionable silence watching the fire. By 11pm, they were both yawning uncontrollably. No sooner had she voiced concern in regards to Red than they heard a car door shut. They greeted him at the door. He was too exhausted to eat anything. The three of them agreed to wait until morning to view the tape together. With their alarms set for seven, they all went to bed for a good night's sleep.

Chapter Twelve

Rusty and Elsie were awake by six. He was first in the kitchen. He heard her go into the bathroom for a shower. By the time she was in the kitchen, he poured two cups of coffee with cream.

He handed one to her. "Good morning mate."

"Thanks. Good morning to you. Any stirrings from Red?" She said as she sat at the kitchen table.

"Not yet. Maybe the smell of coffee will wake him." He joked.

She nodded in agreement. "What's for breakfast?"

Before he had a chance to answer, they heard the outside door open and shut followed by boot stomps.

"Good morning. Glad to see you're both awake. I thought I'd be eating cinnamon rolls alone." Red said as he walked to the coffee pot.

Seeing the look of confusion they exchanged, he explained. "I've been up for over an hour. Since I wasn't seeing any signs of life from either of your rooms, I figured I'd take care of the horses in the barn."

He opened the oven to reveal a pan with a towel across it, then turned on the oven. "We're having cinnamon buns for breakfast if that suits everyone."

Elsie and Rusty nodded.

"I've already had them rising. After the oven is done heating, they'll take about 25 minutes." Red mimicked Betty Crocker.

The topic of conversation became the pretty little dapple-gray filly born a few days after the hail storm. It didn't take much thought to name her Hailey.

After the rolls were in the oven and the timer was set, Red turned towards the living room. "What are we waiting for?"

Elsie raced back the hall to her room for her notebook and script. When she returned to the living room, the men had gotten the same from the study. Red had the remote. They agreed to not discuss anything until they'd viewed it once. However, pauses to write ideas or comments was allowed. Without disturbing her, both men went into the kitchen when the oven timer buzzed. Red iced the cinnamon rolls to place on plates. Rusty handled getting fresh coffee for the trio. The men retuned to the living room placing the fare on the coffee table. When she started to get up, Rusty waved her back down. Like any good manservant, he carried a plate and cup to where she was seated. He even tucked the napkin in at the neck of her shirt. Without thinking, he patted the napkin against her chest. She looked at him wide eyed as if he were insane. He realized what he had been doing, then backed away from her while making an exaggerated face and holding his hands up in a shrugged apology. She rolled her eyes at him before re-focusing on the film.

There was one scene that was meant to be a real tearjerker. Neither one said anything because they wanted to see her true response.

The scene wasn't quite over when she yelled "Tissues!!"

The men did a high five as they fetched a box of Kleenex. Elsie ignored them as she dried her face. Finally, the story wrapped with the end of the movie. She was still sniffling as she carried her pile of used tissues to the trashcan. The men had gathered the dishes to put in the dishwasher. For a moment, she watched the m. After which she gave each a kiss on the cheek.

"I'm going out to see Hailey", was all she said.

She went to her room to put on her boots. The two men were dumbfounded. They waited to talk about the film until they heard her go outside. It was almost noon when Elsie re-entered the ranch house. Red and Rusty spent the time she was gone very productively. Neither man had noticed that she had taken her notebook along to the barn. Upon her return, she went into the kitchen to get a hot cup of coffee. The two men joined her.

She was ready to chat. "Hailey is a very pretty girl."

Red nodded his thanks.

"Did you two come to a meeting of the minds while I was gone?" She asked hopefully.

Red spoke first. "We had a very productive talk. Overall we are very pleased with it. We are also consistent on the things we do and don't like to this point."

"But?" She interjected.

Rusty spoke this time. "But now instead of going with Red's or my idea for that particular scene, we don't think either approach is right anymore."

She smiled. "Well we all agree then. Do you guys mind if we watch it again after lunch? Then you can fill me in on some of the changes you already know you want to make. We might find the answer while talking about other scenes."

When lunch was ready, they moved to the living room. Red and Rusty couldn't wait to give Elsie their commentary. Quite a few hours later, they were all spent. If they talked or thought about the movie another second, their heads would explode.

"Who would've thought discussing a movie could be so exhausting? I need a break." She said.

"How about a ride to air the cobwebs?" Red suggested.

Rusty readily agreed. She hesitated.

Red understood from her last visit. "Don't worry Elsie; I had Molly brought in from the pasture this morning."

To bring Rusty up to speed, he expounded. "Elsie loves horses, but she's a tenderfoot when it comes to riding. I have quite a few gentle mares. Elsie is partial to Molly."

Rusty had to ask "Why Molly?"

Elsie answered. "It's the name of Sara and Tom's therapy dog. She is one of the sweetest dogs anyone could ever meet. Red's Molly has the same soft brown eyes as malamute Molly. I couldn't ignore synchronicity that strong."

Rusty chuckled. "I suppose if I were in your boots, I'd probably feel the same way."

The trio put on riding accessories—boots, hats, leather gloves and lined coats, then headed for the barn. It was a beautiful day. With a few hours till sunset, they could enjoy a leisurely ride. The big sky immersed their senses.

Pinks and oranges streaked across the sky by the time the trio returned. Each took care of the horse they had ridden prior to moving to the house for dinner. The two men kept a lively conversation going through the meal. Elsie was unusually quiet. Less than an hour from when they adjourned to the living room, she excused herself.

"If you'll excuse me gentlemen, all that fresh air has me falling asleep sitting here." She offered as she stood.

"Elsie you can't go to bed. We haven't had dessert yet." Red tried to coax her into staying. "I had Rusty get a cheesecake for you."

She lightly teased, "You boys enjoy it. And if possible, please leave me a slice."

Then she paused her departure to add, "It was a nice day. Thanks and good night."

"You're welcome. Good night" from Red.

"Sleep well, mate" from Rusty.

The only problem with going to bed early is waking at an odd hour. When Elsie roused at two o'clock, she was wide-awake. After locating the cheesecake, she cut a huge slice of it and poured a glass of milk. She watched the tape once more while she savored every bite of the rich, creamy dessert. An inkling of an idea had worked its way to the forefront of her mind. Not wanting to lose the inspiration, she stopped the DVD without turning off the player. She got herself another slice of cheesecake to nibble on while she outlined a suggestion. It was getting light outside when she finished. The pages waited on the table for Red and Rusty along with a note not to disturb her. When the two men arose, they found it. They both liked the pitch—problem solved. Red called one of his assistants to make the arrangements for her to go home the next day. Not that they wanted to get rid of her. On the contrary, they both wished she could stick around. Unfortunately, she had a separate life on which they had imposed. It was only fair to let her go home since she'd accomplished what she had come to do.

She watched most of a day of filming prior to her departure. Since Rusty wasn't needed for any of the scenes late in the day, he went to the airport with her. The line at the security checkpoint was non-existent. Rusty and Elsie hugged. He stayed while she had her ID verified before stepping through the metal detector.

He called to her. "I'm going to miss you mate."

She laughed. "I doubt it. Good luck with the rest of filming."

One final wave goodbye, then she was on the escalator moving swiftly from sight.

CHAPTER THIRTEEN

RUSTY WOKE TO someone knocking. Looking around the room, he remembered where he was and why. He opened the door wearing the hotel robe he'd donned last night. It was Caleb. The two men hugged. After Rusty was dressed, they set out for breakfast. The brothers talked about nothing of importance. Rusty had already filled Caleb in on Elsie's condition yesterday and there had been no calls informing him of any changes. Another hug, the brothers parted. Caleb started his return trip to the ranch. Rusty walked to the hospital. He spent the morning there. Elsie's condition had improved slightly, but she was still comatose. In his hotel room, he stretched across the bed. A call had to be place to Sara and Tom. If the accident had occurred in the states, Sara would be on her way there. Being half the world away made it very difficult. He couldn't call the states for another couple hours. Maybe he could catnap in the meantime.

After Elsie left the filming in Montana, Rusty had made it a point to call her every couple days. His daily schedule made it difficult to call her at normal hours. She told him to call whenever he found time, particularly since she did her best work at odd hours. He learned she was reviewing a screenplay of one of her books. Her approval was due to the studio executives by the end of the week. They had agreed to let her know their intentions within the month. However, she felt it was bad luck to speculate further until she'd gotten confirmation. At first they talked work, the dogs and the weather. As time went on, they discussed anything that crossed their minds. Since he was somewhat isolated, she took immense pleasure in sharing the latest tabloid stories featuring him.

Red and Rusty shot the last scene the week before Thanksgiving. The wrap party was held in town. Rusty wished Elsie was there. She said it was frivolous to fly out for one night. Plus, she'd didn't relish getting on an airplane again for awhile. Selected members of the production staff stayed through Thanksgiving to assist in the editing process. Red wanted the finished product no later than Christmas. Even though the release wasn't scheduled until summer, he wanted it done.

The final edit was completed a week early. Rusty stayed at the ranch for a few extra days. He flew into LA two days before Christmas. Sherry fetched him from the airport. The lack of a project in the upcoming year was the topic of conversation on the ride from the airport. After dropping his things by, they met her husband Harris for dinner. During dessert they exchanged Christmas presents. Rusty had a 5-day all-inclusive package to a resort in New Mexico for the couple. It had a PGA rated golf course, which suited Harris to a tee. And Sherry would love the spa. Rusty could hardly wait to open his gift. Every year Sherry was creative with what she got for him. When he opened it to discover a book, it was an anti-climax.

Upon seeing his disappointment, she realized he needed enlightenment. "I take it from your face you don't know anything about this novel?"

He raised his eyebrows indicating she continue talking. "It has gotten rave reviews and been on the bestseller list for months. It was sold out everywhere with back orders unavailable until January. The publisher had to do another printing. Harris did some work for one of their executives last year. He was able to pull a few strings to get this one while the glue was still hot."

He appreciated the thought glancing at the back of the book jacket. "It looks interesting. It'll give me something to do over the next few weeks. Thank you."

"Look closer." Sherry poked the front cover.

"Sifting through the Ashes a novel by" Rusty read aloud "E. Endy. Oh. Wow!"

This time he flipped through the pages. An envelope slid out.

Sherry answered his questioning look. "Open it."

It held a round trip airline ticket from Los Angeles to Allentown with a list of available flights over the next two weeks. Handwritten on a slip of paper was an address. He was speechless.

Harris explained. "When I received the FedEx package with the book, I called the fellow to thank him. He asked if I was looking for more clients. When I said 'always', he asked if I would be willing to suggest ways for Ms. Endy to handle her increasing finances and pending contracts. She had asked for recommendations which wouldn't cause a conflict of interest. My name came to mind. If I were interested, he would forward it to her. She called me right away. Thus, the address."

Sherry added. "As for the plane ticket, tell me which flight and I'll call to finalize."

A giggle escaped from Sherry when Rusty jumped up to give her a big hug.

As he sat back down, he said, "I believe you've outdone yourself this time!"

"Don't forget to call Ms. Endy to let her know you'll be coming for a visit." Sherry added.

"Harris, you didn't happen to mention to Elsie that your wife was my assistant, did you?" Rusty questioned.

Harris replied. "No. I answered her questions, but offered no additional information. However, I must add that speaking to her over the last few days I felt as though I was lying by not telling her. She seems like a very nice person. I'm looking forward to meeting her in January. Since I'm flying to New York to meet with another client, I thought I'd take the train into Allentown for an extra day. When I told her Sherry was coming along, she invited us to stay at her place for the weekend and see her quaint little town."

Sherry continued where he stopped. "From the different things she said to Harris, we were able to come to a few conclusions. She lives alone in a very rural area. Her house sounds like a bed-n-breakfast by invitation only. And she has no reservations or closings until we arrive."

She winked at Harris with that last bit.

"So she has no idea I have her address or that I'm going to call her to pick me up at the airport?" Rusty's question reverted to a statement when they both nodded.

An odd feeling came over him.

"How was Elsie going to react when he invited himself to stay with her? And, oh by the way, I'll be there in forty-eight hours." He thought to himself.

Harris and Sherry dropped him at the hotel on their way home from dinner. It was too late to call Elsie. He knew from their last talk that she'd gotten through the screenplay on time. This allowed her a month to catch up on other things before she started working on something else. Unless, she got inspired, instigating a new project. Better to wait for morning to make the call.

Elsie was delighted to hear from him. After the usual amenities, he addressed the reason for the phone call.

"What are your plans for New Year's Eve?" He asked.

She replied "Nothing really. I like to spend it with the dogs. Some of the neighbors go shotgun happy at midnight so I want the dogs safe in the house. What are you doing?"

"I was kind of hoping to spend it with a friend and her dogs." He spoke matter-of-factly.

Total silence followed.

He wanted to fill the gap, but he couldn't think of anything glib to interrupt the long silence.

Finally, she responded with disbelief. "You want to come visit me for New Year's Eve doing nothing?"

He spoke hurriedly. "I thought it might be nice to spend a few days relaxing. Who better than with you? If it's a problem, no big deal, I can stay here in LA."

"No! Er, yes! I mean yes, come visit." She paused a moment to pull her thoughts together before speaking again. "I'll set up the guest bedroom and bathroom. When will you be flying in? What airport? What kind of food do you want? What . . ."

He interrupted. "I'll have to call you back with a definite flight and time. But I was hoping to fly into Allentown the day after Christmas and stay until the third. Is that okay with you? If it's too long a stay, please let me know. I don't want to be an imposition."

It was Elsie's turn to cut him off. "You are more than welcome. You just took me by surprise. And I'm not a very good cruise director."

Rusty chuckled at her rambling. "As far as I'm concerned, whatever you do or don't plan is fine with me. Don't feel you need to entertain me."

Something she did without trying.

"As far as food, why don't we worry about that when I get there?" He didn't want her footing the bill.

Plus, it would give them an excuse to drive around the small town.

They ended their conversation so he could call Sherry. When he called Elsie back that afternoon to give her the flight information, she'd had time to absorb he was going to visit her. This time enthusiastic delight was quite evident in her voice.

CHAPTER FOURTEEN

RUSTY DEPARTED LOS Angeles at 6am the morning after Christmas. He was filled with anticipation at spending eight days with Elsie. To keep himself occupied Christmas Eve and Christmas day, he'd read Elsie's novel. Not at the end yet, he read on the flight and layover. He completed the final chapter on the flight from Pittsburgh to Allentown. He was in awe. To think, the woman he was flying to see had written this story was difficult to fathom. There was a depth to her which she rarely let other than her closest friends see. She was the kind of girl whom people never took a second glance. She was also a genuinely caring person. That was the Elsie he had gotten to know over the last couple of months. To juxtapose that Elsie with the one who wrote the novel in his hands appeared to be diametrically opposed. The tale she had written was a testament to the complexity of her mind. Rusty started to wonder if he was out of his league. The captain's announcement to prepare for landing interrupted his contemplation. His flight had arrived on time—4:30 in the afternoon. With the security changes at airports over the last decade, she was unable to meet him at the gate when he disembarked from the airplane. They agreed to meet at the baggage claim carousel.

He spied her first. Definitely not putting on any heirs, she was wearing hiking boots, jeans, mock t-neck and an oversized sweatshirt. Not that he faired much better in worn jeans, faded polo shirt, discolored penny loafers and a tattered baseball hat. Evidently the baseball hat worked to hide his identity, since Elsie didn't know it was him until he was a few feet in front of her. She had looked his way a few times. It wasn't until he was walking directly towards her the realization dawned on her face into a dazzling smile. He dropped his coat and carryon bag at his feet to free both arms with which to hug her. She dropped her own hat and coat so she could throw her arms around him. Their embrace had to break when his hat fell off. When he bent to get it and his bag, he grabbed her garments as well. On the short walk to the carousel with the flashing light, he playfully plunked the Iditarod emblazoned hat onto her head, then took her hand into his. They chatted about the flight and the weather as they waited for his suitcase. The weather was damp and drizzly. He was feeling chilled on the jaunt across the parking lot to her jeep. It would be almost 6pm till they reached her house.

A sigh of relief escaped as she parked the jeep in her garage. When they opened the door to the screened-in porch, a herald of howls could be heard. She showed Rusty to his room before releasing the dogs from their crates. Normally the dogs would be in their sixteen by six foot kennels outside. Wet dogs are smelly; wet malamutes resemble wet wool. The dogs also believed in exuberant re-acquaintances. A welcoming ritual preferred without muddy paws and drippy hair. The dogs commenced sniffing and rubbing against Rusty as he joined Elsie in the kitchen. By the time she was topping their Irish coffees with whipped cream, the dogs' fervor had been exhausted. Sophie and Tycho lazed on the floor watching for food to drop. Elsie handed Rusty his coffee followed by walking into the living room. He and the dogs followed. She flipped on The Weather Channel. With her feet tucked underneath her, she settled on the sofa. Rather than picking either chair in the living room, Rusty sat on the other end of the sofa. Sophie curled on the cushion between the two people while Tycho claimed the spot under their mistress.

Looking at Rusty, Elsie asked. "Do you mind?"

"Mind what?" He didn't understand.

She sent a pointed look at the large pile of gray fur between them.

"No worries mate." He remarked.

"At least you got her head. I warn you, she might try for some whip cream. They like to see how much other people will let them get away with." She stated. "If she does get on your nerves, tell her 'off' while giving her a push."

Referring to the television, he queried. "When's the rain supposed to stop?"

After swallowing a mouthful of coffee and cream, she answered. "It should stop sometime overnight. Be prepared for feeling like Dorothy on her way to Oz. Winds are supposed to worsen. They can get quite strong. One good thing, it dries everything quickly. First thing tomorrow morning, I'll have to walk around outside to fetch things and check for any damage."

She paused to watch him scratch Sophie's muzzle.

When he looked at her, she continued to the extended forecast. "We should probably go food shopping tomorrow since they're predicting snow for the 29th. And we don't want to be anywhere near a grocery store on the 28th. Everyone makes a mad dash for bread, milk and eggs the day before it snows. It happens whether the prediction is for an inch or a blizzard."

"Sounds like fun. Let's go that day instead." He hid his smirk by taking another drink of the velvety brown liquid.

Her words full of acid. "Then you'll pay for any damage done to my car. And . . ."

He couldn't contain his amusement any longer. His chuckle stopped her indignant little speech. She pulled the pillow from behind her to toss at him. He easily dodged the flying pillow. Their quick movements riled the dogs into standing positions. Before either person could react, Sophie was licking the inside of Rusty's glass mug and whacking Elsie in the face with a wagging tail.

"Sophie! Off!" Elsie gave the insistent dog a shove. "Sorry about that Rusty."

With renewed humor, he responded. "No worries mate. I was done with it anyway."

His cup was empty.

Standing, she asked "Would you like another one?"

Reaching for the licked clean glass mug, she added "In a fresh cup."

Instead of handing it to her, he stood, too. "Yes. Let me help you."

He turned her to face the kitchen, then gave her a little push to get her moving.

As he got the can of whipped cream from the refrigerator, he started talking again. "My assistant Sherry and her husband Harris gave me your book for Christmas."

He paused to see if she would connect the dots.

She didn't miss a beat as she reached for the hot pot of coffee. "I take it your talking about the book that's been so popular. "

She continued verbally unraveling the clues from what he'd said. "I know Sherry is your assistant and that she's married. Her husband's name is Harris. That's new or is it?"

Her eyebrows arched as she looked at Rusty. "Sherry and her husband wouldn't happen to be the same Harris and his wife who will be staying here for a couple days so Harris and I can discuss my business arrangements?"

He started spraying whipped cream onto one of the coffees. "They are."

Seeing her lips purse to contain a biting comment, he explained. "I know we had discussed your need for someone like Harris, but I didn't orchestrate you getting his name. Believe it or not, it was a pleasant coincidence. I only found out when the three of us met for dinner after I flew into LA. I phoned you the very next morning."

Her minor irritation abated, she asked "Why didn't you recommend him?"

"I didn't want you think I was trying to weasel in where I might not be wanted. If you're worried that I don't think he's good at his job, you can stop. Harris gets high marks on both ability and integrity. Even though he tends to be too business oriented and stuffy, he's an okay guy." Rusty replied returning the whipped cream to the refrigerator.

Elsie was satisfied with his answer. "Do you want something to eat with your coffee this time? I have cookies and an almond coffee cake."

"If the rest of your pantry is as stocked, why are we going for groceries?" He couldn't let the tease pass unsaid.

A shy embarrassed filled her face when she answered. "Well, I ran to the bakery this morning for some donuts. The coffee cake looked scrumptious, so I got that too. When I was carrying them in from the car, I felt my cell vibrate. Thinking it might be you, I tried getting it out of my pocket and dropped everything. Anyway, I managed to save the coffee cake. The donuts were smashed. Their edible, but I didn't feel right offering them to a guest. I needed a second item in case you didn't like almonds. Since I had plenty of time, I baked peanut butter and chocolate chip cookies."

With a chuckle, "Not only does she mediate and write books, she can bake too."

He gave her a quick hug. "How about both?"

He'd been with her only a few hours and felt genuinely relaxed. Something he only ever felt at home on the farm.

A small table with two stools was in the center of the kitchen. They chose to use that instead of returning to the living room. He handled turning off the television. Meanwhile, Elsie set the pastry feast on the little table to go along with their Irish coffees. They talked about the book while they nibbled. The dogs fell asleep at sentinel positions. The clock chimed midnight as they were putting the food away. After saying good night, he went to his room. She headed downstairs to run the dogs prior to going to bed.

He wasn't really tired since it was still only 9 o'clock according to his body. Looking around the room, he noted its sparseness. The bed was a queen-size mattress and box spring on a metal frame with no headboard. A cherry dresser, from the early 70s, was against the wall between the windows. A plain off-white ceramic lamp set on a matching nightstand. The window treatments were tasteful—mauve blinds framed by tied back white lace curtains. A pretty pattern was stenciled in mauve at chair rail height. Even the ceiling fan blades and lampshade contained the same stencil pattern. What looked like a wood chair to a dining room set was against the wall opposite the bureau. It was spray painted in off-white, to hide years of scarring. It also exhibited the stencil pattern in mauve. It wasn't until he had finished unpacking his bags and removed them from the bed that he noticed the handmade patchwork quilt doubling as a bedspread. Its base color was dark blue with mauves and creams scattered throughout. Going into the adjoining bathroom, it had the same stenciling on the walls as the bedroom. On the sink was a basket full of soaps, shampoos, lotions, and other sample size sundries. The shower curtain, rugs, towels and washcloths were unadorned solids in colors matching those found in the quilt. Another look around the bedroom, Rusty could see the hominess of Elsie's personal touches, which further invoked a feeling of welcome. With the warmth of that sentiment and the quilt wrapped around him, Rusty drifted into a blissful sleep.

CHAPTER FIFTEEN

AFTER SIX HOURS of sleep, Rusty woke to howling. However, it was difficult to differentiate between the sounds caused by the wind versus the dogs. Wearing only boxers, he shivered under the covers. He heard a door slam, but no scuffing and pounding from the dogs barreling up the stairs. Then it sounded like water was running downstairs. He got up to take a hot shower. Dressed in his warmest clothing, he emerged from his room. This time when he entered the kitchen, the dogs weren't there to greet him. He leaned against the doorway to watch Elsie prepare coffee. Her outfit's only difference from the day before was a fuzzy sweater replacing the sweatshirt. He could smell a sweetness emanating from her.

"There must be a full bath downstairs" he thought to himself.

When Elsie turned from the brewing coffee maker, she gasped in surprise.

"Rusty! Goodness I didn't hear your door open or you come out the hall." She said catching her wits.

"Good morning mate. Where are the dogs?" He said cheerily.

"Good morning. They're in their kennels eating. After breakfast when I go outside to check things, I'll let them out." She replied. "Are French toast and sausage okay for breakfast?"

He nodded. When the coffee maker beeped, he poured them both a cup while she prepared the food. During breakfast, they chatted about the wind and the substantial drop in temperature. He helped her clear prior to donning their coats and gloves to go outside. She also pulled on an ear warmer band. They went outside via the front door to the screened in porch. The same porch they'd passed through from the garage the night before. Outside Rusty was surprised at how much the darkness and rain had distorted things. The house sat back from the road much farther than he'd thought. He hadn't realized the driveway was curved not straight. The garage was actually at an angle pointing towards the back of the house, which explained why the enclosed porch was an odd shape. They continued around the garage to the rear of the house. At the corner of the garage, they walked down a slope towards the back yard. A six-foot high chain link fence surrounded the yard. There were mature trees of all kinds growing in the yard.

Elsie explained as they entered through the gate. "The property is two acres with a full acre fenced in for the dogs."

When the dogs saw them, they began to "woo"—asking to be released from their side-by-side kennels.

She continued checking the house as she walked towards the dogs. Realization struck Rusty looking at the rear of the house. It was built into the landscape—the downstairs opened at yard level. When she released the dogs, she cleaned their kennels. He was expecting the dogs to greet him like the last night. Instead, they only gave him a perfunctory sniff before racing to the far end of the yard. She kept a watchful eye on them as she and Rusty walked along the fencing. Meanwhile, the dogs frolicked with an overabundance of energy. By the time they'd finished walking the perimeter, he was chilly. He wasn't wearing enough layers for this kind of cold.

"Elsie can we go into the house from down here or do we have to walk around to the front?" A shiver could be heard in his voice as he spoke.

She nodded, then whistled for the dogs. After kenneling the furry fiends, they walked towards a set of French doors. He was astonished when they stepped inside. He expected a utility room. It was a master suite; or in this case, a mistress suite. The room was directly under the bedrooms upstairs with their combined size. A wood-burning stove in the corner to the left of the door with a slate hearth forming a triangle heated the space. She sat on the chest to the right of the door to remove her boots. As she removed her coat, she walked across the room to move the mouse on her computer. He shed his coat while standing in front of the stove to get warm. Once his front was toasty, he faced the room. There was a dog bed and a laundry sized basket full of dog toys by the blanket chest on which she had been seated. In the opposite corner from where he stood was a small television. It was flanked on the left by a bookcase and on the right by a modest dresser. A Queen Anne chair covered in creamy brocade with a plaid chenille throw draped across it set a few feet in front. In the corner adjacent to the stove, Elsie's queen-size bed dominated. The comforter matched the snowflake wallpaper border, throw rugs and treatments on the French doors. A quilt rack displaying another handmade quilt hung on the wall over the bed. Limited edition wolf prints and photographs of dogs in show stance decorated the walls. It was cluttered in comparison to the bedroom he was using. With all of the space, it looked lived in rather than chaotic.

She had been watching him take in the room while she perused her email.

When his gaze finally settled on her, she spoke. "Do you approve?"

"It's quite nice. I take it you have a bathroom, too." He responded.

"It's across from the stairs. I also have walk-in closet under the stairs. The door between the stairs and bathroom leads to the furnace, hot water heater, and laundry area that doubles for washing dogs." She said motioning towards the hallway.

He walked over to open the door for a peek.

"That makes sense. The door under the kitchen leads into the utility room." Looking at the ceiling above her bed, he commented further with a mock lecherous leer. "The room I'm in is directly over yours. Hmm."

"Just leave it in your imagination Garnet." She chastised him. "What do you want to do now?"

"Since you're being no fun mate, I guess I'll have to settle for going to a mall to buy something to keep me warm." He said faking a shiver from her cool response.

"You wussy Aussie turned Californian. This kind of weather is great. The only thing missing is the snow." She teased ignoring his sexual innuendo. "We can go to the mall, then stop by the grocery store on the way home."

He donned his coat again as they walked upstairs. On their way to the garage, she grabbed his baseball cap from the coat tree.

"Don't forget your disguise." as she tossed it to him. "By the way, if you get mobbed, I'm leaving you there."

They arrived at the mall as it opened. Luckily, it was fairly sparse. She got a great parking spot. It didn't take too long or too many stores for him to get what he needed. What freaked her was that he carried a huge sum of cash with him. He couldn't really use credit cards or Traveler's checks without drawing attention. But he'd spent four hundred dollars without the easing tension on his plain money clip. At least he had fifties not hundreds, which the stores wouldn't have accepted. The mall had become quite crowded in the last two hours. A few people stared at him as the duo made their way to the exit. The plethora of department and specialty store bags filled half of the cargo space of her jeep. At the grocery store, they bickered like an old married couple about what and how much to buy. The cart was full when they got into the checkout line. Rusty insisted on paying for the groceries. The cashier waited for them to argue it out.

"Rusty, I am not a pauper. You are a guest in my house. I will pay for the groceries." She bristled.

"Elsie, I invited myself to visit and I'm not spending money on a hotel room. I'll pay." He groused back.

"Didn't you spend enough money at the mall you need to wave some more around?!" She hit below the belt.

"That was uncalled for mate." His tone brusque, then it softened. "Please let me pay?"

"You're right that was low." She conceded defeat "How about fifty-fifty?"

"Seventy-thirty and you have a deal." He countered.

"Oh alright!" She quickly calculated the amount to give him, which he added to his cash to pay the cashier.

After loading the groceries, the jeep was packed full.

"You said we have to go to a state store for booze." He reminded her of wanting to get alcohol.

Not only did they stop at a State Store, also a beverage warehouse for case of beer and flat of soda.

Bags were moved to ride on top of the Yuengling Lager and A-Treat. One of the bags of clothing was shoved in a corner against the roof to make room for the champagne and wine.

"When on earth do you expect to drink all of this? I mean, I don't mind the occasional pickling of my liver, but not a constant barrage." She remarked sardonically.

It was a little after two in the afternoon when the car had been unloaded and groceries put away. Elsie put a roast chicken in the oven for the evening meal. She grabbed a beer on her way downstairs to let the dogs run the yard. He also grabbed a beer to stretch in front of the television in the living room. He woke an hour and a half later. After searching the upstairs with no luck for Elsie, he wandered downstairs. Stepping onto the last step, he could hear her talking. Not wanting to intrude upon her phone conversation, he went back upstairs. The aroma from the roast chicken permeated the kitchen. It looked like she hadn't started anything else to serve with it yet. Fifteen minutes later, she discovered him peeling potatoes. The pot on the stove started to boil. He saw her watching him as he slid the last potato into the pot with the others.

"Was your telephone call anything important?" He made conversation as he cleared the potato peels.

She got plates from the cupboard to set the table. "Not really. Sara just wanted to chat. We exchanged gifts Christmas morning at their place. She was happy to hear I already had a chance to use the electric griddle. Plus, she wanted to know if you had arrived safely."

"You told your friends I was coming for a visit?" He asked in a curt tone.

"Don't get cranky. I only told Sara and Tom a friend I met at Red's was visiting." She said without subterfuge.

"I couldn't very well have someone stay over living out here in the boonies and not make sure someone else knew about it. Not to mention, Sara is notorious for stopping by on a whim. If she'd see you before me, she'd call the cops thinking you were an intruder. Can you imagine the fiasco that could lead to? The tabloids would run headlines like 'Rusty Garnet Arrested in Sex Hideaway' or "Rusty Garnet vs. Small Town Justice". Which would you prefer?" She used an obvious trigger.

"Okay mate, point taken." He agreed.

When they were done with dinner, she brought the dogs inside. However, they wouldn't settle. After a half hour of their pacing and unsuccessful attempts to find a comfortable spot, she determined their issue.

"I spend very little time up here. They aren't used to it. I'm going to kennel them." She stated.

Much later in the evening, she put together a tray of snacks similar to last night to go with Irish coffees. He emerged from his room with a big box when as she placed the fare on the coffee table.

"Merry Christmas!" He exclaimed cheerily.

"What? Is that for me?" She was dumbfounded.

"Santa Claus left this in Montana for you." He placed the box on the sofa.

Without saying a word, she dashed down the stairs. Seconds later she returned. She handed him a bow hiding a box.

It was her turn to say "Merry Christmas. You open yours first."

Inside the box was a sterling silver howling wolf head money clip.

"It's lovely. Thank you." He stated heartfelt. "Now yours."

He could tell she had been more excited about his opening the gift from her than the one for her.

She was speechless as she pulled out a pewter blue canvas barn coat sporting the film's logo on its back. She slipped the coat on to check the fit. A DVD and picture frame were in the bottom of the box underneath the coat. The frame held a photograph of Red and Rusty from on the set with a personal note and autograph from each. The DVD had the name of the movie on it along with big block letters stating "BLOOPERS".

Finding her voice, she said. "Thank you Rusty. Can we watch it?"

He put the DVD into the player. Pushing the box aside, they sat on the sofa together.

While they waited for the DVD to load, he commented on her still wearing the coat. "I take it you like it?"

She grinned real big. "It's even the right color. Was this a cast and crew gift set?"

He chuckled at her insight, but could see she was enjoying the package nonetheless. "The coat was. Your picture is only of Red and me. The rest of them got a whole group shot unframed. No one else even knows about the bloopers. Red and I cut it especially for you. The master is locked in Red's safe."

Conversation halted while they watched. It was an hour of gaffes and acting goofy. She laughed so hard tears ran down her face. That alone made the trip worth it, he thought. When they said good night a little before midnight, it included a warm embrace.

The snow that had been predicted amounted to no more than a few inches. It was sufficient for the dogs to go into a frenzy of rolling and digging. He delighted in watching the dogs play from his bedroom window. It was after eight this morning when he finally roused. Upon seeing the snowy layer outside, he thought it best to wear one of the mock t-necks and flannel shirts. Elsie was not in the kitchen when he went for a cup of coffee. He even had to start the coffee maker. Laughter from outside moved him to the large window to view of the backyard. Unfortunately, he couldn't see her. The sound of a door closing echoed up the stairs. He moved back to the kitchen to get them both coffees. When she didn't appear, he carried her cup downstairs.

Without a free hand or a door to knock on, he called for her when he reached the bottom step. "Mate?"

She didn't respond. He continued advancing. When he reached the doorway to her room, the sight caused his breath to catch in his throat. Her back was towards him while she fueled the stove. Her flannel nightshirt many sizes too big stopped at her knees. Socks that matched the yellow plaid in the nightshirt were scrunched around her ankles. Hair stuck in all directions from pulling off a knit hat. The child-like appearance of such a capable woman stunned him. Not wanting her to think he was spying, he reversed from view.

He cleared his throat loudly from the stairwell. "Ahem. Good morning mate."

Her feet shuffled across the floor as she responded. "Come in Rusty. Good morning."

When he offered her one of the cups, she said appreciatively "thank you. I could use something warm on the inside."

"You should've asked for help carrying the wood." He said noticing the stacked woodbin.

She shook her head. "You were asleep. And I'm used to doing it myself. As you can see, I haven't gotten through the shower yet."

Her free hand on his elbow directed him back to the stairs. "So if you don't mind going back upstairs."

"Okay, you don't have to push mate." Before complying, he stopped for a moment. "If you don't let me help the next time, I'll take it as a personal insult."

As he took the stairs two at a time, he smiled at her sound of exasperation.

Later, he joined her to Sara and Tom's to fetch a bail of hay. With a forecast of temperatures dropping into the teens, the dog boxes needed extra bedding. Upon their arrival, he thought there was a pack of wolves nearby from the intensity of howling as she parked. A woman with gray-streaked brown hair tied on her head in Pebbles Flintstone style appeared from below the opening garage door. Both women started chattering at the same time. A black and white dog resembling a stockier version of Tycho ran over wooing at Rusty. Since his ears were flattened giving him a familiar goofy expression, Rusty crouched down to his level. After the requisite face sniffing, the dog trotted away to lift his leg on the closest tree. Elsie made the necessary introductions once they were all in the house. Rusty wasn't sure if she purposefully omitted his last name. Neither Sara nor Tom showed any signs of recognition. It wasn't until Tom and Rusty drove Elsie's jeep to the barn that Tom's demeanor changed slightly. As if something had amused him. Rusty didn't recall saying anything funny while they were conversing about the property. Elsie and Sara were in the backyard when the men returned to the house. Upon joining the women, Rusty discovered what it was like to be the center of attention for seven malamutes. Elsie had warned him that they would be boisterous. However, they were cuddle-bugs at heart. When the dogs huddled around him, he was filled with elation rather than fear. Even as the dogs growled at each other as they vied for a closer position, it didn't bother him.

After a few minutes, the women growled at the dogs "Enough. Go play."

All but two of them obeyed.

Elsie spoke alone this time. "The seal or darker girl is Page. She's Tycho's sister."

He crouched down for the two bitches to greet him properly.

"G'day Page", he said as Page licked his face.

The other bitch was snuffling his ear so he turned to her.

"You do that just like Sophie . . ." his words trailed off.

She looked like Sophie. "But we left you at home."

Elsie and Sara were giggling.

This compelled Tom to enlighten their bewildered newcomer. "You did. Deedles and Sophie are littermates. They've baffled a few judges when they've been in the show ring at the same time. The judge will look from one to the other as if his eyes were playing tricks."

Pointing a thumb in the direction of the gleeful women, he continued. "As you can see for yourself, these two enjoy immensely."

To which they simultaneously stuck their tongues out at him.

Tom gave Rusty a knowing look. "You want a beer?"

Rusty nodded, then followed him into the house. The two men enjoyed their beer while talking about the girls and the dogs. By the time the girls came inside, the men were talking about the adjacent properties.

Rusty had to ask. "Why don't you have any farm animals?"

"I wanted a cow, but Tom said no." Sara answered pouting.

"That's because you would have it sleeping in the bed with us and the dogs!" Tom parried.

They were all laughing now.

Their banter was full of love and respect. He had been more than a little surprised to discover that Sara had a son Elsie's age. Her vivacity made her look younger than her years.

Sara invited them for lunch. "Tom cooked a pot of chili yesterday. There's plenty if you'd like to stay."

Elsie gave Rusty a questioning look. To which he nodded in affirmation. Sara worked on heating it while Elsie grated cheese and sliced a loaf of fresh bread.

"Why don't we watch a movie instead of another football game?" Sara spoke pointedly to her husband.

He relinquished by pulling a movie from the cabinet to place into the DVD player. The girls were still concentrating on the food when he hit play on the menu. It had played long enough for Rusty's name to appear on the screen. Tom stopped and ejected the DVD. He definitely knew the man sitting in his house was the actor Rusty Garnet.

Sara had noticed Tom getting up after being seated for only a few minutes. "Is something wrong?"

Tom tried to answer sensibly. All anyone could hear was muttered gibberish.

He glanced at Rusty who spoke to save them from further discomfort. "I saw that movie a few days ago so I asked if we could switch to another."

"As long as it isn't football." Sara responded vehemently.

After spending a few hours with them, Rusty could see why Elsie spoke about them so much. On the drive home, Rusty wondered how the conversation went when Tom told Sara who Rusty was. He didn't have to wonder too long; they hadn't been through the door five minutes when Elsie's cell played "Who Let the Dogs Out". It was Sara. From what Rusty could see of Elsie's expression, Sara was giving her a rough time for not sharing all of the pertinent facts in regards to her house guest.

Elsie covered the phone to speak to him. "It's going to take a little while to soothe Sara's feathers. Would you please carry the hay to the kennels and let the dogs run?"

When he nodded, she mouthed a "thank you" as she returned her attention to Sara.

He tossed the bail down to the yard from the porch. He went into the house to go through Elsie's room. On his pass through, he couldn't help overhearing her end of the conversation.

"I understand you being miffed. I knew you would react this way and was putting it off. Give me some credit! I gave myself the same lecture numerous times." She finally had a chance to speak. "You know as well as I do that the tabloids stories are someone's overactive imagination spinning a tale from a rumor or chance sighting."

Her voice stopped, but she paced around the living room in agitation.

"Yes, I like him. We are friends, nothing else! I am not deluding myself by thinking we could be anything more than that!" She had gotten loud and her tone turned sarcastic, "yeah right! Like Mr. International hunk who has starlets falling at his feet would think of me in that way!"

Rusty was glad he was at the bottom of the steps where he couldn't hear anymore. On one hand, he was glad to see she was being realistic about their friendship. On the other, her last two comments had stung startlingly. After filling the dog boxes, he brought the dogs into the house with him. He hoped they'd help Elsie feel better from her tiff with Sara. Assuming she was off the telephone. Rusty sighted her cell on the kitchen table when he hung his coat. The dogs were already trotting to the living room. She was sitting on the sofa flipping through the television channels. He could tell by her watery blood shot eyes that she'd been crying. The dogs were trying their best to lick away the evidence. He was sure she wasn't upset with him. The thing he didn't know was whether she was upset with Sara or herself. However, he did feel partially responsible. After the dogs gave up, he knelt in front of her.

"I'm sorry if my visit has caused waves. Is there anything I can do mate?" He asked.

She took a few moments before raising her gaze to his.

"Denounce your throne and have plastic surgery to change your looks." A smile tugged at the corners of her mouth in an attempt to make light of the situation.

Steadily holding her gaze, he didn't let her off the hook. "Are things okay with Sara? "

A sigh escaped as her attempted smile evaporated. "She understands. That doesn't mean she's okay with it. She's worried. It isn't your fault."

He sense her hesitation. "I take it there's more to it than the obvious."

When she started to talk again, he hushed her. "Shh. You don't have to tell me. If you want to talk, I'll listen. But if you're not comfortable, I understand."

Her gaze faltered as her eyelashes fluttered downward. "Forget about it."

She stood as if leaving it behind.

Heading for the kitchen, she stated. "I'm having a bowl of ice cream with lots of Hershey syrup, whipped cream and pecans."

Turning to look at him, she attempted another smile. "Are you joining me? Or do you prefer being morose?"

This time he let her have her way. He was certain she wasn't troubled merely because Sara had been upset with her. There was something else to it which Sara had dredged up. Rusty would have to wait until Elsie resolved it for herself or shared it with him.

The rest of his stay consisted of the same uneventful routine. It was very comfortable and relaxing. He thoroughly enjoyed socializing with the dogs. His greatest pleasure came from learning Elsie's quirks. The way she kept busy—tidying things, preparing an elaborate meal, emptying her sewing basket. Early mornings seemed to be her most peaceful. He would watch her from his window. There were instances she would stand perfectly still watching the dogs frolic. In the afternoons and evenings they would watch movies. She would flip through the movie channels in the same order: HBO, AMC, TBS, TNT, UPN, and SyFy. This was not the cable order; it was her order of preference. Since it was the holidays, "An Affair to Remember" with Cary Grant and Deborah Kerr aired. She started sniffling at the scene in the theatre with "Hello". Another holiday movie was "Desk Set" with Katherine Hepburn and Spencer Tracy. It wasn't a tearjerker, but he could see how she identified with it. When of all things "Halloween:

H2O" aired one afternoon, she insisted on watching it. He obliged by allowing her to hide in his shoulder till the scary scenes were over. Their routine varied slightly New Year's Eve. Instead of Irish coffees and cookies, they had champagne, cold shrimp and stuffed mushrooms to ring in the New Year. And the dogs stayed in the house overnight.

By the morning of his flight, he could tell she was ready for him to be gone. The odd part, it didn't bother him because he understood. During the two weeks over the holidays, she had specifically not done any writing. Her self-imposed restriction was to be lifted New Year's day. It had been extended on his behalf. She was more than ready to get back to work. Also, having not lived with anyone for two years and eight years with someone of the opposite sex, it was not an easy adjustment. Granted the level of comfort they shared made it fairly easy. However, it did infringe on her way of life. And he had demands awaiting his return to California.

Chapter Sixteen

Rusty re-read Elsie's book between his return to California and the string of award ceremonies he was scheduled to attend. For a change, he was anxious to see certain people at the award show parties. With the right adaptation, her novel would make an outstanding movie. The lead role was going to be a challenge to portray. And he wanted it. First, he needed a director who felt as passionate about the story as he did. If Rich Taylor were eager to direct, the rest would fall into place. They hadn't spoken since Rusty split with Celeste and went back to Australia. Rusty asked Sherry to see if Rich would be willing to meet. Before Sherry had a chance to contact Rich's assistant, she called to set an appointment with Rusty. The earliest Rich had available was two days after this weekend's festivities.

At the Golden Globes, Rich and Rusty were seated tables apart. After trading the usual amenities, Rich told Rusty that he would talk with him at the first break. Having had the honor of working together on "Planetary Motion", they understood each other fairly well. Rich knew the actor could be impetuous if not given the opportunity to voice his opinion. Rusty couldn't contain his enthusiasm when Rich waved him over during the break.

"Have you read or heard about the novel 'Sifting through the Ashes'?" Rusty said taking the seat next to Rich.

A smile that would've made the Cheshire cat proud formed on Rich's face. "Yes. Yes, I have read it. And found it most fascinating."

Not into playing games, Rusty revealed his idea. "I think it would make a really good film with the right screenplay adaptation."

"Then that makes is a consensus." Rich commented.

"Does that mean something is in the works?" Rusty asked feeling deflated since the cast had most likely been selected.

"There are too many ears to continue this conversation here. Can you join us for breakfast at seven tomorrow morning?" Rich said scanning the immediate crowd for anyone who might be listening.

"Tomorrow at seven." Rusty accepted as he stood.

The two men shook hands. Rusty mingled his way to his assigned table.

Their breakfast meeting went much different than Rusty had envisioned. He was expecting to be told the basics and that his interest was appreciated, but all parts had been filled. Instead, Rich handed him a screenplay with the main character's name highlighted on the list of characters. Before Rusty could ask any further questions, Rich told him to read as much of it as possible prior to their scheduled meeting the next day. Rich also gave him a projected shooting schedule along with locations. Everything they discussed needed to be kept quiet. Rusty spent the next twelve hours reading. If he had any doubts about playing the lead, they were dissolved upon reading the screenplay. He felt as if it had been tailor-made for him. The part would revitalize his career; thus allowing him to retire from acting with grace. Maybe not stop altogether, but take small supporting roles and cameos. The next morning, he reviewed the shooting schedule with Sherry. By the time he met with Rich, Rusty had enough comments and questions that he hoped they had adequate time. At the end of their meeting, Rusty had his answers. Only final approval of his playing the main character remained. Certain things were still under negotiation with the author. Rich promised he would notify Rusty by the end of the week. Rusty thanked him, then left without telling Rich he knew Elsie. He didn't want to risk a conflict of interest that might ruin the deal for either of them. One thing Rusty knew for certain, he was glad it was Rich, not him, haggling with her.

When Harris returned from his trip east, he was pleasantly surprised. As nice as Elsie was, she was unyielding when it came to business. Coming from Harris it wasn't a complaint, but a high compliment. She had definite goals and expectations. Harris was able to work with these rather than trying to guess what she might want. Rusty had been somewhat annoyed that he didn't know what those were. This had been a source of amusement for Sherry.

A woman whose opinion of Elsie had been simply stated, "I like her."

And nothing further had been said to expand on it.

Rusty couldn't decide if it was good or bad that Sherry had said nothing in regards to Elsie since. He talked to Elsie that Monday. She'd shared the good news that her latest deal was in the end stages. Also, the romance novel due at the end of April had a completed first draft. The anxiety over waiting for news about the film caused her to throw herself into the new book. He wanted to share his news with her, but it would have to wait until all of the details were ironed out.

It took till the end of the week for Rich to call Rusty. He sounded exhausted. They'd spent the last week getting the rest of the cast signed on. Less than an hour ago, they agreed to final terms with the author. The movie was a go. Filming would start in two weeks in New Orleans to catch the end of Mardi Gras. The crew would also travel to the Appalachians, New York City, northern New Jersey, Cambridge, Vermont, and New Mexico. Rusty was the only cast member required at all locations. The rest of the cast would join them per the shooting schedule at their designated scene site. First, he called Sherry to work arrangements with Rich's assistant. Then Rusty called Elsie.

Answering, she babbled with excitement. Her current story had been mailed to her editor that morning. Sara and Tom had agreed to watch the dogs while she was in New Orleans. She had always wanted to go to Mardi Gras. Now she had her chance. Most significantly her first serious book was going to be made into a blockbuster movie. The ultimate compliment came from the celebrities. The majority of side characters important to the storyline could be considered bit parts. When the big stars were asked to play these roles, most of them jumped at the chance because they loved the book. Somewhere in her rambling she mentioned she was looking forward to seeing him again. There would be a minimal allotment of time together with them both being so busy. Rusty wasn't sure if she said that to save him face or if she was giving him the brush off. After they disconnected, he chastised himself for not accepting what she said at face value. Granted, he didn't know everything about her and probably never would. One thing he was sure, she'd been brutally honest with him in the past; there was no reason to stop now.

CHAPTER SEVENTEEN

LYING ON THE hotel bed, Rusty dreaded the telephone call he had to make to the states. He hoped Tom would answer rather than Sara. It took him a few minutes to retrieve their number from Elsie's palm pilot. He programmed it into his cell so he didn't need to repeat that test of his patience. Only the machine answered. Having no choice, Rusty left a message stating there had been an emergency and requested a return call no matter what time. Not knowing what else to do while he waited for the couple to call back, Rusty slipped into the past to be with Elsie.

Mardi Gras didn't disappoint. It was the perfect setting to step into character. A house outside of town had been rented. Rusty, Rich and the minimal film crew set up shop within days of each other. The only one missing was Elsie. It gave them a chance to scope out a few specific locations without wasting her time. Rusty and Rich met her at the train station the day before the official start date. Rusty carried her bags while Rich painted the scenes he envisioned shooting. Since she was starving, they took her to eat at a cafe they wanted to use on Bourbon Street. After brunch, they showed her an alley that looked bright and innocent during the day; at night, took on sinister shadows. Festivities were ongoing, but they didn't grow into an engorged throbbing mass until after dark. Before heading to the house, they strolled along the voodoo shops. They were walking with the crowd when they passed a door with a wolf howling at the moon painted on it. Elsie stopped so quickly Rusty knocked her over. When he'd finished helping her stand, an exotic looking woman dressed in purple amd gold appeared next to them. Without saying a word, she took Elsie's hand.

After a moment, the exotic looking woman said in a soft voice "My name is Madame Marna. Would you please come with me?"

Rusty could see Elsie was hesitant. When she made eye contact with him, he felt it. She had to go with this woman.

Elsie spoke "Is it alright if my friends join us?"

Madame Marna touched the hands of both men for a moment. "Yes, they may join."

They walked through the door with the wolf howling at the moon. Once inside, it looked like any other magic shop they'd seen. A much older woman sat behind the counter. She smiled pleasantly to them as Madam Marna motioned them into a room. A round table with chairs was in the middle.

When Madam Marna faced them from the other side of the table, she spoke again. "Gentlemen, please take a chair and move to the side of the room. Mistress, please be seated across from me."

Elsie stood her ground "What are you going to do and how much will it cost?"

Madame Marna seemed shocked. "Did you not feel it?"

Rusty spoke with an edge. "Feel what?"

Madame Marna looked at him, then to Elsie. "The same force that caused you to stop was what beckoned me outside to find you. I invited you. The only cost is your time. Please sit."

She turned a knob on the wall to dim the lights before sitting.

Rich looked on in fascination while Rusty watched warily. Madame Marna placed her hands out palm side down. Elsie put her hands under Madame Marna's without touching. In a soft tone, the priestess chanted something melodically unintelligible. The space became pressurized and a glow formed around the two women.

"It must be from moving out of the bright sunshine to this darkened room." Rusty thought rubbing his eyes.

The mantra stopped. The two women were smiling at each other as if they'd shared a pleasant childhood experience. Rusty could hear Madame Marna speak. It was too soft for him to distinguish the words. This lasted twenty minutes. The glow that misted the room evaporated. When the women stood, so did both men.

Madame Marna glided gracefully to Rusty.

She took both of his hands in hers, then spoke for only him to hear. "To survive the journey, you'll have to let go of her hand, but never let go of what's in your heart."

Releasing his hands, she stepped away.

Speaking to all three of them, "Peace be with you."

Focusing only on Elsie, the priestess closed with: "Thank you for allowing me to shine light into your darkness."

Elsie replied "May the light shine from you always."

She touched the fingers of her left hand to the center of her forehead, then rested the same hand on her ample chest.

The trio exited through the door which they'd entered.

When they were outside, Rusty asked, "What did she say to you?"

Elsie smiled. "I'd prefer not sharing until it comes true."

Rich finally spoke. "That was incredible! It was a page right out of your book. Guess that's where you got the idea."

"More or less", she commented cryptically.

Rusty sounding unconvinced, "You mean you believe that mumbo jumbo."

She grabbed his arm to stop him.

Facing him, she said boldly. "If I didn't believe it, I couldn't have written the book we are about to film."

Trying to make sense of it, he rebutted. "Your book is based on Jungian philosophy and psychic visions in relation to it, not about fortune tellers."

"Madame Marna may earn a living as a fortune teller, that doesn't mean she lacks a psychic gift. She is a true voodoo high priestess. And there's a difference between plopping down in front of someone and saying 'tell me my fortune' versus a moment of synchronicity or overwhelming feeling that nags you to do something", irritation evident in Elsie's voice.

Rich tried to defuse their argument. "What was that thing you did with your hand at the end? It looked like something Buddhists do."

Elsie turned her attention and a gentler tone towards Rich. "The left hand is used because it's our intuitive side. It is placed on the third eye, where we see all other worldly things, then to rest on our heart in pure love."

"Pure love, voodoo high priestess isn't that a contradiction!" snorted from Rusty.

She faced him, hands on her hips. "True voodoo is similarly based as Wicca. And all of it is essentially the same as what any other religion should be based upon—the divine spirit. It's a way of life, a way of being, not about curses and zombies. But then why would I expect a narrow-minded, pig-headed, self-centered has-been boy-toy actor to think any differently!"

Rich broke their heated exchange. "I think it's time to go to the house to give Elsie time to settle in before we come back into town tonight."

Both Rusty and Elsie nodded in agreement. They walked to the car in silence. Rusty had already realized she'd turned her words on him merely to make a point. It is wise to have the facts, not movie spun hype.

To ease the tension, Rusty pursued a safe topic. "How are the dogs?"

"I know what you're trying to do." She replied good-naturedly. "Don't worry I'm not mad; you will understand one day. The dogs are well, but I miss them already."

She was assigned the corner room on the first floor. Each floor had its own bathroom. The men were on the second floor. She would be sharing the floor with two other females. One was the makeup artist who was flying in that evening. The other was an actress who couldn't fly in until the next afternoon.

The trio didn't go into town until after eight o'clock. There was a night of rampant fun awaiting them. Elsie wore jeans, canvas sneakers, and a familiar peach blouse. Rich and Rusty wore a similar uniform the difference being their shirts were plain cotton, yellow and red, respectively. It only took a couple drinks for Rusty to discover if Elsie wore the same peach bra he remembered. At first, he didn't think it was as provocative as when it was wet. As the night continued, he liked it almost as much dry.

She had no inhibitions when she was asked to flash for a set of beads. After that she didn't bother re-buttoning her top. The psychedelically colored shells nestled in her bountiful cleavage. He felt envious of those beads. She stopped at a vendor selling masks. She found a lacey turquoise one edged in peacock feathers. Rich selected one that made him look like Tweety-bird. When Elsie saw Rusty's lack of interest, she found a red silk mask with horns. His look of displeasure didn't stop her from sliding it onto his face and positioning the horns atop his head. Her smile mirrored his devilish look. Donning her own mask, she motioned to the vendor prior to walking away; leaving Rusty to pay. It wasn't an issue since she had told the two men that the only money she would be carrying was a twenty tucked in a safe place. Rusty had slipped a few more bills into his wolf money clip to accommodate her. He didn't mind. Matter of fact, he was delighted to do it. Especially now seeing the decadent fun she was having. He'd lost count of how many shots she'd consumed. The throngs of people increased as the time neared midnight. It was impossible to move without being groped or pinched. Somehow she managed to keep moving through the crowd. When someone would grab her, she would gracefully slip out of his or her grasp before the person had a chance to take advantage. The two men lacked her nimbleness in passing through the mob. Even if her shirt had been a brighter orange, they would've had trouble spying her. Too many of the other people were on stilts or wearing ornamental headpieces hiding her naturally short stature. A fleeting moment of panic welled inside when he couldn't locate her in the writhing horde thwarting his progress. He managed to make headway towards Rich; who did the same towards Rusty.

"This is ridiculous we'll never find her." Rich yelled to Rusty even though he was right next to him.

"I agree. Let's make our way to the car." Rusty replied at a comparable volume.

Rusty hoped Elsie was lucid enough to remember the pact they had made upon arriving at the festivities. If any of them got split up longer than fifteen minutes, they would rendezvous at a bed-n-breakfast on the city limits. A cab ride would use the twenty dollars. At least she would be away from the swarm of partygoers. She would also have access to a phone. Who could she call? No one was at the house to answer, nor did she have her cell phone with her. He had first hand knowledge, his own hands had been inappropriately placed several times where he'd have noticed a cell phone amidst the enjoyable topography.

It took almost an hour for the two men to return to the car. And twenty minute drive to the bed-n-breakfast. As they parked in front of the building, they saw her on the veranda. She sat with her legs pulled underneath her. The cup in her hands prevented them from moving as she spoke. Quite a few people sat enthralled in a semi-circle around her. Even though the veranda simply used candles for light, it glowed with intensity. When she saw the men coming up the walk, she waved. They could hear her voice as they neared her as she continued speaking to her audience.

"My ride is here, but I want to thank you all very much for the hospitality and listening to my ramblings." Elsie said as she stood.

The small gathering clapped in appreciation.

She repeated the same motions and saying she had with the fortune teller: "May the light shine from you always." She handed her cup to the hostess, then walked to the men.

"Don't stop on our account." Rich said in awe.

The group was heading to their rooms. Elsie smiled and nodded as they disperse. Rusty could see that she had genuinely enjoyed the company of these people. Her demeanor openly relaxed. And he could swear the air surrounding her sparkled.

Basically ignoring what Rich said, Elsie spoke to both of them. "I am so glad to see you two! I'm ready for my pillow and blanket."

"We're ready for sleep, too. From the looks of it, you've been waiting for a while. How'd you get here so quickly?" Rusty asked.

The trio got into the car to continue the trip to the house.

She rambled. "You're not going to believe this. I ran into a guy I worked with several years ago. He hasn't been to Mardi Gras in years. A friend of his got a great deal on a package so he decided this was the year to come back. Anyway, I stumbled and he caught me. When we recognized each other, I turned to introduce you only to discover we'd gotten separated.

Jerry led me to where the taxis were standing. He's joining me for lunch tomorrow at the cafe."

The following giggles were full of girlish glee.

Rusty interrogated her further. "How well do you know this guy?"

She responded with a dreamy lilt in her voice. "When I joined the happy hour crew on Fridays, he was one of the regulars. There were three of us with something in common—over thirty and divorced—that the others didn't understand. The rest of the group was college new hires who thought love could be found on the dance floor. Jerry and Grant had been friends for years. Grant and I had known each other about two years. Jerry and I became fast friends. We'd help each other if someone was being too clingy or to drop a hint our way. It was a very symbiotic relationship."

She continued talking to her self rather than the two men in the front seat. "Gosh, I didn't realize how much I missed him until now. He's one of the good guys. I'm surprised he was alone."

To put a stop to her reverie Rusty spoke curtly. "Just be careful. We don't need any complications."

Rich sent him a surprised look, then returned his attention to driving. Elsie, content in her memories, volleyed no response from the backseat.

The silence continued until she mumbled a happy "good night" as they parted at the staircase for their assigned rooms.

CHAPTER EIGHTEEN

ELSIE DID NOT emerge from her room until time to leave for the cafe. The crew had posted the departure times on the board the previous day. It would give them plenty of time to eat and setup prior to shooting the scene. Rich and Rusty had been awake for a few hours reviewing scenes. Julie, the makeup artist, joined the trio for the drive to the cafe. This was Julie's first assignment alone. She was used to reporting to a head makeup artist. Due to the budgetary and scheduling constraints, she was it. In her late twenties, she had five years of experience working in the industry. Nonetheless, she was nervous making her a bit too effervescent. It didn't take a trained eye to see Elsie was suffering from the over indulgence of alcohol and lateness of last night. Rusty could tell she was having a hard time following Julie's chattering. Her concerted effort paid off when in the course of the conversation she mentioned meeting an old friend. Julie popped open the case she had in the backseat with her.

"You can't go see an old boyfriend not looking your best now can you?!" Julie bubbled.

Elsie put up no fight. Julie was in her element. The chattering had changed to a humming melody of popular tunes. In no time at all, the greenish hue that had infected Elsie's skin was hidden so well, it looked like her natural skin tones. Julie reached into her shoulder bag for a pick and hair gel.

Elsie balked. "Julie, I appreciate the effort, but please go easy. I don't want to spend the day with hair that could put someone's eye out. And he's not an old boyfriend."

"Oh I wasn't going to change the way you have it. I just want to pull out those red highlights." Julie responded as she put barely a dab of gel on her fingertips.

After smearing the gel on her other fingers, Julie plucked at the hair on Elsie's head in a haphazard fashion.

Rich spoke as he pulled up along the cafe. "Ladies, I'm dropping you here and I'll go park. Rusty would you please get Julie's portable table from the trunk?"

Rusty nodded in adherence. He opened the door for Elsie who was seated directly behind him. As she stepped out, she lost her balance. He reached to steady her. Their gazes locked for an instant long enough for him to see her look of uneasiness. He smiled down at her. Unable to help herself, she reacted in warm appreciation. Her smile did more for her face than any amount of make-up could. Once she was safely on the curb, he retrieved Julie's table from the truck. With the table removed, Julie reached for her case dolly. Elsie carried the two stools to the table he was wheeling to where a crewman was waving. They helped Julie stabilize the makeup table, then left her to get organized.

Rich returned with one of the crewmen. Rusty partially listened to them talk while he watched Elsie. She checked her cell phone prior to scanning the cafe. Suddenly she waved, walking to the other end of the patio. He followed the path she was taking to see the man that was watching her. Jerry wasn't very tall, about 5'8", wiry build and a receding hairline. Unfortunately, his flaws weren't what bothered Rusty. It was the perfect smile the man flashed followed by the comfort in which they embraced. Not to mention, the way Elsie looked at ease with him as they ate, talked and touched for the next hour.

Rich walked to where Jerry and Elsie were to inform her they were ready to start. She hugged Jerry good-bye to return with Rich. Her face reflected her delight. Rusty being the consummate professional, pushed the irksome thoughts from the forefront of his mind. They finished at the café on time. The partygoers were beginning to swarm with the sunset. Julie stayed with the trio on the move to the next spot. One case was sufficient for touch-ups. After a few hours, Rich called it a night. Shooting in the middle of the street party became more challenging than anticipated.

Tina Laney, the actress hired for the Mardi Gras scenes was waiting for them upon their return. Having been a Miss America at one time, it didn't take any adornment to improve her appearance. At the moment, she wore a pout on her otherwise flawless face. No one had been at the house to greet or take care of her needs when she arrived. Rich proceeded to apologize and flatter her until they got her settled into her room. The next morning it became apparent to everyone involved that she was going to be high maintenance—lots of fawning and appeasing of her whims.

Since the rest of the shooting was to be done after dark on into the wee hours of the morning, it gave them free time in the mornings and afternoons. For most, mornings were an attempt at six hours of sleep. Elsie and Julie had the least amount of responsibilities so they hung out together. Julie would return to the house to work on Rusty and Tina prior to the evening's shoot. Meanwhile, Elsie would stay in town and supper with Jerry. Rusty spent his time reviewing lines with Tina, then having dinner with her and Rich. The only time Rusty would see Elsie was at the onset of and intermittently throughout the night's filming. Even then, they only spoke if her input was warranted. Her prediction of their time together had been true thus far. But she wasn't making an effort to see him. Then again neither was he. He had an excuse; he was working—putting all of his energy into this role—as he had with every other role.

At the end of the schedule, there was enough filmed for Rich to work with when it came time to edit. Now they were headed to Cambridge, Massachusetts for two weeks. Next weekend they had the Academy Awards in Los Angeles. After Cambridge a month was scheduled in Stowe, Vermont. Elsie gave Rich and Rusty hugs at the airport saying she'd see them in Vermont. It bothered Rusty that he wouldn't see her for such an extended time after their recent lack of contact.

Rusty made a call prior to the flight taking for Boston. "Hello mate. The shoot is hectic, but going well. I need you to do me a favor. Have a gift basket sent to Elsie at home."

Sherry finally had a chance to speak. "Hello Rusty. Glad to hear the film is progressing. As for the gift basket, I don't think that would be a wise idea. Maybe we can come up with something else if you tell me what you did wrong to warrant a gift?"

"I didn't do anything wrong!" He snorted defensively. "We didn't get to spend any time together after the first day. And she met an old friend that she spent all her time with."

His voice turned angry. "Oh hell! Why should I make amends when she was the one with somebody else? It's not like we have a relationship. Never mind!"

"Rusty wait!" Sherry burst out preventing him from hanging up.

"What?!" Rusty remained on the line.

"Did you ever think that she kept herself occupied to prevent from feeling ignored or left out? I'm sure she understands that you need to stay focused. Don't try to bribe her. Just talk to her." Sherry cajoled. "And if the current story splashed across the gossip papers is only partially right, I can see why she was making herself scarce."

"What story?" His anger refueled.

"About you and Tina Laney spending a week at Mardi Gras." Sherry gave him a synopsis of the rag sheet stories. "Nothing was mentioned that you were there filming. But the pictures are fairly incriminating."

"Thanks for the heads up mate. I'll call you from the hotel." Rusty disconnected.

Pushing the button for assistance, he filled Rich in on what Sherry told him. He asked the flight attendant if they or anyone in coach had a copy of the current week's gossip paper. She promised to look for one. When they landed, she apologized for not finding one, but recommended a newsstand he could try on the way to baggage claim. Rich saw it before Rusty. Rusty grabbed a copy of two different tabloids with pictures of Tina and him on the cover. Rich paid for the newspapers. He had to steer Rusty around people as he read on their trek to fetch baggage claim. By the time they stopped to wait for their luggage, Rusty was irate.

"Look at these pictures mate!" He said pointing violently at the pages in his hand. "You were with us in every one of these photos and have been conveniently trimmed out. And look at this one where she's in my arms. That was part of the scene we were filming."

Rich spoke in a low tone. "You need to chill. People are looking at us, including two guys wearing TSA jackets. I don't think you want to become another headline so soon after this one."

He managed to guide Rusty to an area with less of an audience.

Rich continued calming him. "It's their usual story full of misleading pictures. You and I know those dinners were discussing the upcoming scenes. Plus, we did have to give Tina a lot of undivided attention to prevent her hissy-fits."

It worked.

After a few minutes, Rusty asked what he had deduced. "Do you think Tina is why Elsie spent so little time with us?"

A huge grin covered Rich's face. "Rusty old man, I think you got it bad for that lady."

Ignoring the comment, he asked again. "Is that why she stayed away?"

Taking pity on Rusty this time, Rich answered seriously. "I'm sure Elsie tried to keep herself busy when she wasn't needed."

Rusty shot him a cranky expression so Rich continued. "And what woman in the initial stages of a relationship wants to be compared to a beauty queen?! Tina's clinginess had to have been annoying to see. Even if you are just friends, she wasn't about to put herself into a belittling position. Anyway, that's how I see it."

"What about that Jerry fellow she was spending all her time with?" Rusty asked still irked, but no longer yelling and shaking his fist.

Rich maneuvered them back to the baggage claim while he spoke. "That's a question you need to ask Elsie, now isn't it?"

"Sherry said the same thing." Rusty's anger deflated.

"Sounds like a good assistant." Rich smiled more gently. "You know if Janie and I hid things that were bothering us, we'd have never stayed married for the last twenty years. We have our ups and downs, but we keep the lines of communication open as a way to hold onto our love and respect for each other."

Rusty clapped his hand on Rich's shoulder. "Thanks mate."

Elsie didn't answer the phone when he called forcing him to leave the number where he could be reached. Rusty was disappointed she hadn't called him prior to Los Angeles. When he met with Sherry on Saturday, she had a large envelope for him. It was from Elsie. Enclosed was a copy of the tabloid story and pictures. Elsie had added some blurbs of her own—"Beauty Queen or Drag Queen", "Check mate or Stale mate", "Lacks Rich Relationship". Rusty relished her word play. Plus, there was a note.

Rusty,

Enjoy the Oscars. The dogs and I will be watching the pre-show to see if you forgot to zip your fly.

Then we'll be tuning into the Awards show. Maybe one of the cameramen will catch you picking your nose.

Elsie

He chuckled as he shared it with Sherry who also enjoyed the humor in it. He couldn't wait to see Elsie in Vermont. In the meantime, he had an idea for tonight.

He usually arrived late to avoid the pomp of the red carpet parade. Tonight was going to be different. He had Sherry call Lana Ravine to wheedle a surprise for her sister Laura. The Ravine sisters had been around for thirty years. They were infamous for their uncensored fashion commentary. On numerous occasions, Laura called him a major hotty. Normally, it was a source of embarrassment. On this particular occasion, he was going to use it to his advantage. Rusty wanted to let Elsie know he was thinking of her. This was a means to accomplish it. Lana had been more than willing to accommodate his request; especially since it would render her sister speechless. Leaving his fly open was tempting, but could be construed as bad taste. Instead, je went for the fun prank. He arrived in the middle of the procession of stars to help camouflage his presence on his way to where Laura was stationed. Lana had been prompting Laura that she had a surprise for her. One of the station's crew maneuvered him to the on-deck for Laura. He donned the devil mask concealed in his tuxedo jacket pocket. The crewmember distracted Laura's attention from the pageantry long enough for Rusty to move into place directly in front of her.

When Laura faced the red carpet again, Rusty and Lana, who was watching on a viewer at the other end of the red carpet, yelled "surprise!"

It worked! Laura dropped her microphone. Rusty removed the mask to reveal his identity. Laura stuttered his name into the retrieved microphone, then continued to gape at him.

He bent to give Laura a kiss on the cheek. "It was lovely to see you darling! Thanks Lana."

As he stepped away, he blew a kiss towards the camera. "Miss you Mate."

Moving further out of range of the interviewers lined along the perimeter, he smiled at his devilishness.

CHAPTER NINETEEN

RUSTY AND RICH drove together from Massachusetts to Vermont. There was still daylight when they arrived at the hotel. It was two sprawling bungalow type buildings in a clearing of pine trees at the end of a gravel road. They parked in front of the building with a sign painted OFFICE and DINING ROOM with arrows pointing to the appropriate slate walkways. Rich's assistant, Carla, had arrived Saturday to make any final arrangements with the hotel staff. Rich and Rusty walked into the office to identify themselves. A chart of the second building was on an easel next to the counter. The second building contained the guest rooms. All of the rooms except two had names attached to them. Rusty located Elsie's name in a corner room closest to an exit door at the end opposite the designated parking area. He also noted with disappointment that Julie had taken the room next to her. Rich was on the phone with Carla.

Rich spoke as he hung up. "Carla saved the adjoining rooms for us. They are at the far end facing this building. We can leave the door open in between when we need to."

Rusty, still examining the room plan, pointed to the room adjacent to Elsie's. "I'll take the corner and you can have the other one. Okay mate?"

Rich nodded. Rusty wrote their names on the room chart. The older gentleman behind the counter reached for the last two keys.

He spoke with an obvious New England accent as he handed them each their keys. "My name is Jake. My wife Edna and I own the place. If you need anythin', please call. We're happy to oblige. It's quite a pleasant surprise to be full up now that skiin' season is wanin'."

After parking, they grabbed their luggage from the Explorer. Lugging it towards the end of the building, they spotted Elsie with Tycho. Rather,

Tycho spotted Rusty. A drawn out howl caught the attention of the two men. Elsie waved as Tycho tried to drag her closer to them. Keeping him on a taut leash by her side, Elsie intersected with the men at the door. Rusty set his bags down to hug her, then knelt to get a few sloppy kisses from Tycho. Rich embraced Elsie while Tycho was occupied. Before they had time to exchange amenities, Carla was standing in the doorway.

"Rich we only have an hour till dinner and we really should review things prior to your pep talk during the toast." It was a demand, not a request.

Used to Carla's way of handling things, Rich responded amiably. "Okay Carla. I can unpack while we talk. Rusty you need to hear this, too"

"Okay mate." Rusty said to Rich.

Looking at Elsie, he asked "Should I save you a seat at dinner?"

"Yes please." Elsie answered with a girlish smile.

With a final rub behind Tycho's ears, Rusty picked up his bags and entered the building. He'd gotten his toiletries emptied when there was knock on the wall. Looking around the room, he saw the connecting door. Rusty unlocked and opened his side.

Rich said as he walked into Rusty's room. "This was a good idea."

Walking back into his room, Rich spoke to Carla. "Carla please move closer to the doorway to allow Rusty to hear you better."

Rusty continued to unpack, hearing most of what Carla was relaying to Rich. The hotel had no problem complying with serving dinner at six or leaving the room open indefinitely until everyone exited the first night. Subsequently, the menu and meal times would be posted on the board a day in advance. Since they had reserved the whole hotel for the next four weeks, Jake and Edna agreed to close the restaurant for them exclusively. This also enabled them to use the dining room and front of the building for a few shots. The cabin they'd found wouldn't be ready until the end of the following week. Luckily, the ski resort agreed to let them film earlier than scheduled to fill in the gap. All of the crew was accounted. Maci Castle, the actress for this location, had arrived the day before. Carla recommended Rich seat her at the table with him and Rusty. She hoped it would help

Maci feel more comfortable. This was Maci's first big picture. Rusty entered Rich's room by the time Carla was ready to review daily schedules.

It was 15 minutes till dinner when they finished the meeting. Dinner was casual, but Rusty wanted to change his shirt from the one rumpled and smelly from the flight. Elsie was already in the dining room when they entered. She was standing to one side with Julie and Maci.

"It seems Maci latched on to the girls. That should help ease her nervousness." Rich said as he picked a table that was suitable for addressing the group throughout the evening.

Rusty headed for the three women.

"Good evening ladies. Would you care to join us?" He motioned towards the table where Rich was standing.

Rich seated Maci between him and Rusty. Rusty held the other chair next to him for Elsie. Julie giggled when he also held the chair on the other side of Elsie for her to sit. A waitress emerged from the kitchen. With their drink order taken, Maci made a comment about Rusty's antics from the red carpet at the Oscars.

"It'll make great press." Rich said jauntily.

Julie piped up "Guess the devil made you do it!"

During the ensuing laughter, Rusty pushed Elsie's napkin off her lap. He leaned over to help retrieve it at the same time she did.

Then he whispered in her ear, "Actually, you made me do it."

Upon righting herself in her chair, Elsie fussed with her napkin. It was a way to keep her face down to veil the blush that had crept into her cheeks. No one else at the table took notice. They were occupied in a lively discussion regarding the Oscar winners. It didn't take long for the whole crew to arrive. When Carla appeared, Rich waved her to the empty seat next to him.

During the remainder of dinner, Rusty was unable to share further private words with Elsie. Throughout the evening, they would brush knees or arms due to the closeness of the table. Each occurrence caused a renewed pink shine to Elsie's cheeks. Rich gave his pep talk prior to dessert, stayed until eight, and then excused himself. The crew took the signal to not make it a late night. With a 4:30am wake-up call, the group didn't linger. Rusty hoped to walk Elsie to her room. Unfortunately, Julie was busy talking to her. Plus, Maci was asking him questions about a scene. After assuring Maci that the schedule had allotted plenty of time for run-throughs prior to filming, he walked to his room. Unexpectedly, he heard a female voice yell. When he stepped outside, he could hear it was Elsie.

"Sophie baby, come here." Her voice was in a forced high-pitched happy tone, but Rusty could hear the wavering of panic. "Sophie treats!"

As he rounded the corner of the building, he saw why she was panicked. She was holding onto Tycho with one hand and a leash attached to nothing in the other hand. Into the trees quite a distance, he could see Sophie's white plume of a tail bounding about in the moonlight.

"Sophie!" Rusty hollered.

She hadn't seen him earlier like Tycho. Upon hearing him, she came to his beckon at breakneck speed. As he hugged her in greeting, he grabbed hold of her collar. Elsie with Tycho ran to them. Her hands were shaking so much she was having a difficult time hooking the leash. Taking it from her, he clipped the tether to Sophie's collar. Instead of relinquishing the leash to her, he held onto it when he straightened.

Tears were running down Elsie's face when she finally spoke to him.

"Thank you so much Rusty. I must have caught hair in the clip. We were on our way back inside when she heard a noise in the woods. When she pulled, the leash released. I was afraid she'd keep going." Her voice was still noticeably shaking.

He wanted to comfort her with a hug, but with the dogs on leashes he was afraid they would get knotted.

Keeping his voice low in an attempt to calm her, he said, "Glad to be of service love. I'll help you take them to the room."

Once inside her room, he pushed the door shut while she removed leashes.

Elsie spoke as she hung the leashes by her coat. "Rusty, I can't thank you enough. If you wouldn't have shown, I don't know what I would've done to get her to come back. I don't know what I'd do if I lost her too; and on the same day as Tribble."

Rusty tugged her gently into an embrace. Her arms slid inside his unzipped coat. The collage of her aptly named woolly malamute hung over the cedar box containing his ashes in her home. Thinking about what she said, Rusty realized it must be the first anniversary of his death. He rubbed his scruffy face against the top of her head in unison with the rocking motion to soothe her. Finally, Rusty heard her sigh followed her body relaxing. However, Elsie's softness molding into him caused his body to harden. He released her in an attempt to censor his response. After placing a gentle kiss on her lips, he left her room.

Now was not the time or place to escalate their relationship to a sexual level. They cared for each other. He cherished their friendship to where he was concerned if adding intimacy would enhance or destroy it. Plus, there were things she had as of yet not elaborated—namely the fact that she had been married. This bothered him. Did she still believe she wasn't his type? Particularly since he was finding her more alluring each time he was with her. With a 4:30 call to set, he couldn't afford a sleepless night. Reading through his lines for the next day focused his immediate priorities to allow sleep.

As usual Rusty threw himself into his role. The first week went by with only a few "good mornings" and "hellos" exchanged between him and Elsie. If he wanted to know anything about what she was doing, he had only to chat to Julie during make-up or with Maci between scenes. Unlike Tina, Maci sought Elsie's help to understand her character. Elsie also spent a substantial amount of time with Rich on the set. With a two-hour window allotted for each meal, it made it tough for Rusty to catch Elsie for a bite to eat together. She would go to breakfast and lunch first thing while he went later due to wardrobe and makeup. For dinner, he went early or he'd fall asleep in his food. Elsie and Rich appeared long enough to fill plates to eat while reviewing dailies. It was a grueling schedule for everyone the first week.

By the second week, the crew had been able to ease up. There was no relief for Rich and Rusty. Much to his chagrin, Rusty noticed Elsie's friend

Jerry watching filming on Sunday. Starting Monday, Elsie was at lunch late with Jerry in tow. Plus, Jerry would help her walk the dogs.

"Why didn't I think of that?" Rusty growled at himself.

He was angry with himself because Elsie was having a flirtation with another man right under his nose. It was too coincidental the way Jerry left the site before dinner and re-appeared at the hotel around the time Elsie and Rich were done. Rusty did nothing to interfere or make a claim of his own. Worse yet, Elsie acted like nothing between them had changed.

The events Rusty witnessed Friday had him convinced Elsie was like the other women he'd dated—a fraud. He had gone to Julie's room for his morning make-up. There was Jerry leaving Elsie's room to walk Sophie. His appearance disheveled in sweats he hadn't been wearing the prior evening. It bothered Rusty so much that by lunch, he had to talk with Elsie. He headed for her room. Not seeing her outside walking the dogs, he knocked on her door. Instead of Elsie answering, Jerry opened the door wearing only pants. Peering beyond Jerry in the doorway, Rusty could see the dogs were crated and Elsie was under the covers. The second bed was undisturbed. Rusty gripped his hands into fists. Fighting the urge to punch Jerry in the face, he stormed out of the building onto a path leading into the woods. Occasionally along the way, he picked up a stone to hurl at the closest tree. Having gone quite a ways down the path with his anger unabated, he struck the closest tree with his fist. The bark flew. There was a gasp behind him. It was Elsie. She'd called to him, but in his rage he hadn't heard her. He turned to face her, his face full of fury.

He took a step towards her growling, "Why didn't you tell me?"

She started to move backwards away from him. In a few strides, he reached to grab her. While trying to scramble away, she tripped on a fallen branch.

She squeaked "Don't you dare touch me", then held up her arms to protect her face.

The terror he saw on her face made him stop moving altogether. His anger put into check by his concern for her. By this time, Jerry and Julie had made there way along the trail to where Rusty stood over a cowering

Elsie. Rusty looked in their direction trying to make sense of the situation. Julie released Jerry's hand to kneel down next to Elsie.

Jerry yelled at Rusty. "What the hell is the matter with you?"

Still trying to keep his anger contained, he bellowed. "Why were you in her fucking room?"

The other man was quick to offer an answer. "I had used her shower because Maci was in Julie's room having her make-up redone for the afternoon."

Not completely satisfied with his answer, Rusty interrogated further. "What does Julie have to do with this? Why was Elsie in bed at noon?"

Jerry looked at Julie, then at Rusty to respond. "Julie and I are dating. As for still being in bed, Elsie has been sick. She felt worse and thought she'd try to sleep it off."

Releasing an annoyed huff, it was Jerry's turn to interrogate. "Now how about you tell us why you have blood on your hand and Elsie is on the ground?"

Rusty looked at his oozing hand. Jerry's clarification of what Rusty saw dissipated his anger. He knelt in front of Elsie. The terror on her face transformed to wariness.

Sincerity filled his voice, Rusty spoke to Elsie. "Mate, I would never hurt you. No matter how angry I get, I would never hit you."

Her eyes narrowed with skepticism. "Why were you angry at me?"

Rusty rocked back on his heels.

He answered in a lower pitch. "With you and Jerry spending so much time together, I was jealous. Then seeing him come out of your room this morning and again when he answered the door, I thought you two were . . ."

The verbalization of his thoughts was difficult. "I wasn't as angry with you as much as I was with myself at being wrong for thinking that we, you and I . . ."

Admitting it to himself and Elsie had Rusty feeling vulnerable enough, having an audience added to his discomfort.

"Well, important to each other." There, he'd said it.

Her face was strained with a mixture of emotions.

Her voice dripped with bitter sarcasm as her eyes met his. "You were jealous so instead of asking me what was going on, you assumed the worst. I couldn't be very important to you if you didn't trust me enough to talk to me!"

She picked herself up from the ground, shrugging off everyone's attempt to help her.

When she strode back down the path, Jerry stepped in front of Rusty to block him. "In this particular instance, following her would not be a wise idea."

Jerry looked at Julie. "Hon, Rusty and I need to talk. Maybe you should make sure Elsie gets to her room safely without anyone seeing her. Thanks."

Julie's eyes were full of gentleness when she looked at Jerry. "Don't take too long."

Jerry patted her hand, then she went in pursuit of Elsie.

Rusty didn't want to hear a lecture. "Listen mate. I've been trying to talk with her since last week. We've both been too busy to get even a few uninterrupted moments together. I'll get her some flowers to apologize and when I explain it, she'll understand."

Jerry didn't let Rusty's comment dissuade him. "From your reaction to her moment of hysteria, I take it she hasn't told you much about her ex-husband?"

This caused Rusty to pause in his rush along the trail. "Other than an offhanded remark about being divorced, she hasn't said anything. There are times she'll say something or get a look on her face that I know has significance. She'll shrug it off."

"Let's head to your room. I'll clue you in on some of it." Jerry said to continue their progress to the hotel.

"It's going to take a lot to get out of this mess with her. You scared her which was a very bad thing. Her ex-husband was a very controlling and manipulative SOB. He would buy her expensive things, then guilt her into doing things he felt a proper wife should do. When she realized what he was doing, she tried to rebel. That only upped the ante from emotional control to the use of physical force. And he never did it where her bruises were obvious. His apologies were in the form of flowers and gifts which appeared to outsiders that he was being romantic." Jerry delayed his narrative until they were in Rusty's room.

While Rusty washed his hand, Jerry continued. "I know some details, but I believe anything more should come from Elsie directly. I will tell you this though. If I ever met her ex, I would beat the crap out of him. And even then, it wouldn't come remotely close to what he did to her."

Jerry took a drink from the glass Rusty filled from the freshly opened bottle of bourbon.

"Elsie's independence and self-sufficiency have been hard earned where she won't have them taken away again. It can be intimidating. I salute you for not letting it discourage you. Unfortunately, this incident may make things insurmountable. You know the saying 'a woman scorned'?" Finishing his drink, Jerry gave Rusty time to digest what he said.

"She's my favorite person. Her intelligence and sense of humor are worth experiencing. I know she can get irrationally mad over stupid stuff. It's part of who she is. She's a package deal—all or nothing. We have a wonderful friendship. I don't want to rush her and don't know if she feels the same way." Rusty was rambling.

Jerry broke into his disjointed remarks. "If you'd have shared that with her earlier, you wouldn't be in this predicament. Not rushing her is a good thing. Try to talk to her, just don't push too hard. Above all, respect her."

The phone in the room rang. When Rusty answered, it was Rich wanting to know why he wasn't on the set. He said he'd be there shortly. Jerry was leaving the room when Julie popped into the doorway. She reported that Elsie had made it to her room safely. And she needed a ride to the set. Jerry drove while Julie worked on Rusty's make-up. When they arrived on the set, Rich was displeased that Rusty had injured his hand. Not to mention, his screenwriter wasn't there because she was too sick. Maybe in a few days she'd feel well enough to add the injury into scenes to prevent continuity issues. With the bandage removed, they could film around it temporarily.

The final scene for the day required Rusty to chop wood. This was an easy task. He'd done it countless times. When the axe connected with the wood, it shattered causing pieces to fly in all directions. He deflected a projectile heading for his face with his injured hand. By the time Rich was next to him, Rusty had his hand shoved in a mound of snow.

"Are you alright? What happened?" Rich asked anxiously.

Rusty remarked with confusion. "The wood exploded! I've never had that happen before."

Rich picked up one of the logs. He noticed cracks in it. On further examination, it had been glued together. He showed it to Rusty. Then he selected another one—the same thing. Standing to the side of the tree stump, holding a log in his hand Rich smacked it vertically into the stump. It fell apart like he had wielded an axe at it with full force. He motioned to the site crew. After a few minutes, they'd resolved what happened. In an attempt to be useful, one of the new members split the wood and glued it together. He thought that if the actor had never split wood, it would him look like a professional. He hadn't counted on Rusty putting muscle into it. Rusty removed his hand from the snow bank to examine it. Julie wiped away the fresh blood. Rich watched him flex it. It hurt a bit, but didn't appear to be serious. The crew cleared the debris. They also replaced the altered logs with normal ones.

A scene that should have taken no more than a couple hours, drug tediously. Rich wanted it done. They were racing against the setting sun. Turning on lights would cause the snow to noticeably melt. Rusty's hand had gone numb. He kept repeating the scene at Rich's request because he felt partially responsible. The situation with Elsie had been put where it wouldn't distract him. Regrettably, one of Maci's lines brought it all to the forefront. Maci's character had to tell Rusty's character that her life hadn't always been easy or tranquil; her start was when she left her abusive ex-husband. When Maci said the line with her eyelashes fluttering over her big doe eyes—Rusty saw Elsie. He completely forgot his line. All he could think of was what a dolt he'd been because he hadn't pieced it together before now. All of the clues were there. And he had seen Elsie in the character Maci portrayed when he read the book. Aware of everyone staring at him, Rusty apologized blaming it on freezing brain cells. Between his distracted state and Maci's nervousness with their first kiss; Rich yelled cut over and over again before the scene had played its entirety. Eventually, they both focused enough to do it the way Rich wanted.

Everyone went directly to the dining room upon returning to the hotel. Julie removed Rusty and Maci's make-up on the drive back. During dinner, Julie told Rusty she would take food to Elsie while Jerry walked the dogs. Then they would be going to a place in town for some country line dancing. Would it be okay for them to leave the care of Elsie and the dogs to him? Rusty thought this would be a good opportunity to show Elsie he wasn't the same kind of man as her ex-husband. Edna bustled out of the kitchen in response to Julie's request. She was as short and plump as Jake was tall and thin. Julie explained they wanted to take food to Elsie who was feeling under the weather

"I'll get a box from the storeroom to make it easier to carry. Don't forget to take plenty of juice and bottled water. Lots of fluids is what the doctor always says. Would you like us to see if Doc Bauman would be able to stop in?" Edna's accent not as pronounced as her husband's.

Julie replied gratefully. "Thank you for the help. Having a doctor examine Elsie would probably be wise."

Jerry carried the box with the food and utensils. Rusty helped by grabbing another box with juices and bottled water per Edna's recommendation. His hand was beginning to throb. He attributed it to thawing in the warmth of the dining room. In Elsie's room, the dogs wooed a greeting from their crates. Elsie stirred upon hearing the commotion. She was wearing a very crumpled flannel shirt with sweats. Her face was puffy and her eyes blood shot.

She spoke with a scratchy voice. "I know it's past your dinnertime guys. I'll get it as soon as I can focus."

Putting the box he had onto a chair, Rusty spoke firmly. "Stay there. I'll feed the dogs while you eat something."

She said "thank you" on her way to the bathroom.

Julie set a place at the table for Elsie to eat. Knowing Elsie was in capable hands for the moment, he focused on the dogs. He took Sophie; Jerry, Tycho. As expected, Tycho did his business by the end of the first lap around the building. Sophie, on the other hand, was contrary. Reveling in her walk with Rusty, she would extend it as long as possible. Jerry and Tycho completed a second lap prior to heading back to the room. By the time Sophie had given in to nature, Julie and Jerry were coming out of Elsie's room. Rusty waited in the hallway with Sophie to get the room key from Julie.

"I'm concerned. She only ate the applesauce. And she didn't sound that scratchy this morning." Julie's face furrowed with worry. "I swear she fell asleep the second her head hit the pillow."

"We don't have to go into town. If you're that concerned, we should stay here." Jerry offered.

Rusty knew Jerry was leaving in the morning.

"No. You two go have fun. I can sit with her." He highlighted his words with a shooing motion.

Julie's face brightened.

As she handed him the room key, she warned. "Try not to piss her off anymore than you already have."

Rusty made a sad-sack face, which invoked a smile from Julie. The couple went into Julie's room to change for the night's festivities. Rather than risk disturbing Elsie, Rusty took Sophie to his room. He was going to shower, then watch television until it was time for the dogs' "night-night potty". First, Sophie tried to join him in the shower. When he toweled off, she hopped into the tub to eat the soap. He chased her out of the bathroom, shutting the door to keep her from eating any other tasty toiletry item. While he got dressed in flannel drawstring pants and a warm shirt, Sophie rolled around on the unused bed. She eventually snuggled next to him on his bed. Jake phoned to let him know Doc Bauman would stop by the next day. Rusty was so tired he fell asleep. Sophie nosed him awake at ten-thirty. He figured it was time for the dogs' last walk for the night. If Sophie hadn't squatted on the lap around the building, she was going to have to hold it until morning. The hand he'd injured earlier in the day was throbbing. When he squeezed the escape proof latch to open Tycho's crate, his hand cramped. He ignored it until he finished walking the gentle giant. With Tycho crated again, Rusty turned on the light by the bed. He was concerned that she hadn't stirred from Tycho's excited woos. At a closer proximity to her, he could hear her wheezing. Adjusting her pillows to ease her breathing, her flannel shirt was soaked along with the blanket. She needed warm dry clothes. There were flannel shirts hanging on the clothes rack.

"Elsie, you need to change into dry pajamas." He spoke expecting her to wake so he didn't have to undress her.

It wasn't that he didn't want to see her body, but to avoid her feeling violated. She didn't stir. It had to be done. He pulled back the blankets. The exposure to air in combination with her wet shirt initiated goose bumps followed by a wave of shivers. This was enough to rouse Elsie. Even though she was conscious, she seemed dazed.

Rusty asked. "How do you feel mate?"

No response.

He tried again. "You need to take off your wet shirt to put on a dry one."

This time her head bobbed as she moved it to look at him. Her eyes were glazed. The earlier shiver escalated to a case of the chills. With great difficulty, he unbuttoned her wet shirt; keeping it pulled closed. He moved to face her back. From behind, he removed the soaked shirt, replacing it with a dry one. Moving to face her front, he struggled to button the fresh shirt. Through the whole procedure, he explained to her what he was doing in case she became lucid. Pain and frustration with his hand laced his dialogue with cursing. Much to his concern, the chills didn't stop after he had her tucked under a fresh dry blanket. Waiting till tomorrow for a doctor didn't sit well with him. Plus, his swollen cramped hand should probably be x-rayed. Picking up the phone, he called Rich. Rich recommended they take a trip to the nearest emergency room before Rusty could. Rich sent Carla to the front desk for directions while he drove the Explorer to the door by Elsie's room. Rusty carried her to the vehicle. They kept her wrapped in blankets on the backseat. Holding her head and shoulders in his lap, he sat with her to prevent her from rolling off. Carla jumped into the front passenger seat. According to Jake's directions, it would take forty minutes to the hospital. It only took Rich twenty-five. He helped Rusty unload Elsie while Carla went inside to commence the process. Rusty carried Elsie into an emergency room miraculously devoid of patients.

Standing at the desk, Carla completed the necessary forms. She glanced back and forth from the forms to the notebook she carried everywhere. Once she finished with Elsie's form, she handed it to the desk nurse. Who in turn attached the page to a clipboard to walk it back the hall to a man exiting a nearby room. He read while he walked to the waiting room where Rich and Rusty sat with Elsie. Another nurse appeared from behind him with an empty wheelchair.

The doctor finally spoke "Good evenin' gentlemen. Let's get Miss Endy in the wheelchair and have a look see."

She stirred as they placed her in the wheelchair. "Where am I?"

The doctor introduced himself followed by a list of questions like "what day is it?" as she was wheeled into the nearest room.

A few minutes later, the nurse collected Rusty to take x-rays of his hand prior to the doctor examining him.

Rusty had returned to the waiting room when the doctor emerged from where Elsie had been taken. "It appears Miss Endy has a severe case of bronchitis. We'll be takin' a chest x-ray to be sure it hasn't progressed to pneumonia."

Rich and Rusty nodded.

"She'll need complete bed rest for the next three days." Glancing at the clipboard in his hand, then back to Rusty, "Mr. Garnet you're next. Boy that name sure does sound familiar. You have family or somethin' 'round these parts?"

With a negative response from Rusty, the doctor continued, "Let's have a look see at that hand."

Together they walked towards a room next to Elsie's.

An hour later, Rusty and the doctor emerged. Rusty's hand and wrist were encased in a purple fiberglass cast.

The doctor stated. "The cast is to be worn for at least four weeks. At that time, you'll need to have your own personal physician x-ray it again to make sure it has healed properly. I'll have the pharmacy fill a prescription for painkillers."

With that, he shook Rusty's other hand, then returned to the room where Elsie slept.

By the time Rich had finished grumbling about having to work around the cast, the nurse was wheeling Elsie to them.

The doctor spoke from behind them "Okay, no pneumonia, but that doesn't mean if you don't take care that it won't turn into it."

The other nurse supplied two bags. Rusty's bag contained only the painkillers; Elsie's, antibiotics and an expectorant.

"You take care. If you need anythin' call or stop by again. As you can see, we aren't that busy here." Dr. Bauman stated.

The drive to the hotel was quiet except for an occasional wheeze from Elsie. Not only was she feeling terrible physically, but also emotionally for getting them all involved. Most people would have been flattered, Elsie felt like an imposition. Granted, if it had been her doing it for someone else, she'd have done it with no qualms. She could help others. They weren't allowed to help her.

Back at the hotel, only Rich made sure Elsie was tucked safely in her room. As for Rusty, Rich knocked on the door between their rooms before storming in. The dark clouds shrouding his face had nothing to do with lack of sleep.

"You know, I thought you had some gosh darn sense!" Rich's temper flared uncharacteristically. "We have a rough enough schedule and you acting like a bull in rut will jeopardize all our reputations, Elsie's included. How about you back off to give the lady breathing room? No pun intended. Not to mention, provide yourself a healthier perspective!!"

Rich slammed the door upon his departure.

CHAPTER TWENTY

A FEW DAYS later, Elsie appeared on the set. Her voice a quiet rasp thanks to an accompanying bout of laryngitis. She served as a great sounding board with third party perspective, which had a calming affect on people. Rich rarely lost his temper or his calm in chaos. The film's early problems combined with an impossible schedule which constantly needed re-planning and his current irritation with his leading actor—all served to fissure his good-natured demeanor. Her rejoining their daily routine eased the tension lines that had formed on his face during her forced absence

Rusty kept himself on a short leash. He hated to admit it, but Rich had been right. To keep the production going, he would have to put his growing feelings for Elsie on a backburner. Especially since he himself hadn't defined them as of yet. And the last thing he wanted to do was put her in an untenable situation that would end in heartache—for either of them.

Elsie aided Rusty unknowingly by keeping away from the social aspect of filming. Rich needed her to write Rusty's cast into the storyline; not only for their current scenes, but corresponding ones. Unfortunately, story timeline rarely matched succession with the filming schedule. This film was no exception, which meant she had to find ways to avoid seeing his right hand in other scenes. They also needed to work it in to the studio shots linked to the current location shots. There were nights Rich and Elsie would crash the dining room as Edna was leaving. All she asked was that they cleaned up after themselves to prevent mice and lock the door.

Members of the crew found their relationship gossip worthy. It wasn't easy for anyone, including Rusty, to not hear it. Oddly, Rusty didn't let it aggravate him. He had finally thrown himself full force into his character;

he wasn't going to allow unfounded rumors intrude on it. Especially knowing Rich and Elsie had a difficult job to do together. All anyone had to do was think about it logically to determine an affair could hardly be occurring. Their schedules had everyone on the set ready for filming by 6am. This meant most of the crew had to be awake by 4:30am. With barely an hour for lunch, of which Rich would review what they had shot that morning while Elsie went to walk dogs. At dinner, Elsie would put together a plate to take to her room, and take a nap since she was still recovering. Rich would be with the crew partaking of the evening meal. After dinner, Rich would call Rusty to his room to watch dailies. By nine or ten o'clock, they'd wrap things in Rich's room. Rich would call Elsie to see if she wanted to review anything. Rusty would sit on the nearest rock smoking a cigarette before turning in for the night at eleven. He usually spied Elsie walking the dogs along a trail with Julie's assistance. That task would take them approximately a half hour since they'd be chatting the whole time. The nights Elsie and Rich needed to have a creative discussion they went to the dining room so as to not disturb anyone else. One night they'd been in Rich's room hammering out scene discrepancies. Their less than quiet discussion prevented both Rusty and Carla from sleeping. They'd agreed after that to use the dining room. Not to mention, why would one have an affair in a building that had four rather large windows permitting anyone to view. One night Rusty couldn't sleep. He took a walk to see if he could help. Upon peering in to see if they were there, they were even sitting at separate tables with the script spread across each respectively. An easel sat in front of them with a large video screen displaying locale or studio shots. Every once in a while, the video story board would animate to circle his arm with purple or make a blue x on it or with a red draw a coat over it. As they got to the end of each grouping, another set would be displayed for review. Sometimes between boards a lively discussion would erupt. At which point, Rusty felt he'd do better to return to his room. If he stayed, he'd hinder rather than help the creative process. He also understood why Elsie's voice seemed worse some morning's when it had been improving the day prior. An hour with Rich and she'd probably strained her already weakened vocal chords.

Each morning after witnessing the late night meeting, Rusty made sure Elsie had hot tea waiting in the cup holder of her chair. He'd mentioned to Edna how Elsie's throat seemed raspier than it should. As the motherly type, she promised to brew a special tea she'd pour into a take-out cup for Rusty to carry to the set. Elsie peered around wondering if it was for her. As she took a swallow of it, he noted her relish the warm, smooth liquid as it soothed her irritated throat.

As the end of the schedule for this location neared, it became apparent they were going to need a few more days. The crew had earned the upcoming break. Four days off between locations had been allotted for time with their families. He requested Carla, Rusty and Elsie join him for a meeting in the dining room three days prior to wrap up in Vermont.

After dinner, Rusty went to Elsie's room to see if she needed assistance prior to the meeting. She answered the door.

"Hi Rusty, come in. What's up?" She welcomed with the dogs pushing to greet him first.

"I thought you'd like company walking the dogs." He offered.

She smiled in appreciation. "That would be great. I don't want a repeat of the first night here when Sophie took off."

"Oh I don't know. I kind of liked the thank you hug I got." He teased lightly to see if they were okay.

She didn't bother saying anything, her blush said it all.

As usual, he leashed Sophie while Elsie handled Tycho. Not that Rusty didn't like Tycho, he looked forward to rough housing with him like when he stayed at Elsie's at New Year's. Rather Sophie adored him and Tycho was a momma's boy. They walked for a short distance in silence.

Elsie spoke first "do you have any idea why Rich wanted to meet with us tonight?"

"No, I tried a couple times to get it out of him, but he said we'd talk tonight." Rusty responded with frustration. "You have any inkling?"

Her face scrunched as she contemplated it.

"I know when we went over the story boards, he had concerns with whether or not certain scenes were necessary as location shots or if he could do them in the studio. Or maybe he's heard the rumors going around?" Her voice trailed off as if she didn't really want to acknowledge them.

"And which rumors would those be?" Rusty wanted to shield her from the ones about her and Rich if possible.

"Take your pick. Those having affairs: Carla and the head cameraman, Maci and the wardrobe lady, me and Rich. Or those who hate each other: Carla and Maci, you and me. Did I leave any out?" Elsie stopped walking to give Tycho a chance to circle.

Rusty stopped, too.

"So you have heard all of them." Rusty grimaced. "Which one bothers you the most?"

"Most of them I don't really care if they are true or not. The one about Rich and me is laughable—I just hope his wife agrees." She glanced at Rusty.

He smiled. "Whew! I thought you'd be upset when you heard that one."

"No. I take it you weren't either?" She prompted.

He sensed her probing, he took the bait. "At first, it bothered me. I didn't want people talking that way about you. As for it being true, I knew it wasn't."

"What? I'm not tempting enough for a man to want me?" She snapped.

Both dogs froze to look at her thinking they'd done something wrong.

Rusty rolled his eyes. "That's not it! I've known Rich for a long time. He's not the type to cheat. And I know you wouldn't mix business with sex."

A quiet little "oh" escaped.

The dogs went back to sniffing the underbrush as the couple resumed walking.

The remainder of their stroll, they discussed the weather forecast for the next few days.

When they arrived at her room, Elsie invited Rusty to stay. "We still have fifteen minutes till the meeting. Do you want to stay, then we can walk down together?"

He masked his surprise at the offer. "Sure mate."

They unleashed the dogs to get a drink of water and settle into comfortable spots.

Rusty called to her in the bathroom. "Do you want to see what's on the telly?"

She stepped out drying her hands on a towel. "Actually, I wanted to ask you a question regarding one of the other rumors."

He looked at her with raised eyebrows. She hung the towel in the bathroom to stall.

"The one about us hating each other" she stated hurriedly.

Her eyelashes fluttered on her cheeks as she broke eye contact waiting for his answer.

Rusty walked over to stand in front of her. He tilted her chin up with his encased hand to force her to look at him. Instead of verbalizing his response as he had intended, he kissed her. His lips met hers gently. She responded by kissing back with the same tentativeness. Her eyelashes tickled his cheeks. He moved closer, deepening their kiss by opening his mouth. Her tongue met his unabashedly. As she leaned into him, his hands slid to cup her bottom. The clumsiness of the cast he wore completely unnoticed by either of them. When his hands explored higher, she didn't stop him. Her hands were trailing a similar path on his body. His mouth left hers to taste more of her. His week's worth of beard prickling against her skin combined with the velvety sensation of his mouth tantalized her nerve endings. The purring moan she made next to his ear was his undoing. He picked her up to place on the bed, sliding his body on top of hers with ease. This time his mouth covered hers for a ravaging kiss. His body pressed into hers, awakening long dormant desires. Her legs parted to allow his hardness to push into her softness. They both started tugging at their clothing. The frenzy on the bed brought the dogs to alert. Suddenly, a snuffling muzzle appeared on either side of their faces. Rusty tried to shoo them away, but they thought it was a new game causing them to bounce about wooing in playfulness. Both Rusty and Elsie ceased their intentions. Rusty's frustration at the interruption dispelled by the absurdity of the situation. He buried his face in Elsie's chest, then chuckled. Elsie laughed, too.

Glancing towards the clock, Rusty said. "Just in the nick of time. We have five minutes to put ourselves together and walk to the dining room."

He rolled off Elsie to remove himself from the bed. Elsie sat up pulling her legs to block her chest. A movement Rusty caught in the mirror as he stepped into the bathroom. When he looked back, her head rested on her knees.

He returned to the side of the bed. "Mate?"

She didn't stir. She merely blinked in response.

Rusty wasn't sure what to say or do. "Are you okay?"

No verbal response, she merely nodded.

"Why don't I believe you?" He asked warily.

Quietly and calmly she answered. "I haven't been here in such a long time I'm not sure."

"Not sure of . . . ?" He didn't understand.

"You, me, us?" Her voice filled with confusion, not upset. "I don't know what you want? Is it one night, a couple weeks or more?"

"I, um , . . ." He stumbled over his answer.

"Don't panic, I don't even know what I want beyond the last few minutes." She sighed in exasperation.

He stood their feeling impotent.

She slid to the edge of the bed.

"Now is not the time to figure it out; we are going to be late. Get in the bathroom to fix yourself. I need to use it, too." She shoved him towards the bathroom.

The dogs were crated by the time he'd relinquished the bathroom. They walked to the dining room in silence; both with too much on their minds in regards to what had transpired between them.

Rich commented when they walked in five minutes late together, "glad you two could make it."

Then he broke the news to the trio—Carla, Rusty and Elsie. They couldn't shoot everything they needed to by the date scheduled. He wanted suggestions on what they could do to avoid having to return at a later date. They brainstormed for two hours. It came down to reorganizing the scenes to make the most of Maci. There were scenes with only Rusty and extras that could be shot after most of the crew left. They would ask for volunteers from the camera and sound crews to stay as long as needed along with a portion of the equipment. This would mean no break between locations. Julie would have to stay to keep appearances consistent. Carla or Julie could also handle wardrobe with their regular jobs. Even though the dogs were getting stir crazy from being cooped up in a hotel room for four weeks, Elsie agreed to stay since she wasn't scheduled at the next few sites. At breakfast, they explained the situation to everyone. Thankfully, there were enough volunteers who didn't need the break. As for Rich personally, he called his wife last night when he returned to his room to break the news to her. She took it better than he'd anticipated; far better than he was.

Over the next few days, things were non-stop. Meals were sandwiches wherever they were filming at the time. Rusty and Maci stayed one night until 2am for a sequence of shots which they didn't want to lose momentum. They both even made it on time for breakfast the next morning. The last few days were grueling which meant Rusty had no time to spend with Elsie. The only time he thought about her were the few minutes his head met his pillow as he drifted to sleep. Everyone else departed as scheduled. The bunch who stayed worked by schedules delivered to their rooms by the start of each day. Filming continued from dawn till sometime after midnight the first two days. Mid-morning the third day, Carla pulled Rich aside.

"Rich, when I ran back to my room to get my notebook, Jake flagged me down. An emergency phone call came in for you. You need to call home as soon as possible." Carla emphasized her last few words.

"Give me the keys." Rich put out his hand for Carla to place them.

Rich turned around to find Rusty hovering nearby. "I have a family emergency. Can you keep going here while I run to the hotel to call from my cell?"

"Sure mate!" Rusty said confidently. "Hope everything is okay."

Rich rushed to the rental. Once the Explorer was out of sight, Rusty and Carla called the group together.

Rusty spoke first. "Gang, we'll be on our own for the rest of the day. Rich's wife is paying him a surprise visit at the hotel. Any issues or concerns, please let Carla or I know. Let's get this scene wrapped so we can eat lunch."

While they filmed another shot, Elsie waved Carla over to her.

"Carla, how did you convince Rich's wife to come?" Elsie asked.

"We didn't, it was her idea." Carla explained. "She'll fly with Rich from here to the next location to stay for a couple days before heading home."

"Do you think he'll be gone the whole rest of the day?" Elsie sounded skeptical.

Carla laughed. "You know, I had the same response. Janie assured me it was a safe bet. Also, she said Rich trusts Rusty. We really lucked out that the cell phones don't work on this side of the mountain."

Elsie smiled in agreement.

The rest of the day went without a hitch. Rich did not reappear. He even left a copy of the next day's schedule at the front desk with a note telling Carla and Rusty to revise. He expected his copy stuck to his door by midnight.

The next morning at breakfast, Rich and his wife were holding hands and smiling giddily. Rusty felt happiness mixed with jealousy at their genuinely loving relationship. Something he thought he had once, but had been a charade. Here he was again on the verge of feeling as if someone could love him for him and vice versa. Could it be possible or mere fantasy?

With Rich's anxious tension relieved, the crew felt revitalized. By the end of the extra days, they had enough, including a few extra, takes. The last day, Elsie was nowhere to be found. On his return to the hotel, he discovered why—she had departed. He asked Rich if there had been an emergency that she left without saying goodbye. The only thing Rich had to say was that had been her agreement with him the night of their rescheduling meeting. Upon further interrogation, Rich shared no other information. She'd gone without saying good-bye. It was a good thing he only had to catch a flight the next day. Rusty emptied the bottle of bourbon. Thankfully, he packed while he was drinking. When his alarm went off the next morning, he just rolled out of bed. He didn't care one iota when people, including Rich and Janie, looked at him like he had grown horns and a tail overnight. On the airplane, he had a few more drinks to abate the hangover.

Rich pulled him aside at the arrival gate to for another round of constructive criticism.

"Rusty old boy, you better stop drinking or we are sunk. We shoot first thing in the morning!" Rich's voice stern. "Don't get involved in anything that could be splashed across the tabloids in a negative way."

Rusty grumbled in agreement.

Unfortunately, it had been too late a warning. Photographs had already been snapped of him in his current condition.

Less than a week later captions read: "Rusty Garnet Ricocheted—on the Rebound Again" and "Garnet Loses Another to his Drinking".

Pictures of him from that day were printed alongside photographs of Tina Laney skimpily clad in a tight embrace with her latest beau. His grotesquely tight stomach and clean shaven face noticeably indicating he was not Rusty. Carla tossed the tabloid running the front page story into Rusty's lap while Julie applied his makeup. The rest of the day he tried to not think about the ensuing lecture from Rich. By the end of the day when they'd returned to their trailers, Rich had made no comment on the subject. The next day still nothing said. The third day Rusty pulled Carla aside.

"Carla what's going on? I mean, I should be glad Rich hasn't said anything about the headline, but it's not like him. Is something else wrong?" He asked pointedly.

She glanced around to see if anyone else was listening before answering. "Actually, yes. It seems Tina Laney made some rather discourteous remarks in regards to you when she was asked to comment on the story."

Rusty didn't understand. "So how is that a problem for us? Not like I haven't been bashed by a starlit or the media."

Once again, she scanned their close proximity. "I haven't seen the interview myself. Apparently it was sufficiently over the top to cause both Rich and the producer to want to fire her ass. Even though they have enough to say she broke her contract, they aren't sure how to get the location shots redone with a replacement. But doing the scenes on set with her will be terribly tense. Rich is concerned the animosity will be noticeable. After all, you two have a seriously steamy scene coming up."

He recalled the scenes yet to be filmed with the haughty actress. "That scene is strictly a sex scene. It is supposed to be devoid of emotion. Her character thinks she can manipulate my character with sex. Since my character is lonely and lacks direction in his life, she thinks she can win him over to use his powers for her own selfish use."

"I bet Rich hasn't analyzed it that far. His temper certainly has the better of him in this instance." A smile formed on her face easing the stress. "Thanks Rusty! I'm going to have a powwow with him to see if he agrees."

"No worries mate." Rusty was glad to have helped.

As Carla scurried away to find Rich, another worry slid into the forefront of his mind. "Why hadn't he heard from Elsie?"

It had been well over a week since they'd last talked. This latest headline should have her itching to send him her play on words for it.

CHAPTER TWENTY-ONE

ONLY A COUPLE of days passed before Rusty couldn't wait any longer. First, he phoned Sherry to make sure she wasn't holding out on him. She assured him she had not received anything from Elsie. Matter of fact, Harris had spoken to her only yesterday. The conversation had been cut short due to an urgent issue on his end. Rusty put his pride aside long enough to dial her cell number.

"Hello Rusty!" Elsie answered cheerfully.

"Hello mate." Allowing her cheeriness to be infectious, he responded similarly. "How are things on the farm?"

Playing along, she contained her giggles "the cows are milked, the pigs slopped, but those hens only want a man's hands sliding under their hoo-hahs to collect eggs."

The silliness of her answer made him chuckle.

Slipping on his best hillbilly impersonation: "Well nah apple-dumplin' I'll jest have ta see if them thar city fellars will lit me git on home ta take care of ma ladies. Sounds like yu're in need of a good cock."

Elsie couldn't hold her mirth any longer, she bust out laughing.

When she was able to catch her breath she said, "Bravo! You too can play the double entendre."

"But of course mate, I learned from an expert—you." Thriving on her lightheartedness, he teased further. "Anything else you'd like to teach me?"

He heard only silence. "Elsie?"

No response, "Elsie?"

He looked at the window of his cell phone. It indicated they were no longer connected. He still had a good signal with a full battery. He pressed re-dial.

"Rusty?" She greeted cautiously.

"What happened? My signal is good. You aren't driving are you?" He tried to fill in the reason.

"No, I'm standing at the upstairs window watching the dogs play. What about you?" She prompted.

"Sitting in my trailer talking to my favorite mate", He wanted her back in a mischievous mood.

Again, he was met by silence. "Elsie?"

This was getting ridiculous. He pressed dial again.

"Rusty what is going on? I'm starting to take these hang-ups personally" her patience clearly wearing thin.

"I don't know. I'm not doing it on purpose." His own frustration also thinly veiled.

"I know you aren't", her tone not as sharp. "How's it . . ."

They were cut off yet again. He examined the cell phone. His settings didn't have a timer set to automatically disconnect. As he moved it around in his hand, he noticed how it would slide into the groove of his cast between his index finger and thumb. The part of the cast at his thumb had been bent in towards his palm. This was due to him using his injured hand far more than most people with a similar break. This out jutting had been pushing the END button as the phone would shift in his hand while he talked. Switching the phone to his other hand, he selected Elsie's name on the phone list. Her phone only rang once, then switched immediately to voice mail. Either she had been mad enough to turn her phone off or she was on the phone with someone else.

He chose to believe the latter as he left a short message. "Hey mate! Calling back again; sorry about before. I need to not hold the cell in my right hand. The cast was hitting the disconnect button. Miss you."

He hoped she would return his call soon. Two hours later, hope faded. He poured himself a drink and switched channels on the television to find the late show with tonight's guest Tina Laney. He wanted to be prepared if she launched another attack. Of course, the host baited her perfectly. Her comments regarding the film and Rich were polite. Then the host asked her specifically what it was like to play opposite such a dynamic actor as Rusty.

Tina pounced. "I don't know why everyone thinks he's had all of those other actresses. From my time with him, he was an inarticulate plodding oaf. And he must have learned to kiss from a kangaroo. We still have to tape a bedroom scene in the studio. I won't be surprised if he turns out to be a dildo with dead batteries."

Tina's commentary infuriated him. He sent his drink flying across the room, striking the wall next to the television. His cell phone rang.

Seeing it was Elsie, he answered it gruffly. "Hello!"

"Rusty? Did I wake you?" She asked.

"If I had been asleep, I wouldn't have bothered answering." He was still stinging from her not answering earlier and the current situation.

"O-kaaay" her tone suspiciously tense. "Are you mad at me or were you watching the interview with Tina Laney?"

"Both!" He snarled.

"Let's start with why you're mad at me." She forced the topic.

"Well, Mate!" Biting off his words. "You ignored my last phone call."

There was a pause before she responded.

"I spent the last two hours at the vet so forgive me for not being at your beckon call!" Her tone denoted her resentment with his temper tantrum.

He quickly pushed his anger aside for concern. "What happened? Which one is hurt?"

"Actually neither; Sara had to rush Deedles to the vet. Tom is out of town so she called me for help." Elsie used the guilt card and won.

He asked with concern. "Is she alright?"

"She needed a few stitches and we brought her home." Elsie eased his conscience. "After Sara had a glass of wine, she settled, too."

"What happened?" He continued curiously.

"She tried to wiggle her way out of the kennel between her dog house and end panel. Even though she got snagged on the chain linking she saw her way to freedom."

"I don't understand. Instead of crying and waiting for help, she kept going with the obvious pain involved?" He questioned.

"Malamutes are more or less impervious to pain when they want something. But they can be such wusses at getting their nails trimmed. For something major, they are stoic." Elsie explained.

He followed the rationale. "But she's alright now?"

"No worries mate." She used his colloquialism. "Now for the real thorn in your side—one Ms. Tina Laney."

"That bitch!" Was all he could manage without leading into a string of profanities he'd rather not use while speaking to a woman of grace.

"Well that was far milder than I expected." She replied sardonically.

He muttered a few more expletives under his breath. However, it translated to cranky gibberish over the line to her.

"Rusty—did you happen to notice the eloquence in which Tina delivered her little speech?" She prodded.

"Matter of fact I did. Rather surprising since she seemed to rank fairly low on the IQ scale when Rich and I would discuss scenes with her." He didn't know where Elsie was going with this. "What's your point mate?"

"Her speech was scripted." She answered confidently. "She merely had to wait for the inevitable question from the host to play the part of the petulant prima donna."

"Why?" He didn't understand.

"It gets her publicity. 'Worn-out Rusty Garnet shuns the talented Tina Laney' is one headline." Elsie paused. "There's also another tactic she could taking."

"And that would be?" His ears were burning.

"Her comment was meant to provoke you." He could hear Elsie chewing on her bottom lip which meant she was uneasy.

""Don't hold back now mate." It was his turn to prod.

"Think about her words 'dildo with a dead battery'." The discomfort with the topic was evident in her voice.

"Elsie, get to the point!" He exclaimed impatiently.

She rushed her words on command. "She wants you to prove her wrong!"

"What?!" His tone outraged. "Are you crazy? The woman hates me!"

"No Rusty, she wants to be the next notch on your bedpost, rather you on hers." She said flatly.

He tossed her words around his head. It couldn't be possible Tina Laney found anything attractive about him; except the publicity that encompassed him at every turn. There was absolutely nothing in her he found desirable. She was a plastic surgeon's masterpiece; that's all she was—plastic, inside and out.

He realized it had been a long stretch of silence. "Mate, are you still there?'

"Yes Rusty, as long as you want me to be", her tone unfamiliar to him.

"You are referring to more than this phone call aren't you?" He needed to be sure.

"That depends on what you want to hear." She was being evasive.

"I want to hear what you want!" The game was wearing thin.

"What I want is never important enough to anyone. Just do what you're going to do with Tina Laney! I'm tired and going to bed. Good-bye." Her speech done, Elsie hung up without any further utterance from Rusty.

Shocked by her outburst, he couldn't think of anything quick enough to keep her on the phone. If he didn't know any better, he'd have sworn her tone relayed disappointment. If he called her back, she'd interrupt him causing him to leave something out. He opted for composing an email. His laptop still in his carry-on bag from when he'd arrived days ago. Once it was set up, he had his thoughts organized. He typed in exactly what he'd been thinking in regards to Tina Laney's plastic personality and equally fake looks.

Then he added "when I decide to pursue a serious romantic relationship, you will be the first to know".

Chapter Twenty-Two

RUSTY WOKE TO his cell phone ringing. He glanced around the hotel room trying to orient himself.

"Hello Rusty, this is Sara. What's wrong?" echoed a female voice through phone.

"Hello Sara. What's wrong?" He repeated dazedly in a thick, scratchy voice.

"Rusty, are you asleep or drunk?" Sara's voice steely with frustration.

"Asleep." Glancing at the clock on the nightstand, he said trying for coherency. "It's 5am here."

"You left a message on both the answering machine and cell phone saying it was an emergency. That we were supposed to call no matter what time it was in Australia." She clarified why she was calling. "Is Elsie alright?"

Rusty sat up groaning as the memory of the last 48 hours once again played center stage.

His groan ignited Sara's anxiety. "Oh my God, tell me!"

Rusty relayed to her how they had gone riding with friends. They encountered a snake. The high-spirited horse reared in response to the potential danger. Elsie was thrown, landing in a group of fallen trees. The snake, thankfully, slithered off in the other direction as the horse high-tailed it back to the ranch. Elsie had been flown to the hospital in Sydney. She had contusions, abrasions, broken ribs, fractured wrist and head injury which had her in a coma; her prognosis undetermined. By the time Rusty finished the story, tears ran down his face.

Tom's voice came through the phone. "What do you need us to do?"

In the background, Sara's sobs could be heard.

"Tom, I only called because Elsie would have wanted me to . . ." his voice cracked with emotion " . . . I honestly don't know."

Both ends of the line were silent except for the shared tears of worry. Finally, Tom disturbed the quiet.

His voice also lacking its usual strength, "We'll call in a few hours for a status. In the meantime, please call us any time day or night if Elsie's condition changes for the better or worse. And if she does wake up, tell her the kids are good and that we love her."

"Okay mate, will do." He replied.

They hung up. Rusty flipped his cell onto the bed. He rested his head in his hands for a few minutes. It was too early for visiting hours. Still he moved to the bathroom for a shower. Afterwards, he decided to call Sherry so her husband was aware of his client's circumstances. It was late afternoon on the west coast. Sherry didn't answer; he left a detailed message. Then he dialed Rich.

"Hey Rusty, how's Elsie taking to Down Under?" Rich greeted.

Rusty kept a tight lid on his emotions as he filled Rich in on Elsie's accident.

"Good God Rusty!!" Rich exclaimed in horror. "I don't know what to say."

"That makes everyone at this point." Rusty sounded deflated. "Elsie would want you and Janie to know. And even though I haven't encountered any reporters, thought you should be prepared in case it does get out."

"I still can't believe you two have been there for almost three weeks with no reports. Maybe this won't be noticed either. Poor Elsie, is there anything we can do?" Rich offered.

"Pray . . ." was all Rusty could say.

Hew decided to go to the hospital anyway. If nothing else, he'd get breakfast in the cafeteria. As suspected, due to the earliness of the hour, the grill hadn't opened. However, fresh coffee and pastry were available. Rusty had brought the newspaper provided by the hotel to pass the time. He selected a corner table to partake of the morning fare. Upon refilling his coffee cup at the counter, a female voice spoke from behind him.

"Good Morning Mr. Garnet. Please tell me your early arrival is due to good news on Ms. Endy's condition?" It was Dr. Edwards.

Rusty smiled cordially. "There has been no change since the first day. I spoke with her family in the states this morning and didn't see any point in going back to sleep. Figured I'd loiter around the cafeteria till visiting hours."

"Do you mind?" Dr. Edwards motioned towards one of the chairs at his table.

"Please do" he offered. "On your way in or out?"

She answered "In. The last two days were my days off. I wanted to make a few extra rounds before the ER gets busy."

Rusty merely nodded.

Dr. Edwards slid the front section of the newspaper to the place on the table in front of her. They both remained silent reading and drinking coffee. When Dr. Edwards drank the last swallow of caffeine, she arose.

"Mr. Garnet, one of my extra rounds this morning is to check on Ms. Endy. If you'd care to join me?" She asked matter of fact.

He quickly collected his newspaper together "yes ma'am I would."

"Then I'll make the trip to her room first." The doctor said as she pushed the button for the elevator.

"Thank you Dr. Edwards." He responded gratefully.

"Please call me Jaime." The doctor suggested amiably.

"In that case Jaime, call me Rusty." He returned similarly.

"Well Rusty, that would be a pleasure." Her response purred with femininity.

Even in his current state, Rusty noted the change in her demeanor. Not sure of what to say, he said nothing to prevent encouraging more of the same from the female doctor. It wasn't that she was unattractive. She was actually quite attractive with her tall litheness and long raven hair braided away from her heart shaped face and pouty lips—his perusal of her merely objective. Any inclination she might have in his direction would be met with failure.

Unfortunately that didn't mean she wasn't going to make an attempt. "So Rusty, how long will you be staying in the city?"

"As long as it takes for Elsie to recover" he kept his answer short.

"Are you two engaged or something?" her voice innocent, her intentions quite contrary.

"Or something" should have been enough of a rebuttal.

Jaime would not let it go "Something permanent or something temporary?"

Thankfully, he didn't have time to answer before the doors opened to allow others to enter the lift. At Elsie's floor, he waited for Jaime to step out first. It was a gentlemanly gesture merely to prevent the doctor from ogling his butt. They walked to Elsie's room. Once inside, Rusty grasped Elsie's placid hand; an action which reminded Jaime of her position. Dr. Edwards reviewed the patient's chart.

When she completed her examination, she spoke. "There appears to be no relevant changes to Ms. Endy's condition. Based on the nature of her fall, it isn't surprising. At least no other serious injuries have surfaced."

"So what does that mean?" He wanted something good to share with the others.

"She hasn't gotten any worse. As for the long term prognosis, it seems to be between Elsie and God." Dr. Edwards moved to the door.

Seeing him start to stand, she stopped him. "There's no reason for you to leave. The nurses won't bother with you. Her neurologist should be by this morning, you might want to talk further with him. G'day Mr. Garnet."

He called out a "thank you" as she closed the door behind her.

What was he supposed to tell Sara and Tom when they phoned? No sooner had the thought crossed his mind, the phone by Elsie's bed began to ring.

"Hello?" He answered warily.

"Rusty, it's Tom. I tried your cell, but when it went right to voice mail, I figured you were at the hospital. Has there been a change in her condition?" His voice sounded hopeful.

Rusty responded wishing he had better news. "No change."

"What is your game plan?" Tom didn't want to push, but Sara wouldn't be satisfied with Rusty's previous answer.

"Her neurologist is supposed to be here this morning. I'd like to talk to him about a few things." Rusty hedged.

"Are you thinking about flying her to the states?" Tom knew the answer already.

"Yes, I feel she would do better at home. Which hospital and the length of the flight are questionable." He stated.

"As for the hospital, that's a no brainer—Lehigh Valley Hospital. It's ranked top ten in the US. But I agree the flight is a major concern. Even with short stays in Hawaii and LA that's an awful lot of jostling." Tom remarked.

"That's why I want to talk to the doctor to see what he thinks. If she would just wake up . . ." His voice trailed off at realizing what he'd said.

"Yeah well, that would be the answer we're all looking for isn't it." Tom could hear the frustration in Rusty's voice.

Frustration fueled by feeling completely helpless.

"Listen Rusty, call when you have concrete answers. Sara is pushing for me to book a flight to Sydney. I don't want her to be an added burden for you. Unfortunately, we both can't leave. I will hold her at bay as long as I can."

"Good luck mate", Rusty replied.

"To you too ol' boy" Tom said.

Rusty took hold of Elsie's hand again as he sat in the chair. He leaned forward, laying his head and chest on the bed. His head nestled between her torso and hand. While he waited for the neurologist, he wondered why women acted the way Dr. Edwards did towards him. Was it because of him or what they thought he was or could do for them? He knew Elsie cared for whom he really was, not the image. Matter of fact, his notoriety placed her in painful situations that other women never face. The Tina Laney incident replayed in his mind.

Chapter Twenty-Three

THEY HAD MOVED production of "Sifting through the Ashes" to the studio in mid-July. They still had two location shoots to complete. West Virginia was scheduled for late September for autumnal shots. New Mexico required night shots in the desert. Those were slotted for the weeks between filming at the studio and West Virginia. Rich wanted to complete as much of the studio scenes as possible. The end of filming was supposed to be West Virginia. This allowed two months for editing and any re-shoots before the proposed premiere date of December 24th.

With the studio in California, it fit nicely into the premiere of the film Rusty made with Red: "Mountains Majesty". It also meant he'd get to see Elsie after two and a half months apart. They'd spoke on the phone every day even if it was only to say good night before going to sleep. The topic of Tina Laney remained closed since the night on Leno. Both seemed more than happy to sweep that unpleasant conversation under the rug. Elsie would be spending a few days with him. He'd even convinced her to stay in the guest room of the condominium he owned nearby. The dogs would not be making the trip.

The first week at the studio was for Rusty alone. A few days prior to Elsie's arrival marked Tina Laney's. The tension could've been cut with a knife. Rich, Rusty and Carla waited for her venom. Even Julie was concerned with the high probability that Tina's temper would erupt. Tina shocked them by acting uncharacteristically professional towards all of them.

Had Rusty not been required on the set, he'd have fetched Elsie from the airport. Instead, Harris met her. Since he needed her to sign a few papers, it worked for everyone's benefit. Sherry was waiting at the condominium to get Elsie settled in before Rusty returned home.

Thankfully, they took a break between takes to allow him to make a quick call. "Hey Mate. Is Elsie there or did her flight get delayed again?"

"They just arrived. He's carrying her bags up to the guest bedroom." Sherry replied happily.

"Before you to put her on the phone, I really want to thank you for being such a sport." Rusty spoke sincerely. "Please thank Harris, too. Especially since her flight was delayed. What did you two find to do for two hours while you waited?"

Sherry couldn't contain a girlish giggle as she answered. "Oh, we found a couple of things to do to pass the time."

"Please tell me you weren't at my place for your, er um, activities?" Her innuendo did not go unnoticed.

"Technically, yes." Her voice filled with mirth.

"I don't want to know." He sighed in mock exasperation.

"To put your mind at rest, the backseat of a Mercedes is very roomy." Sherry giggled again at the thought.

"I told you, I didn't want to know!" Rusty exclaimed.

"Just thought you should, in case your neighbors make reference to it." Her voice contained no remorse.

Rusty merely groaned at the thought of the reaction from his nosey neighbors.

Sherry couldn't prevent a loud laugh from escaping. "Don't fret, we pulled into the garage."

"Are you done making a mockery of me?" Rusty asked in a half serious growl.

"I think so." Sherry's mirth spent. "Here's Elsie."

"Hello?" It was Elsie.

"Hello Mate. Other than the delay, how was the flight?" His tone much chipper at hearing her voice.

"Hi Rusty, it was okay." She answered lightheartedly. "I can't believe I didn't sleep a wink on it."

"Maybe you were excited about seeing me?" he teased.

"Fishing for a compliment? You must be having a tough day with Tina Laney." She remarked deftly side-stepping his intention.

"She's still on her best behavior. But we haven't gotten to the bedroom scene yet." His voice tainted with skepticism.

"Oh, when will that be taped?" she asked.

"Not tomorrow, but the next day" he answered normally.

"It's not going to interfere with the premiere of 'Mountain's Majesty', right?" She questioned with concern.

"Why would it?" he asked bewildered by her questioning.

"A weird occurrence with my dress—I'll tell you later." She replied cryptically.

"Okay mate. We'll talk tonight when I get home. Rich is waving at me." He said distracted.

"When will that be?" Her voice sounded strained.

"We should be done by ten. Gotta go love. See you around eleven." He hung up without waiting for her good-bye.

Rusty didn't arrive home until midnight. He couldn't tell if Tina had been difficult on purpose or was honestly having an issue with the last scene. Odd too, she seemed to handle the run-through prior to the break with ease. It should've taken them less than the two hours slotted to get everything Rich wanted. It took three hours.

Upon opening the door, Rusty heard the television. Perhaps Elsie had managed to stay awake. As he peered over the sofa, he couldn't help smiling. There she lay, on her stomach with her face buried between two throw pillows. From the twisted disarray of her pajamas and hair, he guessed she'd been asleep for quite awhile. It wasn't really any wonder. Her body, still on Eastern Standard Time, felt it was three in the morning. He didn't want to disturb her. If she slept the night in that position, she'd pay for it. Without thinking any further, he scooped her into his arms. The throw that had tangled around her legs came along for the ride. Once in her room, he tugged the bedspread back to slide her underneath it. It didn't go as planned. After he put her on the bed, he attempted to stand only to find his arms knotted in the throw. The more he tried to disentangle himself, the less it appeared to work. His right hand still encased in the cast hindered him further. His frustration grew to where he fought with the knot so much as to cause him to lose his balance. Crashing on top of Elsie woke her.

"What . . . ?" She mumbled sleepily in the dark room.

His answer muffled by the pillow in which his face landed.

Suddenly, she started pushing at him. "Get off!"

Still in an awkward position, he couldn't seem to move one way or the other. This caused her to panic. Her pushing turned to hitting and clawing. In her frantic movements, she managed to loosen the fabric binding his arms. As he got his bearings, he grabbed her arms. This only scared her further. The kick to his groin forced him to release her and roll off the bed. As he endured the excruciating pain, he reached for the light switch. Once the room was lit, she stilled. He watched her from the far side of the room. She blinked a few times while looking around the room. When she realized she wasn't alone, her immediate reaction was to pull her legs up in a defensive action. As she looked in his direction, her eyes seemed to register who he was. At making full eye contact with him, he could tell she'd regained coherency.

He quickly spoke before she misinterpreted what had transpired. "I carried you here because I wanted you to be comfortable. My cast got tangled in the covers."

The recognition of the actual event rather than her distorted sleep state made her start to cry. "I'm sorry Rusty. I didn't realize it was you."

The tears turned into sobs. He immediately closed the distance between them.

He sat on the bed, putting his hand on her shoulder. "It's okay mate. You don't have to cry, it was an honest mistake the way I startled you awake."

She flung herself into his arms, burying her face in his chest.

She stopped long enough between gulps of air to say "You don't understand! I thought you were him . . ."

The adrenalin rush aided his summation abilities.

"No worries. You are exhausted and in unknown surroundings. Then I fall on top of you." He tried using her trick of logic to douse her flash pan of emotions.

It worked. A few shuddering breaths quieted her tears. Rusty could see her peering at him through her wet eyelashes.

"What's going on in that overactive brain of yours Love?" He asked with a tinge of trepidation.

She buried her face in his chest again, making her response incomprehensive.

He found her chin with his hand to gently move her to look at him. "Please, I want to know."

She maintained eye contact with him even though he could tell she would have preferred not. "You'll never want to get near me now."

He looked at her, then at their proximity. "Mate, short of stripping naked, we couldn't get much closer than this."

He could see her taking in their current positioning. They both sat facing each other on the bed. Her legs were wrapped around his waist pulling their torsos together. Add their embrace; there wasn't enough room between them to take a breath without the other feeling it. By the time she finished evaluating this, her face brightened with a new shade of pink. All of a sudden, he also, grasped the true awkwardness of it when his manhood rose to the occasion. Considering the blow it had taken a few minutes prior, it took him by surprise. He abruptly set her away from him to retreat from the bed. The decorative throw which had caused the whole predicament lay unencumbered within reach. He deftly pulled it in front of him as he stood slightly hunched over from both the painful and pleasurable physical response to their contact.

"We're both tired. Let's forget about this and start fresh in the morning. Okay mate?" He said brusquely.

With her nod he left her room, pulling the door closed behind him. Stepping into his room, he balled the fabric in anger to throw at the chair. Without bothering to turn on any lights, he strode into the adjoining bath. After rinsing his face with cold water, he stripped to his boxers and fell across the bed. For as exhausted as he was, he got very little sleep. His dreams were images of Elsie's terrified face and an unknown assailant. The dreams started with her smiling with arms open wide only to end in terrified betrayal. The one he had as the alarm announced morning shook him to his core. It started with Elsie's welcoming stance to him.

As she looked passed him, she said "they can't see us together".

Then she ran from the building towards an open field. He pursued, calling her name. She stopped at beautiful wild flowers edging a plush field. When she turned to face him, he morphed into the shadowy assailant with a plain gold wedding band glinting on his left hand as it rose to strike.

Rolling to a sitting position, his head pounded. Rusty took a very hot shower. The steam didn't evaporate his headache. Along with taking his morning vitamins, he popped two over the counter caplets. 5:30 was too early to wake Elsie to review the day's schedule. He wrote her a note detailing it:

> Good Morning Elsie
> Today's agenda

filming	6-4
Red's arrival	1:30
Dinner delivery	2
limo	5:30
red carpet	7
movie	8-10:30
post-party	11-1

> You and Red eat.
> I'll eat while I'm changing into my tux.
> Rusty

He thought to add a comment regarding their late night fiasco, but changed his mind. For all he knew, she might not remember any of it. He stood the note between an empty cup and the coffee beans. As he walked to the door to leave, he turned off the television that had been on all night.

Things at the studio appeared calm enough at his arrival. When Rich saw him, it only hinted at how the rest of the day would unfold.

"What happened to you?" Rich asked somewhere between concern and irritation.

"Didn't sleep well", Rusty answered about the dark circles under his eyes. "Julie's a whiz; she'll make me look well rested."

"She better have a way to hide those scratches on your neck too." With a raised eyebrow, Rich walked away.

Rusty was glad when he saw Julie had arrived a little earlier than usual. He waved to her. As always, Julie's perkiness at this hour helped jump start Rusty. Rich paused a few moments next to her. Her face held its smile while her eyes darted back to Rusty still standing at the other end of the morning buffet. As soon as Rich moved on, Julie made a beeline for Rusty.

"Goodness Rusty! What happened?" She chirped with concern as she led him to the makeup area.

He knew she would understand since she and Elsie had become friends. Plus, what Jerry knew of Elsie's past had most likely been relayed to her as well. He took a chance.

Once seated, Rusty began his tale of woe. "When I got in last night, Elsie was asleep on the sofa. I carried her to her room, got twisted in the blankets and startled her awake."

He ended with a sigh of desperation.

Julie perused his face, as if looking for other noticeable battle wounds. "Oh dear, how was she when she realized it was you?"

He skirted the intimate details, "I tried to explain to her it was okay. All I could do was stay till she stopped crying."

"Is that why she didn't join you this morning?" Julie didn't pry for specifics.

"I didn't want to disturb her again, so I left her sleep." He replied.

"Rusty! She's going to think you are mad at her." She chastised.

"I left her a note." He quickly covered.

"That was sweet." In her romantic naivety, she did not realize it wasn't anywhere near the love note imagined.

He kept his mouth firmly shut over the matter for the remainder of her administering his makeup.

The morning's filming went in the same manner as the previous evening. Rich yelled cut time after time. One take, Tina even broke into tears. This was totally unexpected in relation to her usual hissy fits. Rusty eagerly relinquished its handling to Rich.

"Okay Tina, why the waterworks?" Rich asked flatly.

"Like any of you care. All you've been doing is yelling since last night. All of you hate me." Then she ran to her dressing room with her hands hiding her face.

Rich, Rusty, Carla and Julie stood there looking to each other for acknowledgement of the bizarre episode to which they'd witnessed.

Rich ran his hand through the barely there hair on the top of his head. "Carla, would you please go find out what the problem is?"

Carla did as Rich requested. It didn't take very long for her to return with an answer.

"It would seem Ms. Laney finds it difficult acting when no one around here likes her. She says she's nervous enough regarding the upcoming bedroom scene, but with no one to talk to she feels ostracized." Carla took a breath to continue in her dry monotone. "Nor has anyone asked her to join them for dinner or anything else for that matter."

This particular comment had Carla looking directly at Rusty.

"Thank you Carla. I will be back in a few minutes." Rich turned away from the group, making long strides for the exit.

Rusty figured Rich needed to clear his head. He went back to his own dressing room to give Elsie a call. He dialed her cell, no answer. He phoned his home. No answer there either. He left a message on both expecting her to respond. He hoped she wasn't still upset over last night. Hell, why should she be mad at him? It wasn't like he'd done it intentionally. The last dream he'd had, nagged at him. Was she falling for him? Could she want more than he could give? The last thing he'd ever want to do was hurt her. Maybe having her stay with him had been a mistake. He couldn't risk letting her get too close. It would only mean heartache. How could he make that clear to her? These thoughts were only making his headache worse. His cell phone vibrated on the dressing table.

He saw it was Rich. "What do you need mate?"

Rich's tone terse "meet me outside now."

"Be right there." He complied.

When Rusty stepped outside, Rich waved him over to a deserted studio across the alleyway. Inside this building, Rich called out if anyone was there. Getting no response, he turned to face Rusty.

"Let me start with apologizing for what I'm going to ask you to do. I see no other way and it's too late in filming to replace Tina." He stopped talking; dug his hands in his pockets in search of another answer.

His hands finding nothing, he continued. "Please ask Tina to tonight's premiere?"

"What?!" Rusty erupted. "You can't be serious that I take her instead of Elsie!"

"There's no other option." Rich shrugged. "She wants special attention—specifically from you."

The director held up his hands to prevent interruption. "I'm not pimping you out. Just be pleasant to her for the next couple of days, nothing more than that."

"This night was supposed to be special for Elsie, her first premiere." As the words left his mouth, Rusty realized he was the one who'd become too attached.

Why else would he want to make it a special evening?

Rich cajoled. "Rusty pal, you know I wouldn't ask . . ."

Rusty cut him off. "I'll do it."

Taken aback by the abruptness of the one-eighty Rusty did on the matter, Rich questioned. "What about Elsie?"

"I'll handle it. Give me ten minutes to invite Tina and to call Elsie with the change in plans." Rusty strode away full of determination.

Returning to their building, Rusty went straight to Tina's dressing room. He knocked twice.

"Yes, who is it?" a wan voice sounded from inside.

"Tina, its Rusty" his voice full of forced cordialness.

There was a bit of rustling, then Tina opened the door dabbing at her moist eyelashes. "Come in."

"No need. I wanted to know if you'd like to join me for the premiere of 'Mountain's Majesty' this evening?" He deserved an Oscar for this performance.

"Yes, I would gladly be your date." Tina answered sweetly.

"We will be sharing the limo with Red Roget and Elsie Endy. We will pick you up at 6 o'clock." He stated his terms.

She pouted as she replied "shame we have to share."

He ignored her innuendo. "Are you ready to return to the set?"

"My makeup is such a mess." Tina continued pouting for his benefit.

"No worries, Julie can fix it with a few minor brush strokes here and there." He took Tina by the elbow to steer her to the set.

His offhanded compliment and gentlemanly gesture put Tina in an amiable frame of mind for the remainder of the day. They managed to complete everything Rich had scheduled. During a wardrobe change, Rusty called Red.

"Hey Rusty, Elsie was showing me around the place." Red answered.

"Good, glad you got there safely mate." Rusty paused a moment before putting Red on the spot. "Red, I need you to do me a favor."

The older gentlemen offered. "Sure Rusty, what is it?"

Rusty clarified the other man's status for the evening's event. "You don't have a date tonight right?"

"That would be correct. What are you gittin' at pal?" the apprehension in Red's voice could be heard.

"Would you please be Elsie's escort for the evening?" There he said it.

"Of course I will. I'd be a fool not to. But why aren't you going to be by her side?" Red replied masking his personal opinion.

"Change of agenda. Thanks, I'll see you in a couple hours." Rusty tried to end the call.

Red was too quick for him. "Hold on there pal! You better tell Elsie yourself. Here she is."

"Hey Rusty, Red says you need to talk to me" her voice chirpy with anticipation.

"Yes, there's been a change in priorities and Red will be your escort for the premiere. I'll be taking Tina Laney." He felt like a grade-A schmuck, but it had to be done.

The quicker, the less painful—like removing a band-aid.

"Oh." It took a few moments for Elsie to conceal her disappointment. "Guess that's how it is in show business, constantly changing one's priorities."

He caught onto her accentuating his words.

"Anything else?" She added.

"No, that's it. See you later." He would have preferred yelling instead of her cool response.

It was after 5 o'clock when he arrived home. He purposefully stayed longer at the studio with Rich. The lesser the chance of alone time with Elsie, the easier to hold onto his resolve to keep her at arms length.

Red greeted him from the kitchen. "Hey pal. How'd filming go today?"

"After smoothing things with Tina Laney, we managed to get everything needed for the day." Rusty answered while filling a plate.

"Uh huh" emitted from Red.

Rusty ignored the noise as he sat at the table to eat his meal. It would only take him a half hour to shower and dress. He couldn't shave because of the needed continuity for filming. Originally, he'd been happy to oblige since Elsie preferred him with a beard. At the moment, it itched.

"Rusty, can we talk?" Red interrupted his reverie.

"Sure mate, shoot." Rusty continued eating.

"Are you going to explain to Elsie why you are escorting Tina Laney instead of her?" His tone relayed disapproval.

"Why should I explain? It's not like Elsie and I are a couple or anything." Rusty put an edge on his words hoping to prevent Red from pursuing the topic.

Red shook his head. "Guess I read it all wrong with the lengths you were going to for her. Then again so did our little lady. She took it terribly hard."

He paused to see if he'd gotten a reaction from his host.

None noticed; he kept talking. "You know, we were sitting here eating and chatting when you called. After she got off the phone, she scraped her food into the trash, then went to her room. Before she went, she actually tried to make me feel better about taking her. She even said 'need a little extra time to get ready for my special date'. She's been up there ever since. No woman takes three hours to get ready for anything."

Rusty placed his fork gently on the plate belying his inner turmoil. "What do you want me to do about it? I didn't ask her to like me. Rather she learns what I am now than after it's too late."

The older man shrugged his shoulders. "It's never too late to find happiness and love."

With that said, he walked to the powder room; lifting his tuxedo off the door as he closed it.

Rusty wanted to use his plate like a Frisbee. Instead, he placed it in the sink, then opened the liquor cabinet. After downing a tumbler of scotch, he headed upstairs to prepare for the evening's pomp and circumstance. By the time he was dressed in his formal attire, his headache had spread to include his neck. He grabbed a bottle of prescription pain killers from the medicine cabinet. Not sure if taking one would be enough, he slipped the bottle into his jacket pocket. He paused at Elsie's door, his hand raised to knock.

It was for naught when he heard her voice echo up the stairs from the entry way. "Thank you Red. It's not often I receive such an honest compliment."

Rusty followed the sound of her voice. She wore the same dress she'd worn to the party with him those many months ago. On her, silk brocade was as versatile as the coveted perfect little black dress. He couldn't help himself when a low whistle slipped from between his lips.

"Isn't that nice of Rusty to whistle at how sexy you look in your tuxedo Red?" She deflected his admiration.

Red played along with her. "To think, I wasn't sure about the cowboy boots. But they are so dang comfortable."

Rusty said nothing, merely ushered them to the waiting limousine. They rode in silence to Tina Laney's hotel. At the hotel, Rusty had to go into the lobby to collect her. She wore an elegant full length dress in jade green chintz. It appeared as though getting in and out of the limousine would be a challenge. As she stepped in, the slit front and back went high enough for him to see Tina was wearing nothing underneath. Red and Elsie both said good evening to Tina as she joined them. Rusty settled onto the seat next to Tina. They had at least a 45 minute ride to the theatre. Rusty poured himself and Red a scotch from the bar. Elsie helped herself to the amaretto ordered along with the scotch when Sherry reserved the limousine. Red and Rusty discussed Red's flight in and happenings at the ranch.

Elsie showed her interest in the conversation with little "oh"s, nodding and occasionally patting Red's leg.

Tina couldn't have acted more bored if she'd tried. When the boys' club conversation died, Tina relayed how awful her hotel was. This led to the trials and tribulations of deciding on a dress for the evening. Five were flown in from a New York designer yesterday. Each had one thing or another wrong with it that she couldn't choose. At the last minute, they made alterations to the one she was currently wearing to make her look absolutely perfect.

Elsie piped up at this point. "Your dresses were on the same flight as me. When we were leaving the airplane, the man in charge of them grabbed my dress, too. The flight attendant had to chase after him to retrieve it."

For an undisclosed reason, Tina found this remarkably funny. She was laughing so much it took a while for her to say anything.

And when she did . . . "Oh honey, your dress must have gotten slipped in the middle of mine because there's no way anyone looking at them would have made that mistake."

Poor Red choked on his drink. Rusty realized if it hadn't been for her focus on Red, Elsie would have had a stinging remark for Tina. Instead, Elsie sent daggers with her eyes at Rusty. Soon enough, they were in the line of limousines waiting to unload at the red carpet leading into the theatre. The lead actor and actress were a few cars ahead of them.

"Rusty since everyone wants to see you and Ms. Laney, you should step out first." Red directed.

"Thanks mate. Are you sure you won't have a problem with this low vehicle and your back?" Rusty showed his concern for the older man.

Red chuckled. "To use your phrase: 'no worries'. The thought of escorting this sweet young lady in front of those cameras has given me quite an adrenalin rush where I'm feeling no pain."

Jealousy filled Rusty. It should be him floating on that cloud. The limousine stopped at the red carpet. An usher opened the door. Time to put on his game face and pay the piper—Rusty emerged. He waved to the crowd before turning to give a hand to aid Tina Laney's entrance. Flashbulbs popped from every direction. Strangers hollered to them. The lights of the television cameras in front were blinding. They posed for a few still shots. Rusty glanced towards the limousine to ensure Red and Elsie had no problems. Elsie had a death grip on Red's hand. She smiled, but he could see the fear in her eyes. Tina pulled at his arm to move into the theatre. Thankfully, there were only a few reporters to contend with inside the lobby. After interviews, they made their way to their reserved seats. It was at this moment Rusty realized he'd made a serious faux pas. They had only reserved three seats. The four of them waited for an usher.

Rusty said under his breath to Red, "There are four of us. We only have three seats."

Red replied "Elsie called Sherry to handle it."

The usher showed them to their seats.

Rusty motioned for Tina to sit first.

As way of explanation, he said. "Red needs the aisle seat for his knees."

Tina didn't argue. However, she was less than pleased when Elsie sat on the other side of Rusty. The first tear jerker scene, Elsie retrieved tissues from her purse. Knowing the ending, she started crying early. By the time the last scene played, she had depleted her supply of dry tissues. Red and Rusty handed her their handkerchiefs simultaneously. She snatched both, covering each eye. From next to him, he heard Tina's overacted huff. It wasn't like she needed it; she hadn't shed a single tear. Rusty wondered if she'd even enjoyed the film. When the lights brightened, Elsie returned the damp, mascara streaked hankies.

Turning to Red, Elsie asked. "How do I look? I mean, from crying, did my mascara smear too much?"

Red beamed as he answered. "You look absolutely beautiful."

The compliment evidently flabbergasted her as much as it did Rusty. At standing, all of the used tissues in her lap fell to the floor. Elsie and Rusty both knelt to fetch them.

Without thinking, he whispered "He's right. You are beautiful."

Not taking him seriously, she retorted "it's the dress".

He touched her hand to tell her "no, you truly are a beautiful woman".

But Tina's whine from behind him shattered the moment. "I'm ready to go."

Rusty shoved the used tissues into his pocket to dispose of in the lobby. They received praise from the rest of the elite audience while they waited for their limousine. Red gushed with enthusiasm at how well the film had been received. Rusty too, was exceptionally proud of how quickly he was accepted back into the fold. Even if he did say so himself; he did a wonderful job with the supporting role. Plus, Red's knack with editing at exacting moments put dimensions into a scene that Rusty had overlooked.

At the party, the two couples separated. By midnight, Rusty was ready to leave the festivities. Red was still working the crowd as he'd learned from decades ago. Rusty watched how Elsie remained by Red's side. Red played the role of the perfect date. Ever attentive to include her in the conversation or wander to the buffet table when her food or drink lacked. He'd gotten into the part to the point of kissing her on the cheek when she excused herself to the ladies' room. The amount of class she exhibited all evening after what an arrogant ass Rusty had been at the last minute, amazed him. However, the stress of the constant crowd could be noticed in the amount of her fidgeting. To the average onlooker, it appeared no different than a woman casually smoothing her dress or removing fuzz from her date's jacket. As Rusty observed her motions, he could see her swirling the ice cubes in her drink or folding and unfolding her napkin along with the other movements steadily increasing. He could understand. The evening was wearing thin for him. Being away from it for the last few years had decreased his tolerance for the superficiality of it all. Listening to Tina Laney's incessant self-indulgence renewed his headache with a vengeance. He slipped away for a few minutes to take two more pills.

At 12:30, Rusty flagged Red down. He pointed to his watch. Red glanced at Elsie by his side to nod in agreement. Rusty collected Tina Laney.

Her displeasure at leaving early was apparent as she sniped "if I had know you would tire this easily, I'd have ordered my own car."

Rusty chose to ignore her remark. As it was, the earliest they would get home would be almost two. Rich, having been to enough of his own premieres, gave them till noon to arrive on the set. Once the limousine started moving, Elsie curled on the seat. Her head rested in Red's lap. It only took a few miles for her to be sound asleep. Rusty poured himself the last of the scotch without bothering to offer any to Red. His glass emptied in one large swallow. Tina Laney's chattering droned incoherently as Rusty slipped into drug induced bliss.

CHAPTER TWENTY-FOUR

RUSTY WOKE LYING across his bed wearing only boxers. At least he prayed it was his bed. Upon rolling over, he could see the light shining from his bathroom. His tuxedo had been draped carefully across the sitting chair. The lighted clock indicated the time of 5:40. He stood and stretched on his way to the bathroom. Not a hint of the headache remained. Not to mention, he felt surprisingly well rested. After taking a shower, he headed downstairs. His stomach's grumbling echoed its emptiness. The smell of the grill made his mouth water. Red did like a hearty breakfast. However, Rusty didn't expect anyone else to be awake yet. Then again Red was used to getting up at the crack of dawn in a time zone an hour earlier. Surprisingly, Elsie stood at the far side of the deck in the bright sunshine. She turned when she heard Rusty slide open the glass door to join them.

"Good morning sleeping beauty. Are you feeling better?" She asked far cheerier than he'd anticipated.

"Good morning. I can't believe you are awake already." He answered.

Red looked at him like he'd grown a second head. Elsie cocked her head with a peculiar expression on her face.

Rusty surmised the odd looks were from his impoliteness at not answering Elsie's question. "Oh I'm sorry; I didn't remember telling you about my headache. But yes, it finally went away."

Red spoke. "Elsie darlin', you were right. He doesn't remember any of it."

"Remember what?" Rusty was at a loss.

Elsie moved to stand in front of him. "You have a choice: Red or me?'

Too confused to answer, Rusty looked from one to the other.

"You tell him. I'm going inside to make the eggs." She pushed passed him, shutting the door with extra force.

"What is going on mate?" He didn't follow.

Red shook his head as he explained. "For starters, it is 6 in the evening, not morning. Secondly, you are damn lucky that lady is still speaking to you."

He paused to let that much register. "It took both of us to get you inside and up the stairs to your room. Then we stripped you down to your skivvies. She fetched you a cool cloth while I put your suit over the chair. I noticed Elsie's tissues still in your pocket. When I pulled them out to throw away, your pills fell onto the floor. Elsie asked what they were. I tried to brush them off as prescription strength Tylenol. You know Elsie; she took the bottle from me to read. Then the fireworks started."

Again, Red waited a few minutes before continuing. "Let's just say, the lady used some mighty colorful language. But I have to agree with her in asking: 'what possessed you to take those with a chaser of scotch?'"

By now, Rusty had taken a seat at the patio table. How did he explain to Red why he did it? He was having enough problems justifying it.

The only thing he could do was apologize. "Mate, I apologize. It was stupid."

"You don't owe me an apology. I spent plenty of time at the bottom of a bottle, both kinds, in my younger years. I hope you come to grips with what's really at the heart of it before it's too late." He grasped Rusty's shoulder for a few moments. "Why don't you fetch plates for the table?"

"Thanks Red." Before opening the glass slider, he asked "how much hot water am I in with her?"

Red shrugged. "You drop her for Tina Laney and then you OD. You tell me."

"Krikey!! What about Rich and filming?" Rusty panicked as it dawned on him he'd missed the day's filming.

"Don't worry. I spoke to Rich. Everything is smooth on that front." Red started whistling a tune from the Wizard of Oz.

Rusty could hear the words "if I only had a brain" playing in his head as he stepped into the house. Rusty gathered everything in which to set the table. Elsie continued preparing the eggs and hash browns. Neither spoke. Still not comfortable with how to broach the subject, he went back outside. After the table was set, he had to talk to Elsie or he wouldn't be able to eat.

Returning inside, he cleared his throat "ahem, Elsie could I talk to you for a minute?"

Elsie turned off the two burners, then looked at him. "You have one minute."

"I wanted to apologize for last night." He said it quickly.

"Go ahead." She was not making it easy for him.

"Elsie?" He realized he had to say it. "I am sorry for mixing alcohol with the vicadin."

"Is that all?" Her tone unchanged.

"And for you guys having to take care of me." He felt confident he'd covered it.

She returned to preparing the food. "Taking care of you is no big deal, that's what friends do. As for the booze and pills, it's your life, but don't expect me to turn a blind eye."

She moved the food from the pans to serving dishes.

He didn't feel like he'd been forgiven for his transgression. "Why do I get the distinct feeling I'm not out of the dog house?"

"Because you apologized for something that didn't get you there to begin with." She handed him one of the dishes to carry outside.

Red set the platter of steaks in the center of the table. As the other dishes of food arrived, they sat to dine. The two men discussed possible projects Red was investigating. Elsie's silence continued throughout the meal. Red and Rusty cleared the dishes. She remained outside dangling her feet in the hot tub. When Rusty joined her, he turned on the tub's jets. Red busied himself in the kitchen.

The tension between Rusty and Elsie seemed to be widening into a chasm. Rusty was stymied. The cool look on her face indicated mere tolerance of his presence. Shouldn't she understand the Tina Laney date? After all, he and Elsie were friends. She should accept him for who he is. Getting his career back on track was his number one goal. If he wanted female companionship, he could find it anywhere. Couldn't he? Or at least that's what everyone else thought. But then why hadn't he taking advantage of his new found fame? Why was he fixating on Elsie? He turned off the noise in his head. He didn't want to have to answer the far too intrusive questions his psyche was asking.

"Elsie, why don't you put on your suit and climb in?" It was a shallow attempt to make nice.

Her response lacked any emotion. "I don't own a swimsuit."

Not entirely sure if he should ask why not, Rusty chose to be playful. "No worries mate, you can use your birthday suit."

Her expression was nothing short of incredulous.

Rusty interpreted it incorrectly. "If it'll make you feel better, I'll do the same."

He pulled off his t-shirt to show his amiability. "C'mon mate, it'll help you relax."

Surprisingly she acquiesced. "Climb in, I'll get towels."

He finished stripping to step into the hot tub. She watched his every move. He sat on the far side of the tub. The sound of the slider informed him that she entered the house. He could hardly believe she agreed to go naked in the hot tub with him. He must've done something right. He had completely relaxed by the time he realized it was taking Elsie an awfully long time to fetch towels. He had the distinct impression he was being stood up. Apparently, she was still miffed with him. As he climbed out, he turned off the jets. Standing on the deck, he looked at the empty spot where he'd piled his clothes. So she was a little more than miffed. Dripping his way across the deck to the sliding door, it didn't slide. He tried a second time. It was locked. There was no key hidden on the patio for this door. He banged on it. If Red went to his room, he'd never hear the noise. This left only one alternative. Walk around to the front door where he did have a key hidden. However, there was nothing on the deck Rusty could use to conceal his manly parts. The walk required passing through two other yards and along the sidewalk. Okay . . . , Elsie was really pissed.

None of his neighbors were outside to witness his naked jaunt. Once inside the house, he found his clothing draped on the banister. Donning his boxers, he grabbed the rest of his clothing on the way up the stairs.

Normally a stunt like that would've caused him to blow his stack. In this case, he deserved it. He knocked on Elsie's door. She didn't answer. He knocked again.

"Elsie?" He called softly.

Still no answer; he tried the knob—locked.

"Elsie, please?" The pleading in his voice sounded pathetic even to him. "Mate, please let me in? I'm not angry. I just want to talk."

Her lack of acknowledgment added to the already seriously humbling experience. With head hung, he went to his room. Instead of wallowing in a fifth of scotch, he read the script for the next day of shooting till he fell asleep.

4am Rusty's alarm blared. By 4:30, he was out the door.

He slipped a quick note under Elsie's door on his way by:

Love—Please?

What can I do to make it up to you for messing up premiere night?

Rusty

The morning's filming was going relatively smooth. Tina Laney was frostier than usual. Rusty couldn't care less. Rich seemed pleased with what the camera caught. Shortly before nine o'clock, there was a loud crash from somewhere behind Rich.

He yelled "Cut! What the devil was that?"

A familiar female voice chirped from behind the studio lights. "Sorry, I was busy watching the scene and bumped into whatever that was."

"Elsie dear, you finally joined us." He announced playfully.

Any annoyance at the incident quickly dispelled. Emerging from the shadows, she smiled sheepishly.

He greeted her with a big hug. "I am glad to see you. I was heartbroken thinking that I wouldn't get to see you this trip."

Teasingly she replied, "Careful, your wife might get jealous."

As he released her, "that's okay, she already knows what a huge crush I have on you."

The director loved to banter.

"But when it comes to my men," she looked directly at Rusty as she said at a much louder volume than necessary, " . . . I don't share."

She was challenging him. After the last few days, perhaps it was time he showed her he could handle it. They continued with the scene until Rich had what he wanted prior to calling for a break. Both Tina and Rusty needed wardrobe changes. While Rusty was changing his pants, he heard a quiet knock on the door.

As he responded with "just a minute" a familiar piece of paper slid under the door.

He retrieved it as he opened the door for Elsie. She wasn't there. He shut the door to read her response.

There were no words, only "XO".

Evidently, she'd finally forgiven him. He wanted to start over with his original intention of making this trip special for her. Unfortunately, it was her last day. Elsie's flight left at 8am the next morning. He'd have to ponder this at lunch. He tucked the note in his pocket, hoping to think of further correspondence. At the moment, he needed to be on set. On his way, he paused at Tina's door. As a way to keep her less testy, they had all agreed to pay extra courtesy towards her until the end of filming.

He knocked, then said loudly "Tina, I'm on my way to set."

"Rusty wait" she called.

He waited for the door to open. "Yes?"

But it wasn't Tina, it was Julie. "I'm sorry Rusty; I didn't get to your room yet for touch up."

"No worries mate. We can do it on the set." He smiled warmly at Julie.

Tina's grating voice interceded. "Or she can do it here so we don't have another accident with my wardrobe."

"Okay Tina." Rusty conceded.

He raised an eyebrow towards Julie as he sat in the nearest chair. Her face had turned the same bright pink as Tina's lipstick. It only took a couple minutes for Julie to refresh Rusty's makeup. The three of them left Tina's room together. On set, they were waiting. There were only two scenes remaining to film with Tina. Both were rather steamy. The first one was with clothes on; the second, a pivotal scene to the plot. It didn't bode well with the first shot when Rich became perturbed with Rusty.

"Cut!" Rich barked. "Rusty, empty your pockets."

Rusty looked down at his pants. The note he'd written to Elsie protruded from his pants pocket. He pulled it out the rest of the way. Glancing around, he saw a bright silk robe hanging on the bedpost. He slipped the note into its pocket figuring he'd retrieve it from the prop later. After three hours, Rich had every possible shot and angle he could need. Rich was being exceptionally diligent; he wanted to avoid requesting Tina Laney at a later date for so much as a voice over.

Rich spoke to the staff. "Okay gang, we have an hour for lunch. Let's not be late this afternoon. Thanks."

Rusty caught Elsie's attention while he headed for his dressing room. When she looked at him, Rusty raised his eyebrows questioningly as he cocked his head for her to follow. She barely hid a smile as she nodded in acknowledgement.

As soon as he entered the dressing room, he discarded his shirt. He was about to remove his pants when there was a knock on the door.

Expecting Elsie, he invited "Come in Love, just getting changed."

With his back towards the door, he removed his pants exposing his boxers. Without warning, a pair of female hands slid inside his boxers to stroke his manhood. Kissing and nibbling commenced on his bare back. Physically, it felt wonderful; emotionally, something didn't feel right.

Surprising even himself, he pulled the soft hands out of his shorts into his own hands. "Love, we need to talk first."

He turned to look at Elsie, to discover Tina Laney. The only thing she wore was a selfishly proud smile. She'd finally gotten him to succumb to her ultimate beauty. A fuchsia silk robe lay crumpled around her feet. An audible gasp sounded from behind Tina. Looking over her shoulder, he caught a glimpse of Elsie at the door, then she was gone. He pushed Tina aside to chase after Elsie. Half way across the set he stopped, searching the soundstage. He didn't care that the crew stood at the buffet staring at him. No sign of Elsie, he sprinted for the door to the studio alleyway. There he ran smack into Rich.

"Where are you going in such a hurry in your boxers?" Rich asked in a terse tone.

Rusty looked up and down the alley. "Did you see where Elsie went?"

"Carla took her to the condo because she wasn't feeling well." Rich stated.

"How did you know she'd want to leave this quickly?" Rusty asked temperamentally.

"We had agreed to go to lunch. Carla called for the car while Elsie went to see if you wanted to go along. When she met me here, she said she wasn't feeling well and wanted to go back to your place." Rich explained to Rusty's satisfaction.

"Mate, would you please have someone get my car while I put pants on?" Rusty asked.

"Why?" Rich asked suspiciously.

"I have to talk to her!" Rusty answered frantically.

As Rich had suspected, "no, we have to finish this scene with Tina today!"

"But we've had a misunderstanding that I need to fix!" Rusty sounded desperate.

"Rusty, what you need to do is think seriously about what you both want before you go off half-cocked yet again!" The director demanded.

His patience obviously worn thin over Rusty's inability to commit to how he felt towards a woman who deserved far more than any man had ever treated her.

"C'mon mate . . . ?" Rusty pleaded.

"Don't do this to her. Let her go until you figure it out or you will continue with these misunderstandings." Rich remained unyielding.

The look of doubt on Rusty's face gave Rich the edge.

"Go clean up whatever mess you've made in your dressing room. Get dressed. Grab a bite to eat. Be ready to go in a half hour." The director had spoken.

As Rusty returned dejected to his dressing room, he heard Rich announce that lunch had been shortened.

In his dressing room, Tina Laney lounged on the chaise in the corner. When he opened the door, she opened her robe to expose her fully naked form. In that moment, Rusty knew he could never be with a woman like her after feeling Elsie's softness.

Clearing his throat of the emotion welling inside, "Rich has called a short lunch."

Purring with gloat "Lover, I'm sure I could fit you in before we need to be on set."

He had to find a tactful way out of this situation. Or he'd ruin the film by pissing off Tina Laney prior to her last and pivotal scene.

"I missed breakfast and really need to eat something to be at my best." It sounded like a trite line from a soap opera.

However, it worked. Pouting with disappointment, she pulled a familiar piece of paper from her robe pocket.

"As long as you make it up to me later, lover." She tucked it into the front of his boxers as she slinked by him on the way to her room.

Rusty pushed the door shut-shutting out the world for a few minutes. He didn't have the luxury of deciphering his feelings for Elsie. He had a job to do. A job if he did extremely well, would do especially well for her. He pulled himself together along with pulling on his clothing.

The crew seemed unusually quiet while he filled a plate of food at the buffet. Rich waved him to the table where he sat eating. They reviewed the finer points of the upcoming scene. The topic of Elsie was never broached. Once filming re-started, Rusty lost track of time. Each take went perfectly. But with the necessary angles and subtle differences in approach, it was after 6 till they wrapped for the day. And to keep things pleasant with Tina Laney, Rich had Carla put together a little going away party for her. Unfortunately, Rusty had no polite excuse to leave until the rest of the crew said their good-byes. As if a time clock bell rang, the entire crew left at 7. Rusty took advantage of the group exodus. Poor Rich would be left to deal with Tina over his disappearance. But he needed to get home to Elsie.

The condominium was oddly dark when he arrived home. The door to Elsie's room had been left open. Its contents looked exactly as they had the day prior to her arrival. He checked the rest of the house. No note, no message, no sign of her anywhere except in his heart. Sherry called the airlines to see if Elsie had changed flights. He would lose his temper if he did it himself. An hour later, she had verification for what he'd already concluded. Elsie switched her flight home from tomorrow morning to one that departed two hours ago. Moving to the bar, he poured a tumbler of scotch.

There was nothing left for him to do. The thought of hopping on the next flight east crossed his mind. He couldn't do that to Rich. They still had a couple weeks left at the studio, then six weeks of gathering the final location shots. Even if he explained the situation with Tina, what good would it do? Being apart was hardly conducive to a relationship. If he was going to be with someone, he wanted it full time, not when it was convenient. Then again, it was his schedule and lifestyle that made it as such. In his heart, Rusty knew Elsie would compromise a great deal to make a relationship work. But there were a few things to which she would never waver. Oddly, they were things he understood and would never ask her to compromise. Those were also things that made him love her all the more. Then why couldn't he just tell her how important she was to him? And how much he loved her? Why did he keep letting other things get in the way? Why did he keep having these thoughts, but never finding answers?

Chapter Twenty-Five

"Mr. Garnet . . . Rusty . . . wake up . . ." A female voice interrupted his memories.

When Rusty opened his eyes, the round face of Nurse Katie Smythe smiled at him.

He sat up. Still holding Elsie's hand, he ran his free hand through his hair.

As she documented Elsie's vitals, she chatted with him. "When my shift started, the overnight nurse told me you were here already. I popped in earlier to let you know the neurologist had an emergency and wouldn't be here until noon. But you were sleeping so soundly, I didn't want to wake you."

"Thank you Katie." He glanced around the room looking for something; what, he did not know.

Nurse Katie watched him. "Dearie, did you lose something?"

It was the wrong question to ask. Tears sprang from his eyes as he swallowed the sobs that desperately needed release.

"Oh my! I'm so sorry to have asked such a question." Nurse Smythe became equally emotional at her faux pas.

"I meant did you misplace something in here, not, oh dearie!" She wrapped her pudgy arms around his shoulders.

The sobs broke loose for a moment. "I love her so much!"

As quick as the torrent hit, it subsided as equally. He reached for the tissues on the nightstand. He offered one to Nurse Katie.

She dabbed at the wet spots on her cheeks as she shuffled out the door. "Buzz if you need anything."

Rusty went into the bathroom to splash water on his face. Staring in the mirror, he couldn't believe this was all happening. He had no idea what to do. Elsie liked to refer to him as her Rock of Gibraltar when it came to things of this nature. What she, and even he, hadn't acknowledged was how much she had become his lighthouse in the worst of storms.

If she had been standing behind him looking in the same mirror, she would have remarked "who is that?".

His scruffy look that she loved had turned unkempt. Add to it his blood shot haunted eyes with dark puffy circles under each. He'd seen this reflection too many times before. It scared him far more than any of those prior. This time he had far more to lose than he had ever hoped or imagined could have been possible. The last time he'd met this part of himself, had been when he'd decided to chase the rainbow which was now in jeopardy of disappearing. The pot of gold he'd found held a woman with a heart of gold—a treasure far more valuable than anything else in the world. Staring into his eyes in the mirror, he could feel the past engulfing him.

After the Tina Laney fiasco, Rusty didn't know what to do about Elsie. Since a plan of action didn't come to mind, he did nothing. He continued working on the film. Days rolled into each other as if the project would never end. They stayed on schedule. Mid-September filming would end in the mountains of West Virginia. A deserted resort from the 1970s served as their location. The years of neglect aided the crew in creating a rustic look. However, since the plumbing no longer functioned, RVs served as housing. Everyone shared except Rich and Rusty. The other actors had bit parts. These scenes focused on Rusty's character.

Even though they were in the final stretch, Rich didn't relax. Matter of fact, he became an unyielding task master. The vision of the final product Rich held allowed no wiggle room. Nothing dared go wrong. When he appeared the first day glowering at everything, Rusty thought the rumor he'd heard to be true. Elsie had decided to not come for the final filming. Rusty felt it was his fault. After all, he hadn't tried contacting her anytime over the last few weeks. And he owed her an explanation. Why?—He wasn't sure; but that he did. The matter had become moot since she wouldn't be coming.

Two days into shooting, Rich left Rusty in charge for a couple hours while he handled an urgent business matter pertaining to the film. When Rich returned, he had Elsie in tow. Upon seeing her, Rusty completely forgot his line. Only Elsie was oblivious to how uncharacteristic that was for him. His usual reaction was to fill in the blanks along the way. A few of his flubs worked such that they became the film version. In this case, nothing came, but stupefied silence.

To make matters worse, Rich jibed him about it. "What's the matter Rusty? Cat got your tongue?"

Elsie said a few words to Rich which appeared to be in reference to leaving. Not getting more than a few steps, she stopped. Rich was talking to her in low tones; too low for Rusty to distinguish words. Whatever it was, Elsie returned to her chair. Determination displayed in the posture of her shoulders as she sat. Rusty took her cue to finish the day without further incident.

At the evening meal, the lack of Elsie's presence would've caused Rusty to feel unsettled had Rich also not been present. He had hoped to get a chance to talk to her during the meal. The crew had been dissipating when Rich and Elsie finally arrived. Rich steered her directly to where Rusty was seated.

"Hey pal, mind if we join you?" Rich asked.

"Have a seat mate, trying to decide on coffee and dessert or going back to my trailer." Rusty responded.

Elsie didn't acknowledge him on her way to the buffet.

"We'll grab our food first so the caterer can start clearing." Rich explained.

Elsie returned to the table first. She sat a third of the way around the round table from Rusty.

Not sure what to say to her, he merely said "Hello Elsie, good to see you."

"Rusty." And that was it from her.

He saw she didn't have anything to drink. "What do you want to drink?"

He stood as he continued. "They have bottled water, soda and ice tea."

The surprised smile on her face at his politeness was quickly concealed by placing a forkful of food in her mouth. This prevented a forthcoming answer.

"Not sure Love, that's okay I'll surprise you." He said in an overly accommodating tone.

At the beverage table, Rich smirked. "Are you two making nice?"

"Mate, I don't know what to do to make nice with her." He admitted.

"Treating her like a queen by waiting on her is always a good place to start." Rich collected two bottles of water. "In case you forgot, raspberry ice tea."

"I didn't forget. But there's only plain ice tea." He muttered.

"There are raspberries on the fruit and cheese tray." With that said, Rich went to join her at the table.

After making the flavored tea, Rusty placed it next to Elsie's plate.

Elsie murmured a "thank you".

As she sipped the tea, another surprised look crossed her face at realizing the flavor.

After swallowing the sweet liquid, she stated a much louder "thank you Rusty".

Rich and Rusty discussed tomorrow's shots. Even though Elsie didn't interject into their conversation, didn't mean she hadn't been listening intently. The catering staff collected the dishes. Before heading to their trailers, Rich waved to the one server. The server brought a few food saver containers to the table—one for Rich, two for Elsie.

The server spoke "Did you need anything else Mr. Taylor?

Rich looked across the table. "Elsie, do you need anything else for tonight?"

She shook her head. "Not that I can think of, this should be good."

"No and thanks for putting these together for us." Rich released the server.

"Doggy bag?" Rusty surmised.

She merely collected her containers. Rusty rushed to get the door for her. Both men walked her to her trailer. It sat the furthest distance from Rusty's on the far side of their film crew community.

Standing on the step, she dismissed them with "goodnight gentlemen."

In unison, the men replied "goodnight Elsie".

The next morning, Rusty didn't see Elsie. After wolfing down his croissant, he put together a little breakfast box for her. It included two croissants and a large coffee with extra cream. He had enough time to deliver it to her trailer. His first knock received no answer. He tried again, calling out her name. This time he heard shuffling around inside the RV.

She answered the door with her hair mashed to one side and pillow creases on her cheek. "What?"

Rusty smiled brightly. "Good morning Love, brought you breakfast."

"What do you want?" She grumbled.

"It's 6:30 am, time to be on the set." He announced full of cheer.

"Go away." She said, then pulled the door shut with a bang.

Rusty heard the click denoting the door had been locked. He left the fare he'd brought on the step. Elsie could be very cranky when disturbed after a rough night. New place, not quite comfortable—he could understand her not getting enough sleep. He went to work.

A few hours later, Elsie appeared on set. Her disposition much improved. She was light and cheery with the crew. Rusty managed to make eye contact with her for a few seconds during a prop reset. Her nod in response left him wondering what else was wrong. He knew her well enough to know she used happy-go-lucky for those who didn't really know her. But for those that did, the ice wall went up.

The day went far into the night. Since they had momentum, Rich kept shooting. The crew took shifts grabbing dinner. Rich and Rusty couldn't be bothered. Elsie disappeared for a few hours, then returned with her laptop. While they worked, she seemed miles away on her laptop. The clear, crisp autumn evening made for an incredible run of night shots. In a few days the moon would be full, making it large and bright. At 1am, Rich called it a day. The rest of the crew headed for their RVs while Rich held Rusty back.

"Thank you for your performance tonight. How those last few scenes would play had been a concern until I saw you through the monitor." Rich didn't often make singled out compliments such as this.

"You're welcome." Rusty yawned.

"Get a good night's sleep. We'll have another long day tomorrow if this weather continues." Rich clapped him on the shoulder as he headed in the direction of his own trailer.

"G'night mate." Rusty remained.

Elsie typed a few keys prior to closing the lid on her laptop.

He stepped towards her chair as she stood. "Love, I'm here to escort you safely to your trailer."

"Oh Rusty, thank you. I thought Rich wanted to talk, but I guess he changed his mind." She appeared disoriented.

As they walked, he tried to melt the glacier. "How are Sophie and Tycho?"

"Doing well. They like staying at home instead of being jockeyed around." She replied easily.

"That's why I didn't hear or see them this morning." He remarked lamely.

She stopped walking suddenly. He turned to see why.

"That wasn't a dream this morning?" Her face scrunched.

He could see her bemusement. "Yes, I didn't see you at breakfast so I brought you coffee and croissant."

"Oh dear, I was up all night working and had only fallen asleep around 5:30. The story line, dream world and reality were befuddled when you knocked. You're lucky the worst I did was slam the door in your face."

"I take it the heroine in your latest story is having man troubles?" He knew she used things going on her life or friends' lives as catalysts for things in her books.

She took a deep breath before plunging into her latest novel. "Yes, the man in question is one of her best friends. She's had less than pleasant relationships with men in the past. So when he starts making romantic and sexual gestures towards her, she becomes confused. But then he suddenly begins sleeping with a materialistic, conniving woman who's only using him to further her career. My lead feels stupid for thinking a man like him would want to be with her. At the moment, she can't decide if she should stay friends with the shmuck or tell him to take a flying leap."

They had reached her trailer as she completed the synopsis.

He had to think quickly. "Did you establish with fact that the schmuck had really been sleeping with the other woman? Or had it merely been circumstantial?"

Her tone contained a sharp edge as they stepped into the RV. "Well, she caught him in the arms of the other woman. He was in his boxers and the other woman was nude."

"Perhaps it was a case of mistaken identity. He may have been expecting his girl, but the other woman entered uninvited. And he didn't realize it was her till he turned to face her." He explained the Tina Laney incident.

"Riiiight, he couldn't tell the difference between a stick figure and pleasingly plump." Sarcasm denoting her lack of belief.

His patience with this pussyfoot game gone with her last comment. "You are not plump! You have soft curves that a man can enjoy. I was expecting you and didn't give it a second thought that it was anyone else."

"And I'm supposed to believe that after you dumped me for her the night of the premiere?" Ire notable in the way she had her teeth clenched to prevent from announcing their argument to the entire encampment.

"I'm sorry about that night. I had to be extra nice to her or she would have caused a stoppage in filming with her temper tantrums." He ran his hand through his hair trying to keep his own agitation under control. "And we were getting too close. I figured a harmless date with Tina Laney would take care of it."

Her eyes squinted in the darkness to study his face.

"What was wrong with us getting close?" She asked the straightforward question.

He had no forthcoming answer even though he'd asked himself the very same question numerous times over the weeks they hadn't spoken. The sounds of the night filled in the silent gap.

"Rusty?" She asked with her large eyes peering up at him and her hand gently resting on the middle of his chest.

A guttural growl escaped as he pulled her roughly into his arms coupled with an open-mouth kiss full of unsated desire. While his mouth ravaged her lips and neck, his hands plundered her soft curves. As quick as he'd grabbed her, he set her away from him with force.

"G'night." He snarled striding into the darkness.

What was he thinking that would accomplish?! He chastised himself the entire walk across the compound. Inside his trailer, he threw non-breakable items to vent his anger at his rash action. He went in search of the bottle of scotch. Usually the sound of the seal crackling under his grip fed his anticipation of the amber liquid. Instead, Elsie's moan as his lips had teased the sensitive spot on the nape of her neck reverberated in his ears. He poured into the closest glass. Merely thinking of how wonderful she felt in his arms caused his boxers to become restrictive. He stripped the few feet which led to the bedroom. The coolness of the sheets was a blessing.

Two hours later, Rusty woke soaked in sweat saying Elsie's name. He stepped into the bathroom to splash cold water on his face and wipe down. His blood shot eyes staring back at him mirrored the demons chasing him. In the kitchenette, he opened the refrigerator to get a bottle of water. He eyed the untouched glass of scotch still setting on the counter. Instead, he drank the water in one long draught—its icy sluicing welcome. Back in bed, he couldn't ease the ache to feel Elsie lying with him. Thankfully, the grueling schedule they'd been under took its toll.

The next morning Rusty felt the lack of a restful sleep. Still wrestling with his actions at the end of the night and his other related thoughts, he was anxious to see Elsie. When he opened the door to his trailer, he had a surprising sight before him. She stood there holding a box with two cups of coffee and croissants.

Smiling hesitantly, she spoke. "Good morning mate."

"G'morning Love." He took the box from her, motioning her into the RV.

He placed their morning fare onto the counter while she entered.

He wrapped his arms around her in a bear hug.

Her voice tinged with concern. "What's wrong?"

Not letting go of her, "Why would you think anything is wrong?"

Pushing backwards in his arms to look at his face, "Number one—you look like hell. Number two—this is one fierce hug. Not that I mind, matter of fact, I like it immensely; just not your style mate."

"Not a very restful sleep; plagued by dreams I can't remember" answering as honestly as he could without exposing himself completely. "As for the hug, it's more my style than anyone knows."

To emphasize his point, he gave her another squeeze. "Mate, I've missed you terribly since LA."

I quiet little "oh" emitted from her.

Yet another quick squeeze, then he released her. "How about that coffee on the way to makeup? Julie will need a little extra time to hide these dark circles."

The rest of the day went wonderfully for Rusty. Elsie stayed on set the entire day. Between takes, he would go to her for opinions and suggestions. Of which, she would smile indulgently at his silliness. After all, he'd been in the business for decades; she mere months. Plus, he'd been this character for the last six months, it's not like he needed her input this late in the filming. Everyone noticed his schoolboy attempts. No one on the set mentioned it. Even Rich held his tongue, in hopes that this time Rusty wouldn't screw it up.

The day turned into a week. Rusty and Elsie spent every spare moment together. They shared hugs, thoughts and glances. As for any further advances, Rusty kept himself in check. Not that it was easy. Until filming had completed to allow him time to work through his feelings for her; he couldn't get either of their hopes up.

A week later, the last scenes to be filmed revolved around a barn dance. Rich decided to roll the crew in as extras. It became a sort of an expanded wrap party. Rich coerced Elsie into wardrobe. Rusty asked Elsie to dance. Rich filmed it originally on a whim, but then kept it liking the chemistry and wholesomeness of the scene.

When the music started, Rusty had Elsie on the dance floor. Getting a bit carried away, there were a few times Rusty swung Elsie with such exuberance her feet didn't touch the floor. When they stopped with the music, her cotton skirt was still swaying about her calves. She didn't have time to catch her breath till the next song started and he was twirling her around on the dance floor again. Pure joy mirrored from his face to hers. It was a scene reminiscent of the "King and I" with Yul Brynner and Deborah Kerr. This time it occurred in the depressed backwoods of the Appalachians in West Virginia. Rich felt like he was in the "Twilight Zone" when he ran the take later that evening. It was exactly how Elsie had written it in the book. It had been omitted from the screenplay thinking it would be too difficult to recreate. The love between Rusty and Elsie had been tangible to everyone in the room that night. Watching it on film, Rich was amazed at the emotion caused by their auras sparkling iridescently with synergy at their magical bond. Rich wondered what it would take for Rusty to see how much Elsie loved him and how much he truly did love her. He'd known for some time that Elsie was in love with Rusty. All of the little things she did to make him feel comfortable. Moreover, she loved the real Rusty, not the one everyone else thought they knew. Rich had been one of the few people Rusty allowed into the real him. It was no surprise to either man that they enjoyed working together. For Rusty to allow a woman into that part of him, after the conniving schemes of his ex-wife amazed Rich. Of course, Rich had the luxury of getting to know Elsie, too. Her unique personality: quirky, deeply caring, sweet, true blue—all with an ice bitch veneer that sent most men running away covering their genitalia. She was exactly what Rusty needed to put his head on straight and find his heart full of love. How to get that message across to Rusty was quite another story . . .

Rich had hinted at it enough times to Rusty only to meet the repeated rote response of "you're wrong mate—we are strictly friends".

While Rich reviewed the day's shots, Rusty and Elsie went for a walk in the moonlight. The reds, yellows and oranges of the season's finale were illuminated by the full moon. They hadn't walked very far when they came upon a small clearing. A fallen tree on the perimeter served as a bench. Rusty opened the bottle of champagne he'd brought. Elsie held two papers cups for him to pour into. They toasted to the film making a respectable showing. Otherwise, they enjoyed each other's company while listening to the sounds of the night. An owl they heard hooting nearby soon appeared circling in wide arcs in the sky above them. It was late. Rusty stood, offering his hand to Elsie. The rest of the crew was still relishing in revelry when the couple returned to the RVs. Not interested in the group party, he led her into his trailer. Neither of them spoke. She placed the empty bottle in the trash, then gazed through the window over the sink. His arms slid around her waist. His mouth found her ear and neck, nibbling gently to create goose bumps on her skin. She turned in his arms to deliver a passionate kiss of her own. When he slid his hands under her shirt she froze. Before he had a chance to say anything, she pushed him back the hall to his bed. Once there, she unbuttoned her shirt, dropping it on the floor where she had stopped. Unsure of where this was going, he did the same with his own flannel shirt. She slipped off her jeans leaving her clad only in a flowered camisole top with matching panties. Again, he followed her lead by disposing of his pants. She pulled back the blankets before sliding onto the bed. He didn't know if he should continue. Heck of thing to have doubts at such a crucial juncture. It wasn't that he didn't want her; because God knew he ached to feel her naked body next to his. He didn't want to hurt her. She perched awkwardly unsure waiting for him. It was then he realized that she was offering something. If he didn't make a move, she would feel undesirable. He yanked his t-shirt over his head, then tugged off his boxers exposing a very hard illustration of how much he desired her. As he moved towards her, she removed her camisole. He sat on the bed next to her. His hands roamed freely over her bare skin. When she relaxed in response to his touch, he eased her into a laying position. His lips began tracing the same path as his hands. He lingered at her nipples, his tongue tantalizing the tips. Her deep moan indicated he could move closer. He shifted his body fully on top of hers. His tongue danced with hers in an erotic kiss. Her body opened to his. The feel of skin on skin fueled their desire. The only thing preventing complete union was her cotton panties. When her pelvis pushed against him he could feel her readiness. Not wanting to wait any longer, he separated long enough to tug off her final undergarment.

Gazing into her eyes, he lowered himself on top of her. As he did, he slowly entered her inviting wetness. The feel of her spongy warmth enveloping him took his breath away for an instant. Holding himself in check, he used small tender thrusts to give her time to adjust to him inside her. When her hips arched pulling him in farther, he couldn't keep control. He gripped her buttocks to push deeper. Her moaning in a lower pitch as she cried out his name declared her climax. Hearing and feeling her peak surged him to the same height instantly. Her name left his lips in a groan of pure pleasure.

He shifted to lie next to her. Keeping his arm across her waist, he buried his face into her neck. Her hand found its way to his, their fingers linked. A light kiss brushed his forehead. He cuddled closer to her. This must be what paradise feels like. In a blissful state, he drifted into a peaceful slumber.

Around midnight, he woke to the moon shining in through the skylights overhead. It illuminated her in an ethereal glow. As if signifying she was the angel sent to save him. She slept serenely curled against him. Her cute little butt snuggled into his groin. Replaying their earlier lovemaking in his mind roused his body to wanting more. He nuzzled her nape while lightly tickling her inner thighs. It didn't take long for her to stir to his attention.

"Mm, that feels good," her voice husky with passion.

Murmuring into her neck, he asked, "Are you ready for it to feel even better?"

"Depends if you are up for it", she teased.

Shifting slightly to allow his manhood to press against her, he responded: "what do you think?"

"Then what are you waiting for big boy?" To make her point, she shifted to allow him access to her femininity.

It took little effort for him to fit into her causing her to gasp with pleasure.

Reaching his hand to the front of where they were joined, he slid his fingers lower to massage.

Whispering into her ear, "Boys don't know to do this."

Much to his excitement, he was rewarded with a squeal of delight as he focused on her need. Wanting it to last longer for both of them, his stroking was slow and tender. However from this angle, the stimulation he was receiving made it difficult to hold out.

"Oh Elsie, I want to come" he groaned.

Her voice in throaty pants, "please Rusty . . . I want to feel you come . . ."

Pushing firmer with his hand from the front along with thrusting harder and deeper a few times from the rear, Rusty reached rapturous release. As he finished, Elsie's body shuddered with contractions of ecstasy. They lay still joined in the moonlight. An involuntary sigh of utter contentment escaped from him with an equally peaceful sigh echoing from her.

Chapter Twenty-Six

THE ALARM ANNOUNCED 4am. He hit snooze to spend a few minutes cuddling with Elsie before they had to start the day. When he rolled over, he found empty space. Getting out of bed, he searched the rest of the RV for her. The spot on the floor where her clothing had fallen last night was bare. He even knocked on the bathroom door supposing she needed a few moments of privacy to dress—also empty. Rusty didn't know what to think. Had she woken and realized she'd made a mistake? Before that thought could run amuck, his alarm reminded him of work. Time for him to face the day; it was the final day of filming. After which, he would address Elsie. For some reason, his stomach was doing somersaults. He blamed it on last day nerves even though he'd never suffered from them previously. Feeling it best to avoid breakfast, he headed directly to make-up.

As always, Julie greeted him effervescently. "Good morning."

"G'morning." He answered gruffly.

Nothing else said by either. He concentrated on his lines.

On set, Rusty and Rich reviewed last minute direction. Elsie stayed to the side talking with Julie; Elsie's smile outshining the morning sun.

"Good morning Elsie." Rich called to her. "You look well, good night's sleep?"

"Good morning Rich." Elsie joined them. "Guess you could say that."

Including Rusty, she turned to him. "Good morning Rusty."

If she felt any discomfort, she masked it well.

Staying on task, he merely replied, "G'day Mate."

Rusty convinced Rich not to break for a full lunch. While the two men reviewed one of the final takes, sandwiches cut into quarters appeared on a tray next to them. Elsie hovered nearby. Finally, Rich motioned for her

Before His Eyes

to watch, too. One shot in particular didn't sit well with the director. When she viewed it, she also made a face. They started brainstorming around Rusty.

He spoke. "Can we finish what we still have left, then come back to this?"

They nodded in agreement. Julie returned from lunch for his touch-ups. In the meanwhile, Rich used his bullhorn to return everyone to work. The last shots went perfectly. By 4 o'clock, they had completed the scheduled scenes. However, both Rich and Elsie insisted they re-take the shot neither had liked. Elsie wrote a few suggestions for Rich. He handed one to Rusty, asking him to ad lib while still incorporating the scripted lines. Each slip of paper got a single chance. By the last one, Rusty realized for what they were searching. As the sun set behind him, he hit the mark. His gut told him he'd found what they wanted.

Rich yelled "cut and wrap!"

Elsie ran over to Rusty, throwing her arms around him. He naturally returned the hug.

"Was it that good?" His question muffled slightly by her hair as his lips searched for her neck.

She pushed back to look him in the eyes. "Most definitely!"

At this point, Rich joined their little celebration. He flung his arms wide to encircle both of them. No words were said. His sigh of relief followed by a chuckle communicated his emotions. After a few minutes, their intimate huddle broke.

Rich grabbed the bullhorn to be heard over the festivities. "Okay gang. First, thank you! Second, let's get this equipment packed. Third, food and drink at six in the big building. See you all there!"

Rich collected his personal equipment and supplies. With nothing to fetch, Elsie remained with Rusty. They followed Julie to her trailer where she removed his make-up. After Rusty had his face scrubbed clean, they headed for Elsie's trailer. On the way, they ran into Rich.

His earlier exuberance deflated. "Rusty could I have a word with you please?"

"Sure mate." Rusty wondered what had dampened the director's mood. "Elsie, I'll catch up with you at dinner."

She merely smiled and nodded. Rich waited till she was outside of earshot before explaining.

"My wife called. My oldest was in a car accident." His voice strained. "Carla is taking me to the airport. We leave in fifteen minutes."

"What do you need?" Rusty rested his hand on his friend's shoulder.

"Someone has to stay to make sure everything is cleaned up here." Rich outlined the task. "Usually Carla stays behind, but she will be handling getting my personal equipment safely home for me."

"No worries mate." Rusty agreed without hesitation. "Consider it done."

His appreciation notable in his voice, "thanks. I'll call you soon."

"Hope that boy of yours isn't too badly hurt." He added as his friend turned to leave.

"Me too", Rich threw over his shoulder as he strode away with purpose.

Rusty's first step was to call Sherry to push his flight a day. Unfortunately, it meant he wouldn't be able to spend time at the airport with Elsie as he planned. Having not said anything, she wouldn't be disappointed. He went to grab a bite to eat with the crew until Carla returned. Sitting at the same table as Elsie and Julie, he clued them in on Rich's premature departure. Other than that, Elsie and Rusty didn't speak privately the rest of the evening. When Carla returned, the two adjourned to Rich's trailer. They emerged around midnight. Rusty went directly to his own trailer. He didn't bother turning on any lights; the moon adequately lit the interior. After his bathroom regimen, he stripped to his boxers to climb into bed. As he stretched for a comfortable a position, he bumped into something—or rather someone. He pulled the covers back to expose the form sharing his bed. Clad in one of his t-shirts, Elsie lay scrunching a pillow sound asleep. He wondered how long she'd waited for him. As much as he wanted to wrap his arms around her, he didn't want to disturb her. She looked so peaceful. Consequently, he stayed on his side of the bed.

When morning came, the other side of the bed was once again empty. He couldn't understand why she'd left this time. They'd slept the night through with no sexual interlude. And she wasn't scheduled to leave for the airport for another five hours. He rushed through the shower to try to catch her.

At the breakfast buffet, he asked if anyone had seen her. The consensus was she hadn't been there yet. He'd surprise her like he tried that first morning.

She answered the door at first knock.

He offered up the breakfast box. "G'morning Love."

She responded "uh huh" as she backed away from the doorway.

Something seemed to be wrong with her face. Once inside, he reached for her. She sidestepped his initial advance. Something wasn't right—he wasn't going to let her get away that easy. Not sure how to grab her, without actually grabbing her. He kept a step behind her until she ran out of space. She had no choice, but to turn towards him. He gently slid his arms around her. She averted her face to prevent his scrutiny.

All he wanted was to kiss her to make whatever it was right. "Elsie, please talk to me."

"What does it matter?" Her response sounded like a pessimistic statement rather than a question.

He didn't want to argue; he didn't want them to ever part on bad terms again. "Okay, what did I do that I don't know was wrong?"

Those words made her look at him, as if assessing his sincerity. Then he saw her eyes were swollen, bloodshot and underscored with blotchy cheeks.

His voice almost a whisper, "please talk to me", emphasized with a light kiss on her cheek.

"Last night . . . we didn't . . . you didn't . . . you don't want . . ." Her response stilted; her eyes darted to and fro with discomfort.

"If I'd have known you were there, I would have cut short the meeting with Carla." Pulling her closer, he explained. "And it had been such a long day; I didn't want to wake you."

Whatever she said muffled in his chest.

He loosened his hold. "What was that Love?"

"I guess that makes sense." Her tone lacked conviction.

He didn't know what else to say. Instead, he kissed her tenderly to show he cared. Even though he wanted more, the kiss remained slow and soft so as to not push her.

When the kiss ended, he directed them to breakfast. "How about coffee?"

She merely nodded. They'd just removed the lids from the cups and his cell phone started ringing. It was Carla; time for him to take charge.

"Sorry Love, gotta go." He gave her a quick kiss. "I'll see you later."

"Bye Rusty." She called after him as he left the RV.

Little had he known that he wouldn't get to say good-bye. He'd been so busy. Hours slipped away causing him to not only fail to make time to talk privately with Elsie, but also miss her departure.

A loud beeping pulled Rusty from the hills of West Virginia to the hospital in Sydney. Nurse Katie Smythe came running into Elsie's room.

She spoke into the intercom. "Ms. Endy is having a seizure."

He stood in the bathroom doorway watching unnoticed. Another nurse wheeled in a cart with supplies followed by the doctor on duty. The doctor stuck a needle in Elsie's IV port. Her convulsions minimized to tremors. They continued checking her vitals. It took a while for the shaking to subside. Another few minutes passed before the doctor gave orders, then left the room. When Nurse Smythe stepped towards the bathroom to get a wet cloth, she finally saw Rusty.

"Oh my Mr. Garnet!" the nurse exclaimed. "Have you been there this whole time?"

He merely nodded. The emotions he felt at that moment warring inside. The only notable sign of the struggle by the way he gripped and twisted the towel he'd been using.

Nurse Katie Smythe relied on her years of experience. "With the type of injury your Elsie has, seizures are not uncommon. All in all, it was a minor one."

He tried to speak, but it sounded strangled.

Clearing his throat he got out "She shook so long after the doctor gave her something."

"Dr. Gallagher diminished the severity of the seizure till it ran its course and her vitals stabilized. We have to be careful with the amount and type of medication given." The kindly nurse explained.

Rusty grunted in response as he moved out of the nurse's way. She filled a basin with water and fetched a washcloth. With tenderly capable hands, she wiped the patient's face, neck and arms.

Pulling away the top sheet, she asked. "Mr. Garnet would you please tell the nurse at the desk I need her assistance?"

"Is there something I could do to help instead?" He needed to feel useful.

Nurse Katie thought for a second. "Yes, yes you can love."

He stood on the opposite side of the bed.

"Since the sheets are damp from the seizure, I need to get them changed. Would you please sit your sweetie up and hold her there till I tell you to lay her back down?" She explained the procedure.

He obeyed. Holding Elsie in his arms made him miss her that much more. Her head didn't snuggle into the side of his neck where it belonged. The nurse stripped the top half of the bed, then remade it with fresh linens. As he held Elsie, he murmured romantic nonsense into her hair.

"Okay dearie, I need to change her gown now." Nurse Katie directed him further as she loosened the back of the hospital garb.

His sharp intake at seeing the large, dark bruises covering Elsie's entire back caused Nurse Katie to question him. "If this is too much, we can buzz for someone else to come in?"

"No, I just hadn't expected them to be that bad", the awe in his voice undeniable.

Nurse Katie finished wiping the patient's back. Without saying a word, he shifted his hold on Elsie to allow Nurse Katie to remove the gown completely. This time his shock was replaced by a stabbing in his chest. The bruises were smaller and much lighter, but they were located on the delicately feminine skin of her bosom. He wanted to tenderly kiss each and every one of them. Instead, he watched as Nurse Katie continued her gentle ministrations. Before dressing her in a clean gown, Nurse Katie patted her skin dry. Then he lifted her prone form long enough for Nurse Smythe to adjust the sheets underneath her buttocks. He carefully laid Elsie against the fresh pillows.

"Thank you dearie, I can handle it from here." Nurse Katie said.

He watched her continue till Elsie's feet had been wiped. As she shook the new sheet to spread over top, the fresh, clean smell chased away the medicinal odor in the room.

With the dirty sheets filling her arms, Katie started to leave the room.

He placed a hand on her arm to pause her departure. "Thank you for taking good care of her."

Nurse Smythe politely replied with "you're welcome love".

In over twenty years as a nurse, she knew not to become emotionally involved. However, from the moment she'd seen them both, she'd cared more than her job required. Everyone recognized Rusty Garnet. Elsie's recognition came from anyone who'd fallen in love with the characters in her books. Having read anything she'd seen about either of these two unique individuals, Katie felt a connection at meeting them. Rumors had surfaced regarding a romantic relationship between the two after the Golden Globes and Academy Awards. They had been titled the "Hermit and the Hedonist" and "Cutie and the Crank". But since then, months had passed with no further reports on the matter. Perhaps Elsie's lack of over the top notoriety didn't peak anyone's interest enough to sell newspapers. Having seen Rusty with Elsie, Katie could see how grounded he'd become. It didn't fit in with his old reputation that got him on the front page of the tabloids on numerous occasions.

In the room, Rusty waited for the neurologist. With Elsie having a neurologically induced episode, it pushed her to the top of the specialist's priorities. Rusty had been asked to leave the room while the doctor did his examination. Afterwards, he led Rusty to the floor office to talk. An hour later, Rusty left with plenty of information, but still no resolution on what to do. The neurologist ordered two specialized tests. They were still in wait mode. If Elsie woke up, her prognosis would be easier to determine. "If" being the operative word. He needed fresh air. First he went into Elsie's room to drop a kiss on her cheek. Next, he stopped by the nurses' station to inform Nurse Smythe they could reach him on his cell phone. Once outside, Rusty took a deep breath, holding it as long as he could to exhale. On his walk, he phoned the states. Thankfully, Sara was running an errand, giving him and Tom time to talk. Rusty relayed all of the information he'd just received. They both agreed there was no point to Sara flying Down Under. The plan was: if Elsie woke up, they would fly back to the states as soon as her condition allowed; if she didn't, nothing would be done for a period of time. In the meanwhile, Tom had the daunting task of making Sara see reason in their decision.

What Rusty felt after West Virginia had been only a fraction of what he felt at this moment. He felt like he was being sucked into a black hole where Elsie no longer existed—a place void of light, happiness and love. A place he thought he'd never have to face again once he'd allowed himself to believe in her love.

When Rusty realized Elsie had left without his having a chance to say goodbye, he thought he'd blown it again. He spent the next twenty-four hours struggling with his feelings as he handled everything on site for Rich. There was no doubt in his mind that he was more than willing to turn his life upside down to be with her and make her happy. Why had he not done that? Because he had other things to do. And she understood his drive. Odd how much they respected about each other's needs. It was difficult to believe someone as beautiful as Elsie could still be alone. She deserved to be taken care of and loved beyond eternity. Why had no one else seen or felt that? Why were those other things he wanted to do mutually exclusive of being with her?

Rich called to let him know his son would be okay. As soon as Rusty arrived in Los Angeles, they began work on the final production. By the 1st of December, the final version had been completed. The weeks in between had been littered with intermittent phone calls and emails to Elsie. Neither of them made reference to the two nights they had slept together. But Rusty wanted to talk about it and how he felt. Over the phone was not conducive to conveying the intensity of his feelings for her. As soon as the studio approved the film, Rusty had Sherry make flight reservations.

The next morning Rusty was on a flight east. This trip there was no preparatory phone call.

CHAPTER TWENTY-SEVEN

RUSTY WALKED FOR over an hour. His growling stomach caused a momentary pause in his reminiscing. He found a restaurant that handled take-out. Maybe the smell would waken Elsie's other senses. Returning to the hospital, he situated himself to eat. There was a bouquet of daisies on the nightstand. The card indicated they were from Rich and his family. While Rusty ate, his eyes fixated on the flowers.

Since the reservations had been made with such short notice, Rusty's flight included multiple airplane changes with an extended layover. Even though he'd departed the West Coast at 2am, it took till early evening for him to arrive in Allentown. Darkness set in on the drive from the airport to her home. The headlights shone across the frosted grass as he made his way along the driveway. Not sure what he'd do if she wasn't at home; he worried when he heard the dogs howling from the backyard. After he rang the doorbell, a wave of relief swept through him as the foyer lit.

When Elsie opened the door, he held a pretty cluster of daisies out to her. "Hello Mate. Per my promise, I'm here to tell you I'm ready to start a serious romantic relationship."

In all sincerity, she asked, "With whom?"

He couldn't believe she didn't know, "With you, my favorite mate."

Since she still hadn't taken the flowers, he placed them on the table in the entry way as he stepped through the door.

Her eyes searched his. "Me?"

"Yes you, Elsie Endy." To emphasize, he tugged her into his arms to give her a long, soft, slow kiss.

When their lips released, he said in a husky voice. "Have I made myself sufficiently clear mate or do you need me to go farther?"

All she could utter was "No, I mean, the door is still open."

He shut the door with his foot, and then continued his heartfelt plea. "I have been falling in love with you over the last year. Would you please give me a chance to make your life easier?"

Her eyes were wide in astonishment. Her mouth moved making no sound.

He chuckled at her loss for words. "Mate, is it possible that you're speechless?"

Blinking caused tears to trickle gently down her cheeks. He tenderly kissed each tear away. Their trail led him to her lips, again. He nibbled, coaxing her to draw him in. Leaning against him, she relinquished by deepening the kiss.

Separating slightly, he teased. "Happy tears?"

Still suffering from the emotional overload, she nodded exuberantly. From that point, a day didn't go by where they either weren't together or hadn't spoken on the phone several times. He made every effort to be with her or make any arrangements necessary to have her with him.

Nurse Katie entered the room to check Elsie's vitals. Rusty cleared away his empty food containers.

The pleasant nurse spoke. "I have to admit that I am a fan of yours."

He merely smiled at the obvious admission.

She tried again. "I mean both of you; particularly when you two became a couple."

He gave her a quizzical look.

Nurse Katie smiled compassionately. "I know you two haven't made a public statement in the papers or anything. But if anyone really watched the two of you at the holiday premiere and award ceremonies, they'd be blind not to have seen it."

Done with her duties in the room, she stated at the door. "And not meaning to be indelicate, it was also hard not to notice the night of the Oscars you seemed to have a difficult time standing to receive your award.

It looked to me as though you were suffering from honeymooner's back strain."

With no utterance from Rusty, Nurse Katie continued to the next patient's room.

His stomach sated, he stretched in the cushioned chair, propping his sock clad feet on the bed near Elsie's—like they would at home when they weren't actually sharing the same piece of furniture. Katie's comments swirled in his head.

Since the studio selected the day before Christmas for the New York premiere of "Sifting though the Ashes", Rusty stayed on the East coast into the New Year.

For this premiere, Rusty didn't disappoint Elsie. They drove to the city that morning. After checking into their suite, they dressed for the evening's event. Arriving at the theatre, they posed for photographers. If any asked for a shot of him alone, he declined. At the after movie party, he stayed well within reaching distance of her. And once back in their hotel room, she showed him how much she appreciated the entire day. The next morning he surprised her by ordering breakfast from room service while she showered. It arrived by the time she stepped into the living room wearing the hotel robe. The look of delight on her face at such a small gesture reminded him that he wanted to see it as much as possible. They returned to Elsie's on Christmas day, then spent the evening with Tom and Sara. New Year's Eve they stayed home with Sophie and Nash.

A few days later, he returned to Los Angeles to take care of business. Their separation made him incredibly nervous. Not that he thought she had another man on the side. Rather, he was concerned she would think it was a ruse to get away from her. Every day he spoke with her numerous times. To demonstrate he wanted to be with her, he made arrangements for the upcoming award shows. Sherry scheduled dress designer and spa appointments. Surprisingly, Elsie cancelled the meetings with the Hollywood designers. Due to the film's anticipated popularity, some of the New York designers made themselves available to her. Since both films were nominated for numerous awards: actor, actress, director, picture, screenplay, clothing design—etiquette required her attendance.

The first test was the Golden Globes. Elsie kept her dress hidden until right before the limousine arrived. The gown was in dark, almost black, blue silk brocade with lavender and white flowers. Its full length with matching low heel slippers would normally have accentuated Elsie's lack of height. However, its low cut neckline and thigh high side slits gave the illusion of a longer torso and legs. Of course, standing next to Rusty her shortness was apparent—not the expected leggy, lithe starlet. As far as he felt, Elsie looked fabulous and she was who he wanted by his side for always. Lots of pictures were snapped of the couple at their arrival. Rusty had been nominated for both films—one in a supporting role, the other as the main actor. The tables assigned for the films had been placed side by side. Thankfully, Tina Laney didn't show because of the lack of a nomination. Amazing everyone, Red attended the event. The last time he'd been at an awards show had been over two and a half decades ago. The biggest surprise of the night was Maci winning her first time out for best supporting actress in "Sifting through the Ashes". When Rusty won best supporting actor for "Mountain's Majesty", he and Elsie hugged, then he and Red. In his acceptance speech, he wanted to make reference to having heeded Elsie's advice to take the part. Especially since her prediction had come true. But he'd promised her they would not spout their relationship. That didn't mean they would hide their affection for each other. Just no statements in referenced to it until they'd worked the kinks from the geographical issues involved. Those that knew them, like Red and Rich, were tickled by the obvious change in the status of their relationship. Neither had to say a word; the giddy smile on the directors' faces each time they caught an intimate gesture between the couple communicated the sentiment.

Elsie skipped some of the lesser award ceremonies. She didn't like leaving the dogs so often. Plus, she still had to make a living. Granted she always took her laptop with her to write on the road. However, working while in California didn't make it high on the priority list. When Elsie had time to spend with Rusty, she wasn't going to ignore him. She'd have plenty of time when they were separated and she'd need to stay busy. Adding to her increasing popularity, she had to strike while it was hot. With everything going on, she finally had to admit she needed a full time assistant. Her friend Trish had been working for her part time handling certain things. When Elsie asked her to go full time, Trish eagerly quit her regular job. Elsie needed to have enough books in the pipeline now that they were selling. The royalties related to the two movies were putting tidy sums in her bank accounts on a regular basis. She had clearly defined goals she wanted to reach. Like buying the farmland neighboring Tom and Sara's property. The farmer would continue living in his family home as the groundskeeper as long as he wanted. A new house would be built for Elsie on the parcel directly adjacent to her friends. Eventually, the original stone farmhouse would be renovated. With Rusty and Elsie's growing relationship, they discussed at length additional possibilities for the property. One of these options included having cattle. Elsie agreed as long as they were free range. He'd been shocked at how quickly she'd adapted to his insertion in her life.

It would have taken illness bordering on death for her to miss going to the Oscars. As she explained to him, this was a chance of a lifetime. He'd tried to convince her they would go next year because he would be a presenter if he won this year. Either way, she arrived in Los Angeles two days before the red carpet ceremony. Once again, he had Sherry schedule spa time for her. A driver transported Elsie from the airport to the appointment.

Upon picking Elsie up at the resort, her face glowed as she slid into the passenger seat of his Range Rover. No sooner had they gotten in the door of his townhouse, she had him in a lip lock. He couldn't determine who tore more at his clothing. Her clothing had already landed on the floor. Unable to wait till they made it to the bedroom, he positioned himself on the stairs. Without hesitation, she straddled him. He couldn't get enough of her; his hands caressed every inch of her as they bucked and rocked together. As climax neared, he grabbed her buttocks pulling her even tighter to him. She cried out his name as he moaned hers.

With her sprawled across him, he asked breathlessly. "Did you miss me, Mate?"

She cocked her head to look at him, then the ridiculous position in which they found themselves. She started to giggle. She tried to muffle it in his chest making him laugh, too. She dismounted, still giggling, to fetch their clothing. He sat up to straighten his back. He watched, still chuckling, as she bent to collect their discarded garments. Her cute little derriere directly in front of him stopped his mirth as desire filled his loins again. Not changing her pose, she glanced around to see why he'd gotten quiet. Without thinking, he stood and threw her over his shoulder.

On his quick ascent, he announced "woman, it's your turn to be ravaged!"

He slammed the bedroom door behind them in emphasis

Around 1AM, he woke to the other side of the bed empty. A moment of déjà vu caused a spark of fear that she'd bolted. Donning his robe, he hurried downstairs. A quick prayer of thanks left his lips when he saw a light on in the kitchen. Elsie, wearing one of his t-shirts, was rummaging in the refrigerator.

He poked his head above the open door.

"Aaiiieee!" She screamed, dropping a jar of kosher dills on her foot, followed by "ow!"

"Love, I'm sorry, I didn't mean to startle you." He apologized.

Catching her breath, "I didn't hear you come downstairs."

They both bent to get the jar rolling across the floor. In doing this, he bumped into her knocking her off balance. She fell into the cabinets with a bang and another "ow".

Placing the offending jar onto the counter, he knelt by her. "Elsie dear, are you okay?"

When she raised her head, she had a goofy smile on her face. "Hey what are a few more bumps and bruises to add to the ones from our earlier activities?"

Completely caught off guard, an emotional knife stabbed him in the chest.

"Mate please, I didn't mean to hurt you! I thought you were enjoying it as much as I was. Why didn't you tell me to stop?" Emotions choked him.

Her face fell.

She scrambled to hug him. "No Rusty, oh God, that wasn't what I meant!"

He peered deeply into her eyes to verify he hadn't hurt her that way. Then he clutched her to him in a fierce embrace.

In that instant, Rusty grasped how much they loved each other. "Marry me!"

"What?" She struggled to see if she'd heard him correctly.

He made eye contact with her. "Elsie love, will you please marry me?"

The look of astonishment on her face answered for her. But he knew it wasn't because she didn't want to marry him. It was the fear everything would change—he would change into someone else or she would have to change for him—making it all go sour.

Speaking with sincerity "no worries Mate, you don't have to answer anytime soon. Just wanted to let you know how I feel."

He kissed her on the cheek, then tried to stand.

She yanked him down again. Unable to speak anything sensible, she gave him a kiss fueled with intensifying emotions. He felt her wanting: wanting him to stay the same, wanting him to love her as she was, wanting to say yes. He could wait as long as it took.

This must have been what Madame Marna had meant with "you will have to let go of her hand, but never let go of her heart".

Rusty had Elsie in his arms needing to be loved and wanted. Opening his robe to expose his naked and fully aroused state, he lifted her on top of him. Instead of her usual squeal of joy, she kissed him fervently. He reached between their legs to shift her panties for access. He delighted in discovering only her femininity hot and wet with anticipation. He was happy to oblige. He groaned in gratification at entering her pulsing passion canal. Her pert nipples through the cotton t-shirt brushed across his chest as they found their rhythm. Her moans and sighs of burgeoning bliss relayed to him when they were ready to climax. After sweet surrender, they lay on the cool tile floor in ecstatic exhaustion.

An hour later, they woke in the same position. Their stomachs grumbled in unison. They smiled at each other knowingly. They needed food after their playful romps had expended an abundance of calories. There was leftover Chinese food from yesterday. A few minutes in the microwave, heated it enough to eat. He opened a beer for each of them.

When that appetite was sated, they headed to the bedroom. They both climbed into bed nude. Her hands wandered across his chest and stomach prior to dipping lower for a few strokes. He reciprocated by fondling her ample bosom and caressing her hips.

He sighed happily at the relaxed intimacy. "Mate, I would gladly continue this, but I am exhausted."

"Me too, just needed a little touchie-feelie." The smile could be heard in her voice.

"Mm." He mumbled.

As they snuggled together, he caught a glimpse of the clock—3:22. Thankfully, they had no plans or appointments which would be affected by sleeping late.

Chapter Twenty-Eight

Rusty stirred six hours later to glorious smells wafting from the kitchen. His back felt stiff and a bit sore as he rolled from bed. He decided to take a hot shower to loosen his muscles before going in search of the origin of the delicious aroma. Her suitcase open on the chair and toiletries setting by the sink indicated she'd already showered. To hurry his progress along, he only towel dried his hair, then threw on a clean t-shirt and pair of jeans.

As the kitchen came into view, Elsie was placing a plate of food on the table.

Looking up she smiled brightly "good morning Mate."

Finding her use of his words cute, he used one of her phrases "back at you babe."

She giggled. "Coffee?"

"Silly question silly girl" he answered with a kiss on her cheek.

"I must be daft, I'm here with you." She volleyed.

He sat by the plate filled with pancakes and sausage links. When he picked up the syrup, it was warm. Elsie brought herself a cup of coffee to the table along with his. Instead of joining him, she returned to the stove. By the time he finished smothering his pancakes; she sat with a plate of her own.

Taking a bite, his taste buds were in heaven. "Love, this is fantastic! What time did you wake up to have all of this done?"

"Around 7:30." She took a sip of coffee.

"I thought for sure you'd have slept longer with yesterday's events." He teased. "You know, all of that flying high."

"Evidently I was less affected than you were old man." She turned the tables on him.

He had to swallow a mouthful of food to banter back. "They say women peak sexually at 40. I don't know how I'm going to keep up in two years. You wear me out!"

She couldn't do anything to hide the bright pink cascading across her face. "Maybe I should have found a 26 year old instead of a 36 year old."

Getting up from his seat, he kneeled by her chair.

Saying in a soft deep baritone full of sincerity, "God help me if you ever find anyone else to take care of you."

At her speechlessness, he planted a lingering kiss on her maple syrup laced lips. Returning to his chair and his breakfast, he was quite satisfied with the dumbfounded look she wore. How he thrived on knowing what made her tick. As much as he loved word play with her, making her go addle-brained was a bonus. Especially since the majority of the time she had the better turn of phrase.

Part way through his plate, he fetched the pot of coffee to refresh their cups.

She mouthed a "thank you" keeping the silence in tact.

After swallowing the last bit from his plate, Rusty belched uncontrollably loud.

"Excuse me mate!" He blurted.

She smothered a giggle before stating: "No worries. Where I grew up, that would be considered a compliment to the cook."

They cleaned the kitchen together. When she washed her hands, he helped. Then they played tug-o-war with the hand towel, which she willingly lost for a kiss. The phone rang. He answered it via the portable setting at the end of the counter. It was Sherry reminding him he had to make a decision about parts he'd been offered.

While still on the phone, Elsie motioned to him.

"Hold on Sherry." Placing his hand over the mouthpiece, "did you need something love?"

"Invite them for dinner tonight." She directed.

"Uh, okay." Speaking to Sherry, "I've just gotten orders that I'm supposed to invite you and your husband for dinner tonight. If that's good for you two, we could discuss this then. What do you say?"

He paused while Sherry agreed.

Looking at Elsie, he raised his eyebrows and mouthed the word "time?"

"Five-thirty." She replied.

Off the phone, he opened the worn walnut roll-top desk at the far end of the living room. He shuffled some papers around to find three drafts. He tossed two of them on the coffee table.

"Mate, would you please skim through these two scripts and let me know what you think?" He asked not expecting anything other than a positive response.

He settled into his overstuffed chair to re-read the one in his hand. She chose the corner of the sofa farthest from him. Resting the script on her raised knees, she propped herself against the arm and a pillow. He repositioned his chair, allowing him to stretch his legs across the unused cushions of the sofa. Their feet touched. Neither of them was wearing socks allowing their toes to play. An hour into it, he refilled their cups, started another pot brewing and loaded the multi-CD player. He resituated himself in the same position as earlier. When the music hit a peppy tune, their toes tapped together to the tempo. They kept reading.

About 1 o'clock he needed a break. He threw the script he was reading onto the coffee table with a bang. She looked questioningly at him with raised eyebrows. A devilish thought crossed his mind with a matching smile on his face. She calmly placed the papers onto the table next to his. With a smile of her own, she parted her jean clad legs by dropping one of her feet to the floor. This exposed a section of sofa which she patted in invitation. He didn't sit with her. Rather he launched himself on top of her with a roar. He wildly nibbled at her neck making her laugh at his silliness. He couldn't contain his mirth either. Giddy and entangled—they rolled off the sofa hitting the floor with a thud. This caused them to laugh harder.

When their glee spent itself, he asked, "How about some food?"

Sitting against the sofa, she answered. "Okay, but not too much since we are having a big meal tonight."

"Yeah and what are we eating? We're having guests in four hours, but nothing is started." He commented as he helped her stand.

"Really? How about you follow me into the kitchen?" She took his hand to lead him there.

She reached into the fridge to reveal a large rectangular casserole dish covered with aluminum foil. Opening an edge of the foil, he saw lasagna ready to pop into the oven.

"When did you have time?" He uttered flabbergasted.

"This morning—it really doesn't take that long." Pride at pleasing him lit her face.

"That's why Sherry brought groceries along with her a couple days ago." He surmised.

"Uh huh", she nodded.

After a few moments of thought, he suggested: "How about veggies and dip for a light lunch?"

"Sounds good", she agreed.

They munched while they read. At four o'clock, she put the lasagna in the oven and set the table prior to going upstairs to freshen up. He soon followed to find her splashing cold water on her face. Leaning against the door frame, he watched. She saw him in the mirror as she let her hair down to brush. He moved behind her, running his fingers through her thick, lustrous mane.

He murmured on her skin, as he kissed her neck. "Your hair is getting long."

"Is that a compliment or complaint?" She queried with uncertainty.

"I'm just letting you know I noticed." He continued nibbling on her nape. "I like it, but I also like your tumbleweed look. Whatever you prefer is okay with me."

She turned to face him. "Good answer."

Their lips met for a tantalizing kiss. After the kiss, she moved away from him into the bedroom. She started undressing. He wanted to assist, but didn't know if she wanted to play or was merely changing for the evening ahead. Only her undergarments were remained. She glanced back at him. Unhooking her bra, she slowly slipped the straps off her shoulders. With a slight jiggle to release the cups the double D duo were free. Keeping her back towards him, she slid the matching bottom from her tight tush. Completely naked, she lay across the bed in a sex kitten pose. So engrossed in the show, he hadn't moved. Rather one part had and now stood at attention. In the couple of strides to the bed, he disposed of his own clothing. No more foreplay was required. She opened her legs inviting him to enter as he hit the bed. It brought new meaning to the fast and the furious. They lay still joined, catching their breath for a few minutes.

Suddenly she squirmed underneath his weight. "Look at the time!"

Glancing at the clock too, he quickly separated from her. Her disheveled appearance needed fixing for their soon to be arriving guests. He remained on the bed staying out of her way. She rushed downstairs to prevent dinner from burning. When he bent to fetch his discarded clothes, he felt a crick in his back. Figuring it was nothing, he didn't bother taking anything for it.

Sherry and Harris brought two bottles of wine and dessert. Rusty poured he and Harris each a pre-dinner scotch. The women finished the open bottle of wine from the refrigerator. Normally, the women would be in the kitchen with the men in the living room. This group could hardly be called normal. All four picked a spot in the kitchen. Harris and Elsie discussed book business while Sherry and Rusty reviewed movie options. During dinner, Sherry purposefully brought up the pending movie parts on which Rusty needed to decide. A lively conversation ensued. Even though Elsie joined, Rusty couldn't tell which way she thought he should go. Dinner officially finished with espresso and tiramisu. They were all enjoying themselves so much that Sherry and Harris stayed until midnight.

After their guests departed, Rusty asked Elsie "Love, what part do you think I should take?"

She didn't stop clearing placing glasses into the dishwasher to answer. "I think you should take the part you want."

This did not please him. "That was not an answer!"

"That's the only answer you are getting." She locked the latch and set the appliance to run.

He poured himself a scotch. "I know you have an opinion and I want to hear it."

"You've been in the industry how many years? Why do you suddenly need me to help you decide?" Her tone flat, giving him no indication.

He took a gulp of the amber liquid. "I want to know what part you think would be better."

She walked to the foot of the stairs.

With one foot on the first step, she turned to state seriously. "If you take my advice and it fails, then you'll blame me. No thank you and good night."

She went upstairs not bothering to hear his rejoinder. He downed what was still in his glass to pour another. He didn't understand. Her response, as logical as it sounded, exasperated him. He sipped absentmindedly at his drink while he tried to decipher her reaction. Twenty minutes later, he had no resolution, but he was not going to bed with this absurdity between them. He took the steps two at a time. He entered the dimly lit room more forcefully than intended. The only light came from the bathroom. She gave him a cautious look from where she sat on her side of the bed.

"We need to discuss this!" He demanded.

She sighed. "Why? It's your career."

Throwing his body down onto the covers next to her, he said, "But it will affect our life together."

She gently stroked his hair. "Nonetheless, you need to make your own decision based on what you want and what's best for you."

Rolling over onto his back, his head rested in her lap. "I don't want to take a part that would cause us to be separated."

Still gently playing with his hair, she countered. "You shouldn't pass on a really good part either."

"But Mate, we should be together." He rubbed his cheek against the softness of her bosom.

Framing his head in her hands, she stilled his motions. "What are you afraid of?"

He closed his eyes without answering. She ran her fingers lightly along his face and neck. In the background, a song from the 80s played from the radio. A ballad from the same era followed, then another. He stood to turn the radio louder. Instead of lying down again, he walked into the bathroom. He readied for bed by tossing his clothing into the hamper and washing his face.

"Rusty?" Her quiet question breached the silence.

She stood in the doorway wearing her usual bedclothes—a cotton camisole and boxers. He noticed his own navy blue boxers with two white paw prints matched hers. She'd given him the ones he was wearing for Christmas. Evidently, she'd bought herself a pair, too. He smiled. She cocked her head in puzzlement. He fingered the paw prints on his shorts, then on hers. A sheepish smile formed on her lips. Using the corner of her boxers, he pulled her towards him. He placed a kiss on her soft lips. After which, he led her to the middle of the room. With the radio still playing 80s love songs, he drew her into a slow dance. After a couple of songs, his hands began a slow erotic dance with her body. She added to his improvisation by gliding her long fingernails across his bare skin. Goosebumps of pleasure rose across his whole body. Her tongue touched the tips of his hardened nubs. He responded involuntarily with a full length shiver. He removed her camisole to return the favor. The matching boxers only survived part way through the next song. Their foreplay lasted for three more songs until they were both panting with such desire they couldn't hear the music. They were closer to the chair than the bed. He picked her up, resting her against its back for support. As he kneeled on the seat, he guided her onto his throbbing member. His full hardness plunging in that deep made her gasp. Her legs hooked around his thighs. An involuntary spasm of desire initiated the longest climax either of them had ever experienced. Both spent, Rusty carried Elsie the few steps to the bed. Under the covers, they curled together. Sleep didn't last long and they were indulging in each other again. The same pattern followed till the wee hours of the morning.

CHAPTER TWENTY-NINE

THEY WERE BOTH still sleeping at noon. Rusty roused first. His back cramping so much he could barely pull himself from bed to use the bathroom. He rummaged through the medicine cabinet for a strong pain killer or muscle relaxant. Unfortunately, after the scotch and vicadin cocktail incident, he'd flushed anything of that nature.

At the side of the bed, he yanked at the blankets. "Elsie . . . ? Elsie!"

With a sleep thickened voice she responded, "Just a few more minutes."

"Mate, please wake up, I need your help." He pleaded.

Fighting through the sleep, she sat. "Rusty, what's wrong?"

"My back", not bothering to conceal the pain.

Now completely awake, she hopped out of bed. "Do you want to go to the emergency room?"

"No! Just help me sit in the chair and find my cell phone." He rejected the suggestion harshly.

She did as commanded. He called his personal physician. If he could hold out for two hours, the doctor could make a house call. Rusty agreed to avoid a herd of photographers at an emergency room. Elsie convinced him to work his way to the hot tub for a long soak. In the warm bubbles, his muscles relaxed. Each time he climbed out, the pain would worsen as it tightened on the walk into the house. He would retrace his steps to the therapeutic tub. With his skin puckering, he had to stay out. She helped him upstairs to wait for the doctor. When the man arrived, Elsie showed him to Rusty, leaving them alone for the exam. The doctor asked Rusty a few questions to aid in determining a diagnosis. Thankfully, the doctor had a good sense of humor when Rusty admitted to his recent exertions. With

Rusty having to attend the award show that night posed a dilemma in the treatment. The doctor gave him a low dosage muscle relaxant for Rusty to stay coherent.

They had an hour to get ready. Since she had showered and fussed with her hair earlier, he could commandeer the bathroom. The mirror in the powder room served for putting on her make-up and fixing her hair. Back in the bedroom, she helped him get into his tuxedo while she dressed. They headed downstairs with ten minutes to spare.

Part way down the steps, he stopped. "Damn!"

Her voice sounded with concern, "Are you in pain?"

"No! Well yes, but I forgot something" his tone plainly cranky.

"Where is it? I'll get it for you." She offered.

"Oh alright, it's in my underwear drawer—a long black velvet box." He wanted to surprise her.

She gave him an odd look as she retraced their steps. He made it to the foyer by the time she rejoined him.

When she handed the velvet box to him, he stated. "No, it's for you; open it."

Her hands shook as she complied.

At seeing the contents, her face filled with astonishment. "It's just on loan right?"

"No, I bought it for you." Pride momentarily dampened the pain.

He removed the contents. "Turn around and lift your hair."

She obeyed his command. He secured the clasp.

Rotating to face him, she hugged him gently. "Thank you Rusty. It is incredibly beautiful!"

The choker of purple amethysts and deep blue sapphires sparkled against her skin.

"You're welcome, but not as beautiful as you." He spoke from his heart.

Elsie glanced about nervously. Rusty wondered if she'd ever hear a compliment in regards to her loveliness, and be comfortable with it.

The door bell announced the arrival of the limousine. Climbing in to the backseat had its challenge with his current condition. She didn't start her nervous fidgeting until they were in line for disembarking onto the red carpet. He worried his back would cramp. The medication had eased the pain to tolerable. The red carpet procession moved along slow enough to conceal his haltingly stiff gait. Occasionally, it did twinge excessively which caused him to clutch her hand. She said nothing. Rich caught them during one of the interviews. He and his wife, Janie, greeted the couple with affection.

Rich said into Rusty's ear as they neared another microphone session. "Why are you walking like an old man?"

"Cause my woman broke me in this weekend." Rusty stated full of male ego.

Rich shook his head and chuckled.

Their last stop was Laura Ravine.

Leave it to Laura to jump all over Rusty escorting Elsie. "So Ms. Endy, I see you and hunky Garnet holding hands. Is there something you'd like to clue our viewers in on? Is this sexy man off the market?"

No one had addressed Elsie directly all night.

Rusty watched her handle it with grace and humor. "Being such a recluse, I am extremely nervous with all of these people. And our big strong hero here has a death grip on my hand so I don't bolt."

Elsie managed play the tabloids labeling her a hermit because she refused to do any interviews in relation to the film. She and Rich had discussed it at length with the decision to leave that for him and Rusty to promote. As for the second part of her comment, it couldn't have been truer.

"Tell me dear, no one asked you at the Golden Globes, who did your dress?" The queen of interviewers pointed out the lack of a new designer gown.

Elsie didn't let Laura's dig rattle her. "My fairy god mother had more important things to take care of and the mice were on vacation. Since we did well at the Globes, I didn't want to tempt fate by wearing a new dress or changing escorts."

Laura gave one of her big laughs. "My dear, you are simply precious. Rusty darling, you would be a fool to let her get away!"

A Cheshire cat grin formed because he had already acted upon that exact sentiment. From then until later in the evening became a blur.

Elsie gripped Rusty's forearm as the nominees for Best Supporting Actor were read. "And the winner is Rusty Garnet in Mountain's Majesty".

He won. He won!

As he struggled to stand, Elsie threw her arms around him in excitement. Rich grabbed him from the other side. What looked merely as congratulatory hugs served as a cover to help Rusty stand with the cameras focused on his reaction. At that moment, he wanted to give her a passionate kiss for the world to see. Instead, he had to concentrate on getting on stage without falling face first. The pain killer had lessened the pain. It also made the world slightly tilted. The associated adrenalin rush enabled him to reach the podium to deliver his acceptance speech without incident. It served him through the backstage interviews immediately afterwards with his usual charm. By the time he returned to his seat, he had missed the Best Screenplay Adaptation. Elsie had not won. Ironically, the screenwriter for her book "Sifting through the Ashes" did win. An hour later, Rich won Best Director with "Sifting through the Ashes". Rich still held the Best Director Oscar in his hand when he stepped from backstage to accept Best Picture.

"Thank you", Rich bowed his head as the applause died.

"Ahem", he cleared his throat to start his prepared acceptance speech. He stopped; mouth parted looking as if he'd forgotten it.

"I can't do this. Elsie! You should be up here. This Oscar is yours because without you this movie would have never happened. Elsie, come up here!" Rich's sincerity and gratitude tangible as Elsie made her way to him.

On stage, he handed her the little gold man, then put his arm around her shoulders pulling her to the podium with him.

"Folks, working with a woman of such intelligence and heart made this movie a new experience for a veteran like me. And for that I will always be grateful." He blew a kiss to his wife before kissing Elsie's cheek.

Rich directed Elsie to hold up her Oscar like he was doing. It made for a great photograph.

Rusty led Rich's wife to the backstage interview spot. Rich and Elsie fielded questions from the reporters. Both of them answered as if they'd taken lessons at the mutual gratification society. If it had been anyone other than Rich, Rusty would have been insanely jealous. At the end of the session, the two couples re-paired.

"Janie, your husband is wonderfully generous and absolutely insane!" Elsie said with tears in her eyes as the evening's events took their toll.

Janie looked into Rich's eyes as she answered Elsie. "Yes, but when you find one like him; it's worth it."

She smiled knowingly towards the other couple. "You'll know what I mean soon enough."

Both couples were picked up by their limousines via the backstage door. Neither went to the after show parties. They preferred to go to their respective homes. On the way, Rusty's back started to spasm. He couldn't find a position to sit or lay on the seat to relieve it. They still had a half hour till they were at his place. Elsie retrieved a prescription bottle from her handbag. Selecting two tablets and fetching a bottle of Evian from the mini refrigerator, she handed them to him.

"Take these." She ordered.

He took them from her with a question. "What are they?"

"On his way out, the doctor told me he called in a strong prescription for after the awards. The pharmacy delivered these while you were showering." She explained.

He swallowed the two potent pills. "Let's hope they work quickly."

They did. By the time they'd gotten home, he was feeling no pain; nor much of anything else for that matter. Climbing from the low vehicle served a different challenge compared to earlier. This time she exited first; giving him her hand to hoist him. At the door, she needed to frisk him for the keys. Of course, he returned the favor. This caused a major distraction for her juggling the two statuettes while searching for the key to unlock the door. Once inside, he finally had a chance to show her his happiness at having her by his side. However, the kiss bordered on adolescent—misdirected full open mouth, sloppy and wet—rather than passionate. She gently pushed his mouth shut from under his chin to give him a peck on the lips. She tucked the two gold figures in each of his coat pockets.

"C'mon, to bed with you." She said tugging at the lapels of his coat.

"Whatever you say Mate!" he responded bawdily.

She stayed just beyond his reach grabbing for her ass. It served as motivation to get him up the stairs. In the bedroom, she went directly into the bathroom and closing the door behind her. He stripped to his boxers. At remembering the Oscars, he took them out of his tuxedo to stand prominently on the center of the dresser.

The bathroom door opened as she exited. She was wearing a pale purple cotton nightgown, her face freshly scrubbed and her neck still bejeweled.

"Be right out mate." He slurred passing her on his way into the bathroom.

It only took him a few minutes. She lay in bed, her eyes closed. He flipped off lights on his way to join her. Sliding beneath the cool sheets, he reached for her. The effort he made felt like she was miles away not mere inches. He snuggled against her to promptly fall sound asleep. He woke a few hours later in the same position. One small difference, his face rubbed a towel rather than her cotton shift. His hands pushed away the terry cloth in search of Elsie. His wandering hand located skin.

"Rusty, do you need something?" She asked.

"You Mate." He grunted.

He tucked her butt against his groin to demonstrate how much. But something didn't feel quite right.

She said in the kindest of voices. "That would be a wonderful idea if it weren't for your back."

"Here Mate, you climb on top so we don't strain it." He rolled onto his back.

She stayed quiet for a few moments prior to pointing out something he'd missed. "There isn't anything to climb onto."

Reaching down to where she had made reference, he discovered the medication had killed more than his pain. He couldn't think of anything to say. The persistent silence lulled him back to sleep.

When he woke later, a feeling of déjà vu swept over him. This time he'd avoided the booze, but these pills packed a bigger wallop. Getting out of bed reminded him why he'd needed them. He wanted to soak in the hot tub. The stairs once again served a challenge.

Elsie sat on the sofa working. She glanced up from her laptop.

With a tentative smile she said "Good morning."

Slightly hunched, he stopped by the couch. "G'day Mate."

He tried to bend over to kiss her; he got stuck part way. "I feel like a rusty hinge!"

She giggled.

"What's so funny?" He grumped.

Stifling her mirth was impossible. "Rusty hinge . . ."

He responded with sarcasm "guess I need some DW 40."

"Would that be DWF 40 or DWM 40?" She asked.

"Huh?" He didn't have a clue he'd transposed the letters.

"Divorced White Female age 40 or Divorced White Male age 40?" She defined the acronyms for him.

He finally caught on. "Since my DWF 40 isn't working for me, maybe I should switch to a DWM."

"The DWF 40 lube was ready. The spray attachment wasn't functioning." She parried playfully.

"Krikey mate! That was a low blow." He spouted at the end of his repartee.

She pouted cutely. "Hmm that's always an option."

It took a minute for that one to sink in—to his disappointment; his manhood didn't even tingle at the thought.

He had to face it. "Love, between the pain and the medication, my libido has gone on walkabout."

Sensing his feelings of dejection, she quickly climbed over the back of the sofa.

Putting her arms gently around him, she said in a low voice. "Have no fear, this won't send me on walkabout."

He made a face at her sappiness. He needed to hear it, but he wasn't going to admit that.

Sinking into the hot tub went easier than anticipated. A half hour later, she stepped onto the deck.

"I brought you something to eat." She announced. "It's here on the table."

He attempted to climb out of the steamy bubbles. He couldn't.

"Elsie!" He called before she closed the sliding door.

"Yes?" She poked her head outside.

Swallowing his pride, he asked. "Mate, would you please help me?"

"Sure thing Love", she answered crossing the redwood planks.

She stepped onto the submerged bench directly behind him. Grabbing him under the arms, she lifted as he stood. He maneuvered the rest with her merely there to keep him steady. His robe draped across the chair in front of the place setting. Putting it on prevented any drafts which might knot his loosened muscles. She disappeared inside. When he brought his empty plate in from outside, he saw her typing away. Not wanting to interrupt her productivity, he headed upstairs to watch the news and make a few phone calls. A massage therapist arrived an hour later to work the kinks.

Early evening, he took another soak. Once again, she had a light meal waiting. This time she joined him. Afterwards, they'd have driven to the beach for a long walk, in his current condition this couldn't occur. She offered sedate activities: cards, scrabble, and monopoly. He rejected the suggestion; sitting for too long made his back cramp. In actuality, he'd been avoiding taking another full dose all day, but he needed to now. She had busied herself by putting dirty dishes in the dishwasher.

He queried as to where she'd put the medication. "Love, where are the pain killers with a knock out punch?"

"Is it that bad again?" She asked with concern.

"Yes Mate." He replied regretfully.

"I believe they are still in the purse I used last night." She supposed. "I'll run up and get them for you."

"No, no." He stopped her. "I'll stay up there. If it hits like last night, I don't want to be far from the bed."

"Okay." She gave him a peck on the lips. "My bag should be on the dresser."

"Thanks." He headed to his room.

Within thirty minutes of taking the potent pills, he fell asleep.

The next two days followed the same pattern. By the fourth day, his back felt better. And with Elsie departing the following morning, he wanted to play again. Unfortunately his system needed to be clear of the medication for a few days for his manhood to be up for a performance.

They took an afternoon drive to the beach for a walk. On the return drive, she yawned repeatedly.

"I'm sorry. I think working till midnight the last few nights has caught up with me." She apologized.

"So you've been falling asleep on the sofa?" He surmised that's why he'd been waking alone.

"No, I've been coming to bed, but by 5am I'm wide awake again." She explained.

He thought a few minutes before making conciliation. "When we get home, take a nap. I'll make dinner."

Two hours later, he heard the shower running upstairs. He went to investigate. Seeing her silhouette through the glass door, he wanted to glide his hands along her sudsy skin. He stripped to join her.

He smothered her surprised shriek with his mouth devouring hers. His mouth moved to do the same to her neck while his hands slid sensuously over her wet body. She gasped in delight as his fingers slipped into her. He chose not to employ them there long enough for her to climax. He continued the blitz on her beautiful body by rubbing his full length against hers. With the suds rinsed away, he turned the water off. They stepped from the shower stall to dry each other. Naked, he led her to lie on the bed. Her nipples were perky and ready to be suckled. With his lips servicing one, his hand massaged the other. Her groans of gratification and hips grinding against his body alerted him she was close. He shifted his whole body to focus on the lower part of her torso. His tongue teased around where his fingers had played earlier. When her hips gyrated, he thrust his tongue inside. She tasted of sweetness. And he was hungry for it as if he'd been starving. He didn't know who got off more from it. If it would've been physically possible for an erection at that moment, it would've been painfully hard. Her hands reached for him. He grasped them with his, feeling her on the brink. She peaked in protracted pulses of pure primal pleasure.

As they lay in their afterglow, she curled into him. She said nothing, but she gazed at him with such wide eyes full of vulnerability. He didn't know what to think. He tucked her closer to him. She dozed. He lay awake not wanting her to leave the next morning. Forty minutes went by prior to her stirring. When she got up to use the bathroom, he went downstairs to finish preparing dinner. Till she joined him, the food was ready and the table set with lit candles.

She murmured a barely audible "thank you" as he held her chair.

Sitting in his own chair, he smiled lovingly at her. Instead of seeing the predictable look of satiety, he saw shy embarrassment.

"Mate, are you okay?" He questioned confused.

She wouldn't look up from her plate, "uh huh".

He blamed it on low blood sugar. Especially after their earlier frenzied frolic. Silence carried on throughout the meal. She ate very little, pushing the food about her plate.

"Don't you like it?" He'd specifically chosen this recipe to make for her.

"It's delicious, not really hungry." Again she spoke to the plate rather than him.

"You haven't eaten since this morning." He knew she was evading the real answer. "And with all of those calories we burned, you should be asking for seconds. So what gives?"

"Nothing that matters", she mumbled.

"Let me decide. Now talk." He wasn't asking anymore.

She glanced quickly at him, then away. He could tell there was a war going on behind her eyes. Getting out of his chair, he moved to kneel beside her.

In the gentlest of voices, "Mate, please tell me what is going on in that head of yours."

Fidgeting with her napkin, she spoke timidly. "What you referred to from earlier."

"What about our play time mate?" He couldn't begin to guess where she was going with this.

Elsie took a deep breath, then rushed out with "What do you want?"

"I don't understand." Confusion twisted his face.

"What do you want in return for that?" This time she held her breath.

The anger rising inside him had to be quelled. Her question must have been invoked from the past.

Keeping his tone as level as possible, "Do you think I pleasured you for a reason other than the fact that I love you and wanted to be with you?"

There were those wide eyes full of vulnerability staring at him. "You didn't. It was only me."

Gently taking her face in his hands, "First, if I didn't like doing it, I wouldn't. Second, I was enjoying every bit of it as much as you were."

Then he asked a question he feared he already knew the answer. "Did he only make you feel good so you would reciprocate with things you didn't want to do or didn't like?"

Since Rusty still held her face, Elsie couldn't turn away. The way her eyes darted to and fro was confirmation enough. He pulled her into his arms. She'd been full of gusto for all, even initiated quite a few, of their sexual experiences. He didn't want to imagine what else that bastard had done to her. It wasn't any wonder she wanted so much to be loved and in the same instance did what she could to sabotage it for fear of the past repeating itself.

Kneeling and holding her, his back started to spasm.

He stated. "Mate, I'm sorry, my back."

She immediately rolled onto her heals with an "oh dear."

He put one hand on the table, the other on the chair. Using them as support, he cautiously pulled himself into a standing position. She also stood. The spasms stopped. He put his arms around her again.

"Mate, I . . . never . . . with you . . . anything you need . . ." His words of comfort and understanding uttered as gibberish.

CHAPTER THIRTY

RUSTY WOKE TO that twinge in his back. No wonder, while he dozed his feet had fallen off Elsie's bed putting him in an oddly twisted position. Straightening in the chair, he checked his watch. Visiting hours were ending. Rubbing the sleep from his eyes, he discovered his cheeks were damp. He returned to the hotel.

Over 72 hours had passed with Elsie still in a coma. The doctors had expected only a 24 to 48 hour time span. They decided to do another CT scan the next morning. It appeared as though the swelling had diminished. On a good note, it hadn't exposed any further injury to the brain which they had been unable to see prior. Why didn't she regain consciousness? How the brain healed itself still remained a mystery in such cases. This did not comfort him. Especially since the way her mind worked made her such a unique individual to those that really got to know her. At this point, when and if she woke, he wondered if she would still be his Elsie. This is what he pondered as he ate a late dinner. Part way through the meal, his cell phone rang. It was the hospital requesting him to return. Elsie had another seizure with adverse effects. He handed money to the waitress on his way for the door. He ran the four blocks to the hospital. The elevator ride seemed to take forever. Stepping from the lift, he didn't see Nurse Katie at the nurses' station. He rushed to Elsie's room. Inside he found the nurse.

She heard him enter the room. "Thank goodness you are here."

"What happened?" Worry furrowing his brow.

"Elsie had another seizure—this one much worse." Nurse Katie fussed with the wires running from Elsie's chest. "We had to use the paddles."

He noted the crash cart in the corner of the room. "How bad?"

"Her vitals won't stabilize. She doesn't appear to be bouncing back." Regrettable sorrow could be heard in her voice.

"But she had been improving." His words sounded contradictory.

Nurse Katie explained. "The doctors are concerned there is brain damage they can't see which is causing her condition to degrade so drastically."

He slumped into the chair.

Nurse Katie could've cried at seeing his hope fade. "I'm so sorry dearie."

He merely nodded. She left him alone. He moved the chair to touch the bed. He rested his head on her hand. After ten minutes of listening to the erratic beeping of her monitor, he knew he had to call Tom and Sara. On his way out, he informed the nurses' station that he had to make a cell call, but would be back in a few minutes.

He paced while he waited for someone to answer on the other end. Tom answered half asleep. By the time Rusty finished telling him the bad news, he'd roused completely. Rusty could hear Sara in the background hysterically questioning her husband.

Tom remained calm as he finished with Rusty. "I'm so sorry Rusty. Please call us when. We'll take care of what we can here."

Dr. Gallagher was waiting for Rusty's return. He informed Rusty in more clinical terms what Nurse Katie had already explained. Rusty strode to Elsie's room. His chair remained in its previous position, beckoning him. No one asked him to leave.

Shortly before midnight, he woke to Elsie's hand moving under his cheek.

The elation he felt bursting open his heart as he lifted his head to look at her. "Mate?"

That quickly his joy shattered—she was having another seizure. The monitor began to beep frantically. Nurses rushed into the room. They held her to prevent from hurting herself. The doctor entered soon thereafter. He checked her vitals, did nothing else.

Seeing Rusty in the room, the doctor ordered. "Mr. Garnet kindly exit the room."

Rusty did not comply. "No! If this is the end, I am staying right here."

"I said . . ."

The doctor was interrupted by Nurse Katie. "Doctor, I can assure you, Mr. Garnet will not get in our way."

The physician's shock at Nurse Smythe's countermand left him speechless. Then the entire room fell completely silent as the monitor stopped beeping. The doctor checked for a pulse.

He looked at Rusty. "I need to know if you want us to continue or stop?"

Never had Rusty been put in such a situation. He thought of what Elsie would want. He knew she didn't deserve to be kept in a state of limbo. The pain in his heart was nothing like he'd ever known, but he couldn't keep her body going if her mind would never return. He took the few steps to her side, grabbing her hand in his. He noticed the hospital staff had backed away to give him a moment of privacy.

"Mate, I will always love you." He bent to kiss her goodbye.

As he touched his lips to hers, a static zap passed between them and the lights flickered. He buried his wet face in her soft chest one last time. His tears sparkled on her exposed skin. As he straightened, he squeezed and kissed her lifeless hand. When he released it, his fingers lingered in hers.

Suddenly, Elsie inhaled deeply as if she'd been drowning. Rusty turned to look at her; her eyes were wide open. The doctor and nurses rushed to the bedside.

The doctor spoke. "Mr. Garnet the monitor is not registering anything. It's not unusual for eyes to open or an involuntary muscle contraction to cause such a gasp."

But it couldn't be. Elsie's fingers were clawing at his hand.

Nurse Katie saw it too. "Doctor, she is grabbing for his hand!"

They all watched, stunned as the patient's eyes opened to dart from side to side. Her mouth moved with no sound. She seemed to be having trouble catching her breath.

Rusty took hold of her hand. "What is it Mate?"

A picture flashed in his mind of when she'd been sick in Vermont. Without thinking, he sat her up. She started to choke, then a gagging cough produced a substantial wad of phlegm and blood. Her breathing eased.

In a quiet, raspy voice Elsie spoke her first words in days. "Thank you."

They all stood staring at her in disbelief. Rusty and Elsie continued clutching hands.

She spoke again. "My mouth tastes awful. May I please have some water?"

Before Rusty could form a coherent response, Nurse Katie poured ice water into a cup for her.

The doctor regained his senses. "Ms. Endy, how do you feel?"

One of the other nurses started checking vitals. Nurse Katie held the cup and straw for Elsie to sip at the water.

Elsie answered the doctor. "Like a rung out dish rag."

They all laughed nervously.

The doctor spoke to Rusty. "Mr. Garnet, please leave while we complete an exam."

Rusty didn't argue this time. He stepped into the waiting room area. He'd share the good news with Tom and Sara as soon as the doctor confirmed it. A few minutes later, Dr. Gallagher approached him.

"Your Elsie appears to be on her way to a successful recovery. Her vitals are strong and steady. We will run another CT scan in the morning to be sure." The professional gave his updated prognosis.

"Doctor, why didn't the monitor register her heartbeat?" This bothered Rusty.

"Evidently when you leaned over her, you somehow disconnected the leads." It sounded plausible.

"And that thing she coughed up?" He grimaced.

"A cranial blood clot must have found its way into the sinus cavity. Just glad it's out." The doctor finally smiled. "We will check for any more to cause a problem. But I have a feeling that was it."

The other nurses left the room. Rusty moved to the doorway to watch Nurse Katie doting on her patient. She saw him waiting.

Moving to where he stood, she whispered to him. "She's all clean. Go ahead dearie."

Rusty didn't move. "Didn't your shift end hours ago?"

"It did. But, call it motherly intuition, I couldn't leave you two tonight." The caring nurse shared.

"Thank you Katie", he kissed her cheek in gratitude.

The care giver's eyes misted as she left.

Only the two of them were in the room. Rusty walked to the side of the bed. Elsie smiled at him. The worst had passed. There she was with eyes shining bright. Relief washed over him causing him to sink to his knees; his head snuggled in her chest.

Elsie gently stroked his hair.

After an extended period, she queried, "Rusty?"

He responded. "No worries Mate. You're back from walkabout."

THE END